# Never Gonna Happen

*New York Times* & *USA Today* Bestselling Author

# CYNTHIA EDEN

# PROLOGUE

"Don't even think about it." Antony Kyle had a warm, charming smile on his face, but his eyes were ice cold.

Antony wasn't normally the icy type. He could be calculating, he could be clinical, he could be an insane genius when he wanted to be, but...

Sebastian Ridgeway forced a laugh. "I have no idea what you're talking about."

"Dude, you're staring way too hard at my sister."

*Shit. Guilty.*

But Sebastian merely lifted a brow. "It's her birthday. She was blowing out her candles. Everyone was staring at her." And, maybe, just maybe...

She was his new favorite thing to look at in the whole world.

"Uh, uh." Antony side-stepped because—hell, Sebastian had just darted his gaze toward Alyssa again. "Don't. That's my one rule, buddy. If we're doing this partnership together, if we are going to be in this—and we are talking about *life-changing* events here—then you follow that rule. You take it to heart. You make it your life mantra if you must."

Sebastian's stare flickered to the plastic cup in Antony's hand. "I think you've had way too much to drink. I'm not interested in your little sister. Hell, I just met her a couple of days ago."

Because this was his first time to be invited into the inner circle that was the Kyle world. A world with a big, bustling family. A world of laughter and hugs and a million other things that Sebastian had never known.

*Freaking birthday parties.* Alyssa had just turned twenty-one. Everyone was celebrating. She was smiling, her plump lips stretching into a wide grin, and her dark eyes gleamed as she turned her head and—

Antony snapped his fingers in front of Sebastian's face. "Hi, there."

*What in the hell is wrong with me?* "Sorry," Sebastian muttered. "I thought I heard her say my name."

"Nope. You didn't. She did not say your name. And here's the deal. You want this shit to work between us? You want us to blow up the industry and take over the world?"

Yes, yes, he did. He had plans. Goals. He'd been working toward this future—a real, solid future—for years. He wasn't like Antony. He didn't have the stable home. The doting mom. The proud dad. Hell, he had no one. No home. He hadn't even known what a friend was, not until he'd stumbled into Antony—quite literally—a few years before. At first, they'd just been acquaintances who happened to share the same talent with computers. Or, more specifically, the same talent for hacking computers. But as time had slid by, they'd grown closer. Antony wasn't the trusting sort, and he didn't usually let people in. Only fair, Sebastian operated the same way.

"If you want all that," Antony continued in his low voice, "then you just follow my one, simple rule."

Sebastian swallowed. He knew exactly where this was going.

"You keep your hands off my sister."

"Not good enough for her, huh?" The words shot out. What was wrong with him? Sebastian put down the plastic cup he'd been holding. What in the hell had Antony's mom put in the punch?

But was it any surprise that Antony thought that way about him? Sebastian knew what he was. He knew the things he'd done, and suddenly getting a new veneer of polish and sophistication because of his business plans with Antony didn't wipe away the past—

"Dumbass, don't say that shit to me. You're good enough for anything."

*But not her?*

"You're too *dangerous* for Alyssa." Antony stepped closer to him. "Alyssa doesn't know what we really do. She can't ever know. She is not made for the world you live in."

He couldn't see Alyssa any longer.

"And it's not like you're going to fall in love with her. You'd break her heart, and then I'd have to try and kick your ass." A despondent sigh. "Which I wouldn't be able to do. You'd just kick my ass. There would be a huge fight. There would be drama, and...let's simply eliminate all that before it happens, shall we?"

*I would so kick your ass.* Antony was right on that score.

"You're my best friend," Antony told him. "So keep your hands off my sister and don't screw this shit up."

Sebastian laughed. "I wasn't planning to put them on her. You have nothing to worry about."

Antony didn't laugh. He didn't even smile.

So much for breaking the tension. "What, man? Do you want it written in blood or something?"

"Or something."

"Fine...I swear..." *Where had Alyssa gone?* He couldn't very well crane his head to look for her, at least, not at that exact moment. "I swear," Sebastian continued grimly, voice roughening, "that I will never, ever put my hands on your sister—" *On her perfect body.*

Antony's shoulders relaxed.

"Well, unless..." Sebastian added—

Alyssa appeared at Antony's side. Oh, damn. She just kind of popped up right there. And her cheeks were stained red. Her eyes gleamed with what sure as hell looked like embarrassed pain.

Sebastian felt as if someone had just punched him in the stomach.

Fuck, fuck, fuck. How much had she overheard?

Her slightly angled chin notched into the air. "I don't remember asking you to put your hands on me."

He looked down. The floor appeared solid, so no chance of it swallowing him any time soon.

"Is that what you thought?" Alyssa's musical voice cracked. "That I met you and started harboring some big crush on you? That I was waiting for you to notice me?"

*No, I was the one with the crush.* He was the one also who'd put pain in her eyes. *On her damn birthday.* Talk about being an asshole. "Happy birthday," Sebastian mumbled.

Her eyes—a warm, amazing brown filled with flecks of gold—narrowed on him.

"I, um, didn't bring a gift." He was so screwing this up worse. "I didn't know it was your birthday, and I—"

"I don't have a crush on you, Sebastian." The red in her cheeks deepened. "And I don't need you to notice me."

*But I do notice you, Alyssa.*

She stepped closer and her amazing scent—some kind of flowery, sweet smell that he couldn't quite identify because he knew shit about flowers—wrapped around him. Sebastian found himself inching toward her, too.

Because she only stood at about five-foot-four, he towered over her. Her thick, dark hair tumbled over her shoulders as she glared up at him.

His hands fisted because he really wanted to touch her.

*Don't do it.*

"I get that you must be used to receiving lots of attention." Her index finger jabbed into his chest. "Let me guess...you flutter those green eyes..."

He fluttered...what?

"And you smile, flashing those dimples..."

She'd noticed his dimples?

"And you get women to do whatever you want because you use that rough, low voice of yours..." Another jab of her index finger—right over his heart.

"Definitely not anything," he murmured.

Her head tilted. "I'm not falling for you."

Antony sidled closer to her. "Uh, Alyssa..." He cleared his throat. Loudly.

Alyssa didn't look at him.

She kept her angry—and, dammit, still hurt—stare on Sebastian as she snapped, "So don't worry. You can rest easy. I won't be around begging for your attention. To be clear, I don't beg for anyone."

No, of course, she didn't. He could all too easily imagine the men begging for her.

Her hand jerked back. "Now, if you don't mind, it's my birthday. I have people waiting for me."

She had the whole world waiting. She turned on her heel and walked away from him like the freaking queen that she was. His gaze slid over her body.

Sweet hell, that ass of hers—

"Jeez, that didn't go so well." Antony slapped a hand on Sebastian's shoulder. "Should have warned you. My sister has a temper."

Suspicion churned through him. "Did you know she was close enough to hear us?"

"Uh, I—"

Sebastian's head turned. His eyes locked on his now squirming business partner.

Antony winced. "I think Alyssa might have been getting a little crush on you. I mean, hell, man, you know women tend to fall for that whole badass thing you have going on." He snatched his hand back and waved vaguely at Sebastian. "Hmm. Maybe we should use it in our promotions. Bet the press would like it, too," he mused.

"Focus." Sebastian waved a hand angrily. "Let me get this straight. You wanted to stop her crush. You wanted *me* to be the villain of the piece. Figured if she saw me as the asshole, she'd lose interest?"

"No..." Antony pushed up his glasses. They hadn't been falling. "I was merely hoping for some boundaries."

"Boundaries, huh?" He unclenched his hands. "You didn't let me finish my promise."

Antony frowned at him. "I didn't?"

"No. You didn't." His gaze slid across the room. Alyssa was standing with two men. Tall, handsome, polished jackasses. "I swear, that I will never, ever put my hands on your sister..."

Alyssa's head turned. Her eyes met his.

"Unless she asks for them," Sebastian finished softly. "Unless she asks for me. In that case..." *I will touch her wherever and whenever she wants.*

Antony laughed. "Oh, that shit is never gonna happen."

Alyssa held Sebastian's stare.

"You never know," Sebastian replied.

# CHAPTER ONE

*Cover blown. Protect my sister. Do anything necessary.*

Sebastian frowned at the text he'd just received from his business partner, Antony Kyle. For a moment, his heart seemed to stop beating.

"Uh, Mr. Ridgeway?" A throat cleared, not so discreetly.

Sebastian's hold on the phone tightened.

"Sir, they are *waiting*."

Sebastian glanced up and straight at an auditorium full of people. He'd been on his way to the podium, and normally, he would never have checked his phone when he was presenting, but that special little ding—that ding had notified him that the message was of some serious code-red emergency status. It was an alert he'd set up to receive only when the shit ever so seriously hit the fan.

Reporters were staring at him. Head honchos in the video gaming field were waiting with bated breath. Social media influencers had their phones up and were recording.

And he really, really needed to get the hell out of there.

*Protect my sister.*

Protect Alyssa Kyle. He pushed the phone back into the pocket of his jeans. Even though he was the headlining speaker, Sebastian wore battered jeans and a loose t-shirt. Some folks in the crowd were wearing expensive, designer suits. They were trying to impress with their money and their clout.

He didn't give a damn about impressing anyone.

Well, maybe *one* person.

"Mr. Ridgeway?" His assistant sidled closer.

"Find Alyssa," he ordered in a low voice. "I want to know exactly where she is, and I want that information in the next minute."

"Minute?" A shocked squeak from Doug Manci. His eyes bulged. "But—"

Sebastian grabbed the podium. He moved his head toward the microphone. "Thanks for coming out today. Our new gaming software is going to blow your mind."

*Cover is blown.*

He flashed a smile to the crowd, deliberately using his dimples because they made him seem charming. He was the face of the company. The one who appeared in all the ads. The one people saw when they thought of Shark Gaming and Design.

*Protect my sister.*

"Protecting our company and our customers has always been my top priority. We want to give them the best experience possible." They had cut out huge chunks of the market in the billion-dollar gaming industry. *We're here to take a bite out of the industry.* He and Antony had kicked ass and taken names, and they weren't even close to being done.

Antony...

The words of the text played through Sebastian's mind. *Do anything necessary.*

The packed crowd waited eagerly. Keeping his voice nice and warm, he said, "But don't just take my word for it. I want you to experience the latest Shark game for yourself. Everyone in this room will be treated to an early look at our latest project."

There was a surprised murmur. Yeah, because this hadn't been on the agenda. Screw that. His agenda had changed.

"I won't stand up here and bore you by running through all the talk of specs and details. That's a waste of everyone's time. Instead, my team will provide you all with exclusive access to our newest game. Trust me on this, you'll find that it's the experience of a lifetime." The VR would blow their minds.

Sebastian turned away from the crowd even as reporters shouted questions at him.

His assistant stood on the sidelines, sweating.

Sebastian headed straight for Doug. "Where is she?"

Sweat dotted Doug's forehead. "She's...she's on a date."

He growled.

"They are scheduled to take in a play at the Langley Theater. You can find her in the company box—"

"Take care of them." He jerked his thumb back toward the shouting crowd.

"But—"

"Don't worry. The rest of the team will help you out." They were waiting in the wings. Sure, he'd just thrown them all a serious curve ball, but they'd handle it. He trained his team very, very well. "I have more pressing business."

Doug hopped closer. "What could possibly be more pressing than *this?*" Once again, his voice was a squeak. His red bow tie had twisted. A habit Doug had. He always wore bow ties, and when he was nervous, he twisted them. "This is a huge deal! A BFD!" Doug yanked at his bow tie. "What is more pressing? Uh, sir?"

*Saving Alyssa.* Saving her was definitely a *big fucking deal.* "It seems I have a date to interrupt." The bastard with her had better not get in Sebastian's way. He was so not in the mood to play.

Doug gaped at him. "You're not serious?"

He was. He was also in a hurry. Sebastian waved to his other team members. They surged up from the background as he marched out. His steps were fast as he headed through the building. He knew his car and driver would be waiting at the front of the building.

When he burst out of the building, the limo was at the curb. The driver jumped to attention. "You're...done early?"

"Get me to the Langley Theater."

The guy rushed to open the door for Sebastian.

"I've got it." Sebastian yanked open the door himself. "If you can get me there in ten minutes, there'll be a big bonus waiting for you."

Moments later, the limo screeched away from the curb. Sebastian pulled out his phone. Stared at the text one more time.

*Cover blown.*

Oh, shit. This was bad. Very, very bad. He fired a quick text back to Antony. *Are you safe?*

He waited for a response. Waited...

But during the ten minutes it took to cut across Asheville, North Carolina, no response came.

Dammit. But at least he'd deliberately used some of Antony's own words from the text in the announcement to the press. Even if Antony had needed to ditch his phone and go dark, Sebastian's announcement would be broadcast everywhere. Antony would see it and pick up on the deliberate language. He'd know that Sebastian had received his message.

He would also know...

*Don't worry about Alyssa. I've got her.*

***

The date had been a serious mistake. Oh, so bad. Dinner at the restaurant had been a long, painful affair. Turned out, Isaac Swain was way more interested in Alyssa's brother than he was in her. Because during the whole long, boring dinner? The dinner that never seemed to end? The guy had been spouting question after question about Antony.

It was downright insulting.

Alyssa's shoulders hunched as they sat in the company's theater box. At least the show would start soon. Then Isaac could *stop* talking her ear off about—

"Your brother is a genius."

"Um." She forced a smile. Like she hadn't heard that line about a time or twenty from people who were awed by what her brother had accomplished. She was awed, too. Alyssa thought her brother was awesome, but she didn't want to talk about him on her date.

"I mean, the way he developed the company from the ground up. Turned into a major player in the industry..."

She tuned him out. Why, oh, why had she thought going on a date with one of the Shark Gaming and Design employees was a good idea? Sure, okay, yes, Isaac was attractive. A transfer from California, he had the whole blond-hair, beach-boy thing going on. Bright blue eyes. Perfectly straight and white teeth. And his body screamed, *I like to work out!* So, yes, okay, fine, maybe she'd agreed to go out with him because he was attractive. Sue her. She'd met him in her brother's office last week when she'd dropped by and—

"He did it all single-handedly, and that is something that most people can't—"

She stiffened, and her attention flew back to Isaac. "That's not correct."

He blinked. His brows—perfectly shaped— *Did he pluck them? Wax them?*—lifted. "I think I know what I'm talking about."

Now she straightened in the chair. Her voice flattened as Alyssa responded, "I think I know my brother's business."

"Yes, well, you don't actually work there, though." He waved one hand vaguely toward her. "You play with your jewelry design."

Oh, the hell, no. He'd just said she *played?* Her back teeth clenched. "My brother didn't create his company alone," Alyssa gritted out. "He has a partner, one you know very well about."

Isaac laughed. She didn't like his laugh. It was high pitched and nasally, and it totally ruined the whole beach boy look. "Please." Isaac shook his head. "You're talking about Sebastian."

"I'm obviously talking about Sebastian Ridgeway. As an employee of the company, you should know who you work for."

He blinked. "The so-called 'bad boy of tech' didn't build the company. He's just the flash. Everyone knows your brother is the real talent."

She could feel her cheeks burning. "Sebastian hates that nickname. If he hears you calling him that, he'll fire you on the spot."

Isaac licked his lips. "Well, good thing he's not here, huh?"

She almost wished he was.

*Wait. Do I think that being with Sebastian is better than being with Isaac?*

"Where is your brother now, Alyssa? I bet he's off researching a new design. I wish I could see how he comes up with his ideas. I would love to know—"

"You should date him."

Isaac blinked.

Whoops. Had she said that last part out loud?

Isaac's perplexed expression told her that, yep, she had.

"Excuse me?" He laughed again.

"You know, Isaac, I think I'm getting a headache." Alyssa glanced around, looking for an escape. She needed one desperately because the idea of spending more time trapped with Isaac was enough to make her shudder. She causally slid the small strap of her purse onto her shoulder. *The better to make a fast getaway.*

"Did I tell you that I moved from California just because I wanted to work for Shark Gaming and Design? I wanted to be just like—"

"Antony?" she finished.

He nodded eagerly and his hand reached for hers. He had a very sweaty hand. "Exactly. I wanted—"

*Please, someone save me.*

But, of course, no one was there. They were alone in the company's theater box. She'd foolishly offered up the box when he'd asked what she'd like to do on their date. Oh, if only she could go back in time and—

The curtains behind Isaac's head flew open.

"I wanted to be like Antony, not like Sebastian. Because come on, who wants to be like that selfish prick?" Isaac laughed his nasally laugh again. "Guy is some kind of Bruce Wayne wanna-be. Trolling around town in his limo. Freaking playboy. What do you think? Does he have a bat cave hidden somewhere?"

*OhmyGod.*

Sebastian was there. He'd just shoved open the curtains. She blinked, wanting to make sure she wasn't imagining things, but no...*still there.*

Sebastian had obviously caught Isaac's comments because one eyebrow lifted up. And he smiled.

It was a killer smile. The kind of smile that a great white shark probably would give to his prey right before his teeth opened up, and he took a big, juicy bite.

"The selfish prick is right behind you," Alyssa whispered.

Isaac seemed to choke. His hold tightened on her hand.

"I'm going to need you to let go of me," Alyssa told him.

He didn't. His fingers *did* move to curl around her wrist.

But his head swung around toward Sebastian and he sputtered, "I-I—"

Sebastian crossed his arms over his chest. "I know you."

"I—yes."

"You work for me."

Isaac still had his fingers wrapped around her wrist. Was she gonna have to pry them off? Sighing, Alyssa stood up.

Isaac rose, too, but didn't let go of her. "I...do," he agreed. "That is, I work for you and Antony. I'm in Research and Development—"

Sebastian stalked forward. "Alyssa, we're leaving."

Any other day—literally, *any* other day—she would have told Sebastian to go screw himself.

She never took orders from him. Not from him, not from any man. But today—this poor, unfortunate day—she almost jumped for joy. "Right. I'm ready." She almost added...*Why the hell are you late?* But she managed to hold that part back because he'd have zero clue what she meant.

Sebastian blinked at her. Then frowned in suspicion. Probably because she never, ever agreed with him on anything. Fighting with him was one of her favorite hobbies, and everyone needed a really good hobby. Driving Sebastian crazy was *her* hobby.

She stepped toward him. Realized that Isaac was *still* touching her. Enough. She jerked her wrist free of his fingers.

Sebastian's gaze fell to her wrist. "Did he fucking bruise you?"

She looked down. There were faint red marks on her wrist.

"You sonofabitch!" Sebastian grabbed for Isaac.

Alyssa stepped between the two men. "No."

Sebastian's glittering green gaze could have scorched anyone else.

She met his stare without flinching. "He didn't bruise me. He just wouldn't let go, so I yanked my hand free. That's all."

"Right. That's all. *That's too fucking much.* He shouldn't have been touching you." A muscle flexed along Sebastian's jaw. "Why the hell are you dating this idiot?"

"Hey, now! Hey!" Isaac stepped around her. Moved closer to Sebastian and puffed up his chest. "Listen, Mr. Ridgeway—"

"Oh, now I'm Mr. Ridgeway?" Sebastian reached for Alyssa's hand. His fingers trailed carefully over her wrist, as if he wanted to soothe the skin. "Because a moment ago, I'm sure I was a selfish prick. Or maybe I was Batman."

"I think it was a selfish prick *and* Bruce Wayne," Alyssa clarified.

Sebastian flashed her a smile.

Isaac's mouth opened. Closed. Opened again. He didn't quite manage speech, though.

Alyssa bit her lower lip as her gaze darted over Sebastian. *Tall, sexy Sebastian.* The devil in the flesh. "I thought...wait, weren't you supposed to be doing your big presentation tonight?"

"Something else came up."

Something else...? She cast a glance at Isaac. He'd closed his mouth again. She wanted to push Sebastian and find out what was happening, but she also didn't exactly want to have this conversation with Isaac watching. Time to leave. "Good night, Isaac."

Sebastian turned away. His fingers were still caressing her wrist, and, as always when he touched her, a surge of warmth spread over her skin. She started to follow him—

"It's like that, huh?" Isaac demanded. "I heard the rumors, but I ignored them."

She dug in her heels. Turned her head around and locked her eyes on Isaac. "Excuse me?" Ice dripped from her voice.

"I was warned that I shouldn't go out with you."

Whoa. Whoa. Isaac had been told not to go out with her? Why the hell didn't someone tell me not to go out with him?

"I was told that your...interest...was somewhere else." Isaac's eyes darted to Sebastian.

And this is not happening. "You were misinformed."

"Was I?" Isaac puffed out his chest. He seemed to do that a lot. It didn't make him look strong. It made him resemble a rooster. "You were just defending him to me!"

Yes, she had been defending Sebastian. "So what?"

"Now you're running away with him! Stories have circulated around the office about—"

"Okay, I don't have time for this shit." Sebastian had turned back around, too. "Let's cut to the chase. You think I'm screwing Alyssa? That what you're talking about?"

Isaac's mouth opened. Closed. Opened.

Did he know that he looked like a fish when he did that?

*A big shark is gonna eat that little fish.*

And the big shark gave his killer grin before he said, "You're right. I am screwing her. Guilty as charged."

No, no, no, no, no, no, no.

But Sebastian wasn't done. "I'm overcome with jealousy at the thought of her being with such a dumbass like you, so I stormed in here tonight. I'm going to carry her out, and I will never, ever let her out of my sight again. I'll spend the next eight to ten hours making wild, passionate love to her, and I'll make sure Alyssa screams my name until she's hoarse."

*Oh, dear Lord.*

Sebastian's voice had been *loud*. So loud that the people in the next box had turned to gape at him.

Alyssa shook her head. "That's not—"

Sebastian stepped closer to Isaac. "And if you ever fucking leave a mark on her again, I will end you. Are we clear?"

There were lots of whispers around them. She was pretty sure someone was even filming with a phone. Because, of course, Sebastian had been recognized.

Everyone else was all fancy for the theater. Isaac was in a suit and tie. She was in her favorite slinky black dress and her red heels because she did love a splash of color, while Sebastian—he looked all rough and dangerous and *sexy*, dammit—in his jeans and t-shirt.

"I-I didn't mean to hurt Alyssa. That was never my intention." Isaac wilted immediately. No more puffed-up rooster chest. "My apologies."

"Good job," Sebastian praised. "You get to keep living."

"*Stop it*," she snapped at Sebastian. What was his deal? He was even more out of control than usual. And that was saying a lot. So much for actually being relieved to see him. She tugged her hand free of his hold.

He immediately let her go.

"I am going home. *Alone,* gentlemen." She sniffed. As if they were gentlemen. Not likely. "I'd love to say it's been a fun night, but it hasn't. Isaac, I don't think we're meant to be."

His brow furrowed.

"And Sebastian..." Her gaze dipped back to him.

He smiled at her. Flashed his sexy dimples.

She ignored the way her stomach dropped. She'd learned—long ago—to ignore her reaction to him. "I'll just skip out on the screaming orgasm tonight, but thanks so much for the offer. Instead, I think I'll go binge watch something." With that, she skirted around him, left the box, and headed for the stairs.

She did not need this level of drama in her life. Alyssa kept her spine straight and her chin up as she exited with what she thought was pretty good composure. Sure, her cheeks were no doubt flushed bright red, and her breathing was way too fast—

*I'll spend the next eight to ten hours making wild, passionate love to her, and I'll make sure Alyssa screams my name until she's hoarse.*

She swallowed. Her knees did a jiggle.

Great. Now she was going to have Sebastian's words replaying in her head all night long.

***

*Sexy as hell.*

Sebastian watched as Alyssa walked away with the grace that he'd always admired. The dress slid over his favorite ass ever, and then his gaze darted down the long expanse of her legs to—

Dammit. She'd worn her red heels? *For this bozo?*

"Am I fired?" Isaac's voice cracked.

"I don't have time for you right now." Alyssa was pissed. He'd have to smooth that over, fast. He bounded after her.

"Are you mad because I called you a selfish prick?"

Sebastian spared a glance over his shoulder. "I am a selfish prick, but, no, dumbass, you don't get to say those things about your boss."

"I—"

"I'm mad because you will not fucking touch Alyssa again, understand? Don't come within ten feet of her."

"Oh." A nod. "So you *are* screwing her—"

"No, I'm not," he snarled. It's just a super, super frequent fantasy.

"But you said—"

Alyssa was gone. Shit. "I don't have time for you now." He rushed after her. As soon as he shot out of the theater box, Sebastian looked to the left, toward the stairwell.

He saw the top of her dark head as she hurried down the stairs. "Alyssa!"

She didn't stop. He was pretty sure she sped up.

If she fell on those stairs...hurrying in her heels...

He wasn't going to chase her down the stairs. That would make her hurry all the more. So he raced into the open elevator and stabbed the button for the first floor. The doors slid closed, and for a moment, he stared at his own reflection.

*Selfish prick.*

Guilty as charged. But he did have one or two soft spots in the world...

Okay, maybe one...

The doors opened. He saw his soft spot. He surged out and stepped right into her path. Alyssa staggered to a sudden stop, and her hands flew out to curl around his shoulders. A quick, startled cry escaped her lips.

"I got you." His fingers closed around her hips.

She huffed out a breath. "Why do you have me?"

"Because you were wobbling on those way too high heels." The sexy heels that she'd wasted on that jerkoff.

Her eyes narrowed.

*If looks could kill.*

His hold tightened on her. "I was worried you might fall."

"Hands. Off."

"Yours or mine? Because I hate to tell you your business—"

"Since when?"

Damn but her eyes were gorgeous. When she was angry, the flecks of gold in her eyes went molten. He wondered if they did the same thing when she was turned on.

"You are always telling me my business! You are always *up in* my business! Just like you are tonight!"

Her lips were red and slick and that full lower lip of hers made him want to take a bite. *Nope. Focus.* "This might shock you, princess, but you're holding pretty tightly to me. I think I can even feel your nails biting into my shirt."

Horror flashed on her face right before she snatched her hands away from him.

He let her go, too. "You're not going to fall? Because I can steady you."

She stepped around him. Double timed it to the exit. Her heels went all *click, click, click*. The doorman hurriedly opened the door for her.

Sebastian followed right behind her. "Alyssa, we need to talk." He nodded to the doorman. The warm air hit Sebastian as soon as he stepped outside. "Look, this is very important and—"

She was already at the corner and attempting to hail a cab.

He sighed, admired the view of her for a moment, but said, "You don't need a cab."

"I do. Isaac picked me up. Since I don't plan to get in his vehicle again, I need a ride home." Her hand kept waving.

"I have my limo waiting." Just steps away. "I can take you home."

A cab slowly headed toward her.

Her suspicious stare darted to Sebastian. "Why did you interrupt my date? Wait, how did you even know where I was?"

He didn't like all the darkness around them. Most folks were in the theater, and the street was too deserted for his piece of mind. "Your brother wanted me to—"

"*Ugh.* Why does everyone want to talk about my brother?" Alyssa shook her head. Took three fast steps away—

And bullets tore through the metal sign behind her, ripped right through it, leaving small holes before they pounded into the bricks that lined the theater's outer wall.

If she hadn't taken those three steps—*those bullets would have hit her.*

For a moment, Alyssa gaped. Then she screamed.

Sebastian scooped her into his arms and ran for the limo. He dove in, with Alyssa cradled in his arms. "*Drive!*" Sebastian yelled. "Get us the hell out of here, now! Take us to my place!"

His body was thrown over Alyssa's and his heart was racing because, holy shit, someone had just taken shots at her! Someone had actually tried to kill Alyssa.

The limo lurched forward. He knew the glass in the windows was bullet-proof because, well, that had been his order. Why not pay for the upgrade? An upgrade that was freaking very useful at that moment.

As his heart thundered in his chest, Sebastian became aware of a few things.

One... Alyssa hadn't made a sound. Not since her terrified scream.

Two... They were sprawled together in the back of the limo. Well, not so much sprawled as...he had her pinned to the seat. His body was on top of hers, he'd grabbed her wrists and anchored them over her head, and his legs were lodged between her spread thighs. Her dress had ridden up. Way, way up.

Three... Adrenaline coursed through his body but, because of their, um, delicate position, so did lust. He was having a rather unmistakable reaction, and he knew that Alyssa had to feel it. Feel him.

His head lifted. "Are you okay?"

Her long lashes slowly rose. Her breath came in quick hitches.

"Alyssa? Ba—" *Nope.* He cut himself off right before he called her baby. That would have been a fatal mistake. "Were you hit?" He didn't think so, but—

"Someone shot at me."

Yes. Actually, someone had shot at her three times. "Were you hit?"

"No." Her voice was low. Breathy.

Her mouth was a few inches from his. It would be so easy to lower his head. To take her lips. To finally taste what he'd wanted for so long.

And, his head did begin to lower. She didn't say anything. The limo was racing down the road and Alyssa was pressed tightly to him, and her mouth—

"What are you doing?" Alyssa's hushed question seemed torn from her.

But it brought him back to reality. Stopped him when his mouth was less than an inch from hers. What was he doing? Sebastian cleared his throat. "Saving your life. Obviously."

# CHAPTER TWO

"I realize I probably just gained superhero status in your eyes," Sebastian continued in that deep, rumbling voice of his, "but do try to control yourself around me, if you can."

Her heart drummed so hard and fast that Alyssa was pretty certain her entire body was shaking. She'd never been shot at in her life. The thunder of those bullets had scared the hell out of her.

And now...

She became aware of a whole lot of things. Mostly...Sebastian. Sebastian being on top of her. Between her legs. She also could have absolutely sworn... "You were going to kiss me."

He laughed. "I saved your life, that's what I did."

"You were just about to kiss me." Okay, yes, the lighting in the back of the limo was dim, but she'd been pretty sure his focus had been on her mouth, and his head had been lowering toward her, and—

"I was trying to make sure you hadn't been hit. You know, being the amazing Good Samaritan that I am."

His mouth was still so close to hers. His body—jeez, the guy was *all* muscle—was above her. He wasn't crushing her with his weight, though. Sebastian always seemed to be conscious of his size and power.

Speaking of size... Her hips shifted a bit. "OhmyGod."

"What?"

"You're...you're turned on." She knew her face had to be blood red. What was worse? Almost getting shot or having *Sebastian Ridgeway* between her thighs...turned *on* between her thighs?

Fine, obviously, nearly getting shot was worse. But having him that way...

"Sorry," he muttered. "It's a reaction to the adrenaline. Nothing personal."

Wait. Had he just told her that his arousal was nothing personal? *Sonofa*— "Get off," she snarled.

"But I'm protecting you. Doing a whole human-shield bit so that you won't get shot and—"

"I bet the limo has bulletproof glass and all kinds of fun little extras." Because Sebastian and her brother always went over the top when it came to transport.

*Although maybe that whole over the top style was more necessary than I thought.*

"Yes," Sebastian told her softly. "It does. Bulletproof glass and plenty of extras."

"Then get *off*."

His hands released hers. His fingers trailed lightly over her wrists, then he pulled back and moved his body to the seat next to her.

She immediately bolted up. Her shaking fingers grabbed her dress and yanked the fabric back *down* over her legs.

"Pity."

Alyssa's head snapped toward Sebastian.

"You've got truly phenomenal legs."

Suspicion had her squinting at him. "Just how well can you see in the dark?"

"It's not completely dark in here. Besides, I've enjoyed the view before."

Her pounding heart wasn't slowing down. "Now is not the time to mess with me."

"Who said I was messing with you? I was giving you a heartfelt compliment. You've got killer legs. I'm sure you know it."

"And I'm sure you are trying to drive me crazy! I'm sure—" But Alyssa broke off because she'd just had a thought hit her. Hard. "I wasn't shot at."

"Um. Yes, you were."

She glanced around the interior of the limo. A bottle of champagne waited in an ice bucket nearby. She grabbed it, popped the cork after some twisting and semi-severe struggles, then chugged some champagne right out of the bottle.

"Alyssa?"

She plunked the bottle back down in the ice bucket and huffed out a breath. "Sorry. Needed that. First the date from hell, then the gunfire."

"Please, help yourself," he invited. "Though you have a little bit right...here." His hand reached out. His fingers slid tenderly over her chin.

Heat surged through her. Dang it. She caught his wrist. "Stop it."

"I was helping."

*Since when?* And he'd totally been BSing earlier. The man was no Good Samaritan. He was a badass, a troublemaker, a heart breaker. Her list could go on and on. Sebastian had enemies for days and... "Obviously, I was not the target tonight."

"Excuse me?"

She let go of his hand and turned to knock on the privacy screen that separated them from the driver. "Hello?"

The driver didn't respond.

"Alyssa, you have to hit the button to lower the screen." Humor slipped beneath Sebastian's words. Humor? Now?

She rummaged around until she found a button that lowered the screen. And as soon as it lowered... "I want to go home."

The driver made no response.

She rattled off her address. "Take me there, now, please." Another thought hit her, and she spun back around toward Sebastian. "We need to call the police!"

"I'll take care of them, *after* I've taken care of you."

"Sebastian, I hate to break this to you, but the last thing I need is for you to take care of me. Wait, scratch that. I don't hate to break it to you. It is my pleasure to inform you," Alyssa crisply corrected, "that I don't need you."

"Then why did you look so happy to see me when I showed up in the theater box?"

"I..." Damn. Because the date was a disaster.

"And, sorry, I guess my memory is a little hazy, but when I saved your life a few moments ago, weren't you pretty happy that I was there with my quick limo that was waiting to whisk you to safety?"

Her eyes narrowed. There was a faint, blue glow in the back of the limo. It ran along the interior, and she was pretty sure that blue glow would transform into party lights with the flick of a switch. Everyone knew how much Sebastian liked to party.

Behind her, she heard the faint whir that told her the privacy screen was sliding back up. Alyssa whipped around and her fist instinctively tapped on the glass. "Hey! You'd better be taking me home!"

"Glass is up," Sebastian told her patiently. "He can't hear a thing."

Then she'd just put that glass right back down. Her fingers flew to the button. She jabbed it, but the screen didn't lower. "You turned it off."

"What?"

"There's another button somewhere back here, and you disabled this one." Her breath huffed out as she glowered toward Sebastian. *Take me home.*

"You're stressed."

*Ya think?*

"Why don't you take a few breaths and try to let some of that tension out?"

"I am always stressed when I'm around you." Truth. She closed her eyes. "But this is worse. A thousand times worse than normal because tonight, I was almost hit when someone tried to take a shot at you."

Silence. Then... "Want to say that again?"

Her eyes flew open. "You are the one with enemies!"

"I have been known to piss off a few people," Sebastian allowed. He didn't sound particularly concerned. Typical Sebastian. "Some would say that's part of my charm."

"No. No, it is not charming to be an asshole. I don't know who told you that—"

"Well, the PR people at the company have mentioned that my—"

"If you tell me that the whole badass persona you have going on sells games, I will scream."

He laughed.

Something else she hated—he always seemed to laugh at her. "No wonder people are shooting at you."

"Uh, don't want to alarm you, but I think those bullets were meant for you."

That made zero sense. "Why would someone be shooting at me?"

He didn't respond.

"Exactly." Yes, sure, Isaac was probably not a super fan of hers at the moment, but she didn't have a long line of enemies. At least, Alyssa didn't think she did. She was kind to animals, she was friendly to children, and she never, ever flirted with another woman's man. The shots must have been intended for Sebastian. "Unless..." Now she considered things from a new angle. "Maybe the shots weren't meant for you or me. Maybe it was all just random."

"That what you going with now? A random event?"

It was an option. "The police will sort this out."

"I'm sure they will."

She edged closer to him. His scent—warm, rich, masculine—teased her. Why did he always smell good? *No, do not be distracted.* "You still buddies with Detective Lewis? I bet he can help. I read an article recently about him and how he's on the fast track to be named chief."

"Yes, I'm still friends with Winston. I'll be putting in a call to him just as soon as I'm sure you're safe."

Her breath expelled. "You mean as soon as you drop me off at my place." Okay, now she was feeling steadier. This whole night had been crazy. And, yes, her fingers were still shaking and her insides were quivering a bit, but that was probably just due to stress. Adrenaline.

*The same adrenaline that had given Sebastian one serious hard-on.*

Her gaze jerked to his lap.

"Just so you know, I can see very, very well in dim lighting. Though, it's really not that dim in here. Not with the blue illumination spilling from all the corners."

In other words, he'd caught her staring at his crotch. Wonderful.

"Something you need?" Sebastian murmured, voice all silky and seductive.

Her stare snapped to his face. "You are an asshole."

"Princess, tell me something I don't know."

"Fine. I'm not your princess, I'm not your anything, and I never will be."

He swallowed. Glanced away. And she had the weirdest, strangest feeling...

*Did I just hurt his feelings?*

She...oh, God. Alyssa had one serious weakness. She hated hurting anyone. Anything. She felt guilty for days if she did that. Even if she accidentally killed a spider. She'd been working on the guilt issue. And so what if Sebastian was hurt? Though she doubted he was. Why would anything she say hurt him? But...

"I'm sorry." Her voice was stilted. "I'm still shaking, and I'm scared, and my head is all over the place." Alyssa pulled in a deep breath and stared down at her lap. "You tried to help me tonight. You got me away as soon as the gunfire started, and you even covered me with your body. That was actually quite heroic of you." Now that she thought about it. "Unnecessary, especially considering the bulletproof limo, but I think your heart was in the right place."

She could feel his gaze on her as he softly said, "And here I thought you believed I didn't have a heart, Alyssa."

Her tongue slid over her lower lip. "I know you have a heart. I just think that—most days—it's frozen in ice."

"Then maybe you can help me melt that ice."

Was he mocking her? She peeked up at him. "I'm trying to both apologize and say thank you."

"Yeah, well, here's the deal." He leaned toward her. Seemed to take up way too much space. Seemed to make her way too aware of him.

"I don't think you ever need to apologize to me. Like you said, I'm a dick."

"I actually said you were an asshole." To clarify.

"You don't need to apologize and you don't need to thank me."

She did. "When someone tries to save your life..." Which, yes, he *had*...

"Fine. Thank me, then."

"I-I *was* just thanking you." Had he hit his head?

"No. Thank me for real. With a kiss."

What?

"If you think I did a good deed, then you can thank me with a kiss. You can keep your lips closed. It can be fast. Just a little peck." She saw him tap his own lips. "Right here."

Had the limo stopped moving? She couldn't tell. "Why do you want a kiss from me?"

"Because maybe I've always been curious about how you taste."

"But if my lips are closed, you won't be tasting much."

"You're right. You can open your mouth. Totally cool with me. I agree to your terms." He slid forward more.

The limo lurched to a stop. Okay, *now* it had stopped moving. Her hand flew up and pressed to Sebastian's chest. "Why do you play with me?"

"Who said I was playing?"

But she plowed right on, saying, "You do one good deed—"

"I've done way more than one. God, your mouth is gorgeous."

"And then you screw things up by being the playboy again. Just when I think I'm seeing the real you."

The back door opened. "Sir." The driver cleared his throat. "We're here."

When the door had opened, more lights had automatically turned on in the limo's interior, and now Alyssa could clearly see Sebastian's face. And...

*Lust.*

His features were hard and tight with a dangerous lust that was directed right at her.

All of the moisture in her mouth dried up.

But in the next instant, a mask seemed to sweep over his features. He smiled, his dimples flashed, and she couldn't read him at all.

"That's the thing," Sebastian rasped. "No one ever sees the real me."

Before she could respond, he caught her hand and tugged her from the limo.

*At least I'm home. At least I'll be able to get away from him soon. At least—*

Alyssa staggered to a stop. "This isn't my house."

"No, it's mine."

She knew that. He was tugging her forward, she was trying to dig in her heels, but it wasn't working and she was having to triple time it in order to keep up with him as Sebastian headed toward the freaking sprawling cabin—*mansion, more like mansion*—that overlooked the Blue Ridge Mountains. A million stars were glittering overhead while the lights blazed inside his home.

The illumination spilled from all of the floor to ceiling windows in the massive structure.

"I don't want to be here," Alyssa huffed. "Sebastian, *stop*."

He whirled toward her. "I will apologize in advance for this."

"What?" Alarm flared through her. "What are you apologizing for?" Before he could respond, she heard the sound of another vehicle approaching. Alyssa glanced back and saw a dark SUV screeching to a stop behind the limo. "Who is that?"

"Security. They will keep an eye on you while I go and talk to the cops—"

"When did you call security?" He hadn't been on the phone in the limo.

"Before I picked you up at the theater."

Shock rolled through Alyssa, and then—

He scooped her up. Tossed her over his shoulder. "I'm really sorry."

"*Stop!*" She surged against him. This was not happening. A million times *not*.

But he tightened his hold on her. Headed for the mansion. Took her *in* the mansion, and this was a bad dream. A nightmare. It had to be because there was no way that Sebastian Ridgeway was carrying her into his house *as she tried to hurtle herself away from him*. Sure, Sebastian was often over the top. The media loved his wild antics.

But this wasn't some PR stunt designed to grab more headlines. This was her life.

This was—

He put her down on the couch. She bounced.

He grimaced. "You are going to be extra pissed about this, aren't you?"

"You have no idea." She blew a lock of hair out of her eyes.

"But at least you'll be alive."

Two men in really bad suits rushed inside.

Sebastian pointed at Alyssa. "You keep her here. You make sure that her skin is not so much as bruised. When I get back, I expect her to be in perfect condition."

She looked at his security goons. Then she looked back at him. "When you get back, I will be gone."

Those dimples...They winked at her. "Want to bet on that, sweet—um, Alyssa?"

She surged off the couch and stood toe-to-toe with him. But since he was so tall, she did have to tip her head back to glare up at him. "This is called kidnapping, and it's illegal. You don't get to hold me captive. That might be your kind of kink, but it's not mine."

Did someone snicker? Maybe a goon?

Sebastian sent a killing glance at the guy. Then his smile—slightly strained—came back to Alyssa. "It's not a kink. Though I'll be happy to tell you about all of the things that turn me on—later. For now, this is about keeping you safe. It's about protecting you. So, be pissed. Hate me, keep right on doing it the way you always have. But you'll be alive. Now, I need to go before the cops get too antsy." He whirled for the door.

"I don't hate you."

Sebastian stopped. Stiffened. "You don't?"

"Well, correction, I am starting to hate you *because you just kidnapped me!*" And if he thought she was going to sit at his place, all calm and cool, he had better think again.

His head turned as he glanced back over his shoulder at her. "I need you to trust me."

No humor. No smirk. No dimples.

Just seriousness. He was hardly ever serious.

"There are things happening that you don't know about. I need you to stay here until I can get a handle on the situation. The reason I came to that theater box tonight—it was because I'd gotten a tip that something might happen to you."

What? Now she could feel the blood leaving her face. *Hello, light-headedness.* She'd wondered why he'd been at the theater, but with everything else happening, Alyssa hadn't exactly gotten the chance to question him hard about that. *Or, heck, did I even ask him about it at all?* Some parts of that limo ride were a bit blurry. Mostly because she'd been nervous, scared, and...turned on.

A deep, dark secret that Alyssa possessed? Sebastian—with this thick hair, his killer grin, and his gorgeous eyes—*always* turned her on.

"I need to investigate now, but I can't leave until I'm certain you're safe. So, please..."

*Please?* Since when did he use that magic word?

"Stay here. Let the guards protect you. You can have the run of the house. Just don't go outside. I have to know you're safe. If I don't, then I won't be able to concentrate on the work that has to be done."

Her gaze flickered around. The guards seemed to hold their breath. Sebastian's square jaw was locked tight. They were all waiting.

*I'd gotten a tip that something might happen to you.*

As far as she knew, Sebastian had never lied to her. His honesty had often been painful for her, especially on a particular birthday that she did *not* like to remember, but... "I'll stay here."

She saw the stark, savage relief on his face.

"*Only* until you get back," Alyssa added quickly. "You go talk to the cops. See if we can get this mess sorted out. Then, when you're done, I expect to go home."

"Of course." A nod. "When it's sorted out, you can go home. Deal."

Wait. That had been too fast. "Sebastian—"

He was running for the door. "Guard her with your fucking lives."

The door slammed shut.

The guards stared at her.

She stared back at them. A terrible thought struck her. "Oh, God. Does he do this a lot?"

One of the guards tilted his head. "Do what?"

Her hands fluttered toward him. "Bring home random women. Get you two to guard them while he runs away."

"Nope," the guard replied cheerfully. "You're the first."

Was that good? Or bad?

# CHAPTER THREE

"Finally came back to the scene of the crime, did you?" Detective Winston Lewis asked as he put his hands on his hips. The movement pulled back his shirt and managed to show both the badge that was clipped to the pocket of his jeans *and* the gun holster beneath his arm. "And here I thought we'd need to track you down."

"I had to take care of an important matter." The place was a freaking zoo. Reporters were everywhere, and all of the folks who had been in the theater before seemed to have already spilled outside. Most of them were filming with their phones.

"Would that important matter by any chance involve Alyssa Kyle?"

Sebastian heaved out a long sigh. "You know it did." He spared a glance for Isaac Swain. The jerk was running his mouth as fast as he could to the uniformed cop beside him. "Guessing Isaac mentioned me?"

"Didn't have to. You're quite the recognizable figure, you know. Probably because you like to put your crazy ass in front of every camera you can find."

Sebastian's arms crossed over his chest. "The cameras are rolling now, and, unfortunately, both of our asses are on them."

Winston shrugged. "That's the way of it. Especially when someone like you is involved in a shooting."

"Okay, Winston, cut me some slack." Sebastian's voice lowered as he edged closer to the detective—and a guy who just happened to be one of his closest friends. "It was *Alyssa*. Someone shot at her. What did you think I was gonna do? Just stand around with her in the street and let the dick try again? I got her out of here as fast as I could. I had to protect her."

Winston rocked back on his heels. "I saw the video footage."

"Street cams? You've already recovered—"

"Got this footage from the helpful folks at the theater. They have lots of security cameras around the building. So I was able to see the whole scene go down." A street lamp glowed overhead, revealing the grimness in Winston's dark eyes and on his face. "Alyssa was lucky."

"Did you see the shooter? Was he in the footage, too?"

"No, but I know where he was when the shots were fired." He turned and pointed to the opposite street corner. "No cameras reached over there, but based on the angle of the bullets and their entry into first the sign, then the building, my team figures he must have been there." His arm fell back to his side. "I saw the bullets miss her, then I saw you grab Alyssa and toss her into your limo. Just like that, you two were gone."

Winston's gaze swung back to Sebastian. "Where is Alyssa right now?"

"My place."

Winston whistled.

"What? Why the hell are you doing that?" Whistles from Winston were bad.

"Why is Alyssa at your place?"

"Because I wanted her *safe*." He looked to the left and saw Isaac pointing at him. Sebastian pointed back with his middle finger. Then he focused on Winston once more. "I have great security at my home. And I left two guards with her. No one will be getting to her tonight."

"Is that a possibility? You think this wasn't a random attack? You think someone was specifically targeting Alyssa?"

*Tread carefully.* "You saw the footage. What did you think?"

Winston rolled his shoulders. Then he gave Sebastian a congenial smile. "I am going to be chief of police here, by the end of the year."

"I know it. Congrats." Every paper in the city had been touting Winston. He was on target to be the youngest chief the city had ever seen. Winston and his mom had emigrated from Jamaica when Winston had been little more than a toddler. His mom had busted ass for him, working hard and doing everything she could to give her son an incredible life. Now that he was grown up, Winston's mission was to make his mother proud.

Sebastian knew he was succeeding at that mission.

"You don't get to be chief by overlooking important facts," Winston informed him.

"I would think not."

"You don't get to be chief by being a dumbass."

"Absolutely not."

"So, my friend, why are you treating me like I'm a dumbass?"

"I—"

"Cut the BS and tell me straight, does this have anything to do with the *other* work that you and Antony are involved with?"

Immediately, Sebastian glanced around. "I need you to not say that shit in public," he growled.

"And I need you to answer the question."

"Dammit, maybe, okay? I need to talk with Antony and figure out more."

Winston whistled. "Is your maybe actually a yes?"

"It...I got a text from Antony, all right? He said he was in trouble and for me to look out for Alyssa, so that's what I'm doing. I'm helping a friend. I'm protecting his sister. I'm—"

"Moving Alyssa into your home?" There was a whole world of meaning in those careful words.

"I have her there just for the night. Just long enough for me to figure out what is happening," he gritted. "Stop trying to make this into something else."

Winston blinked. "It's an attempted murder investigation, why would I possibly make it into anything else? Isn't that more than enough? Or is there something you need to tell me about? You know, something that involves you getting Alyssa into your bed—I mean, your home for the night."

Sebastian gave him a look of disgust. "If I didn't like you, I'd hate you right now."

"Ah, the way Alyssa hates you?"

That was just insulting. "First, she doesn't hate me. And second, I have got to stop oversharing with you when we have guy night."

Winston rubbed his chin. "Since when doesn't she hate you? Because I specifically remember you telling me that Alyssa Kyle hated your guts with a passion." He jerked his chin toward a still-talking Isaac. "But, a few minutes ago, I had that fellow Isaac over there telling me that you interrupted his date like a jealous lover and you dragged Alyssa away from him."

*Back up.* Sebastian's eyes narrowed in suspicion. Was his buddy playing him? "Thought you said Isaac didn't mention me."

"Is that what I said?" Winston seemed to ponder things. "My bad. What I meant was that he told me you stole his date. You know, right before someone tried to shoot Alyssa."

"Protecting her," Sebastian enunciated clearly. "Not stealing. Protecting. That's what I was doing."

"Right." A pause. "By any chance, is this part of *Operation Get Into Alyssa's Good Graces*?"

He scraped a hand over his face. "You would remember that shit."

"Well, you went on about it at length one night. You were going to show her what an awesome guy you were. Going to convince her that you could be counted on. That you were—I believe you called it—uh, hero material?"

"Fuck off."

Winston shook his head. "You can't tell a detective to fuck off. Might make him mad. Might make him cuff you."

"I can tell one of my *best friends* to fuck off when he's pushing too far. And like I explained to you already, Alyssa doesn't hate me."

"How do you know that?"

"Because she told me," Sebastian replied with way too much satisfaction.

"You know, I always thought Operation Get Into Alyssa's Good Graces was really just code for Operation Get Into Alyssa's Pants."

Sebastian surged forward. "It's not like that!"

"It had better not be," Winston said quietly. "Because the last time I looked, you were business partners with her brother. I don't think he'd love to find out that you were screwing his sister. Saying this as one of your *best friends*...maybe having the woman in your home isn't the best idea. Put guards on her, sure, but send her back to her place. It will be a whole lot safer for you that way." What could have been real worry deepened Winston's voice.

The worry caught Sebastian off guard. "Why the sudden concern? Aw, wait, you *do* care—"

"I don't want to see you hurt. I don't want to see Alyssa hurt. The two of you together? That's a recipe for disaster."

*It doesn't have to be. She doesn't hate me. I can keep her safe. I can make this work.* "She doesn't know the kind of danger that she could be facing. *You* don't even know what we could be up against."

"That's because you're a secretive SOB when it comes to your freelance work."

He had to be. "Antony asked me to protect her, and that's exactly what I plan to do." His gaze swept the scene. "I need to be kept in the loop on this investigation. Anything you find out, you'll let me know?"

Winston stared at him.

"Oh, come on. I'm not asking you to break the law—"

"You're asking me to share confidential case information. Yes, yes, that's potentially law breaking. Bending definitely. It's—"

"If you get a suspect, you give me a head's up. Okay? That's all I'm saying." Because he could do plenty of his own investigating through some not-so-necessarily-legal means. He'd gone back to the scene because he knew the cops would be looking for him. The longer he stayed away, the more suspicious things would appear. So he'd gone back for the meet and greet with Winston.

And, shit, how had the guy even remembered *Operation Get Into Alyssa's Good Graces?* Sebastian had been sure that Winston had been drunk off his ass when he'd spilled those details.

*Wait. Maybe I was the one drunk off my ass.* Because Alyssa had been dating that doctor jerk and Antony had mentioned talk of a possible engagement and—*Yep, guilty. I was the drunk one that night.*

Sebastian glanced down at the glowing face of his watch. "I need to get back to her. If you have other questions, call me."

"Oh, I'll have other questions. For you and for her."

Sebastian turned and took a few quick steps—

"Be careful."

He tossed a grin back at his friend. "Worried about me? That is so freaking sweet. Thank you."

Winston didn't smile back. "Watch your ass with her."

*With her.*

Sebastian's grin faded.

"The rest of the world might not know how you feel, but I do. Protect her, fine, do your bit. But be prepared to walk away."

Walk away? From Alyssa? His body tightened. "When she needs me, I'd never walk away." *Never.*

He headed for the limo.

"But what about when she doesn't need you any longer?"

Right the hell then, she *did* need him, and he was going back to her.

*** 

Her phone rang. Alyssa had been staring out at the dark night, her body too tense as she stood in front of the upstairs window in one of Sebastian's *many* guest rooms, and when she heard the quick, hard peal of sound, she jumped.

The phone rang again. Alyssa spun around. When she'd first come into the guest room, she'd ditched her heels and tossed her bag onto the edge of the bed. She grabbed the bag now, fumbling until she got inside and her fingers closed around her phone.

She didn't recognize the number on the screen, but her fingers still swiped across the phone. When her brother traveled for work, he would often call her from different phones, so maybe it was him. "Hello?"

"I missed you."

The voice was low. Rather hard to understand. Had he said *I miss you?* "Antony? Is that you?"

"I missed you," the caller said. The voice was louder. Rougher. Male. And *not Antony*. "But I won't miss next time."

The call ended.

She stared at the screen. Her breath choked in and out. Okay, if that had been a prank call, that shit had not been funny. She immediately dialed the number back. It rang. Once. Twice. Three times.

\*\*\*

When Sebastian slid into the limo, he heard the phone ringing. Since *his* phone was currently in his pocket, the ringing didn't make a whole lot of sense. Then he saw the small phone vibrating on the floorboard. It had been tossed a few feet away from the champagne bucket.

He grabbed the phone. His heart raced as he answered the call. "Hello?" He got ready for a message, an order, something that would change his life. Not like it was the first time his handler had left a burner phone for him to use on a mission.

"Sebastian?"

Alyssa's voice. Most definitely *not* his handler.

"Sebastian? Did you just call me?"

No, he damn well had not called her.

"You called...and said you missed me?"

Ice filled his veins. "Baby, did you just get a phone call from this number?"

A pause. Then..."Did you call me baby?"

Fuck. Yes. "Answer the question."

Another pause. "Yes." Her voice was low. "Someone called me but...his voice wasn't yours. It wasn't Antony's, either."

"What did he say?" Sebastian was searching the limo. Then leaping out. His gaze swept the crowd. His driver was near the front of the vehicle and currently talking to a cop.

"He said that he missed me. But that he wouldn't miss the next time."

Sebastian's gaze jumped to the street sign— the one with three bullet holes in it.

*The bastard is here. He's watching me.*

No, he wasn't just watching. The bastard was taunting Sebastian. He'd called Alyssa, then deliberately left the phone in Sebastian's limo as a message.

*I can get to her. I can get to you.*

Except the SOB was wrong. *You will not hurt her.*

"Are the guards there?" Sebastian demanded.

"Yes, they're downstairs, they—"

"Are they *in* the damn room with you? Can they see you?"

"No, I'm upstairs in a guest room."

*Breathe. She's safe. Breathe.* "I want you to go back downstairs. Stay where the guards can see you. I'll be there as fast as I can."

"Sebastian?" Fear slid into her voice. "What's happening?"

He hated her fear. "Everything is going to be all right. I'll be there before you know it."

He hung up.

Winston hurried toward him. "I thought you were leaving."

"New evidence." Sebastian held up the phone. "Though my prints are now all over it."

The detective frowned at the phone even as he pulled out a small bag from his back pocket. "Learned to keep a spare or two on me, just in case."

"Bastard called Alyssa on this phone. Told her that he was sorry he'd missed her, but that he wouldn't again."

Winston's eyes widened.

"Then he left the phone in the back of my ride. Alyssa called me on it, and I found the phone on the floorboard."

His buddy cursed, low and creatively. Winston's stare cut around the scene. "He's here."

Sebastian looked at the crowd once more. So many people. So many eyes. "He's here now, or at least, he was, a few minutes ago." If the guy was smart, he would have left right after he dropped the phone.

But then again, if the bastard was *really* smart, he never, ever would have made the mistake of coming after Alyssa.

*Because now I'm coming after you.*

"I'll get a check on every camera in the area," Winston told him even as his stare assessed the people hovering nearby. "Maybe one of them caught the guy slipping the phone into your limo."

Maybe. Maybe not. The jerk had avoided the cameras before. "I have to get back to her."

A grim nod from Winston. He'd bagged the phone. "I'll see if we can trace this back to the owner, and we'll go from there." His gaze slid back to Sebastian. "You sure you have Alyssa? Because I can give her police protection. I mean, the phone call pretty much seals the deal, doesn't it? This was no random attack. Someone is after her."

"I have Alyssa." She won't be hurt.

He turned away, but didn't make the mistake of getting back in the limo. Winston would want to search the vehicle, Sebastian knew that. He spoke quickly with the driver, telling him to cooperate fully with the cops, then Sebastian jumped in a taxi.

He wouldn't take the taxi straight back to Alyssa because there was a chance he was being watched. Instead, he gave orders to be deposited at his corporate headquarters. Sebastian kept an extra vehicle there.

Then he sat back and his gaze took in the thick crowd as the taxi drove away.

Was someone in that crowd targeting Alyssa? Was someone trying to hurt her?

If so, the person had made a truly fatal mistake.

Sebastian worked hard not to let the world see who he really was. Beneath the surface, he was cold, hard, and deadly. He didn't mind getting his hands bloody. Hell, he'd done that plenty of times. He could break every rule in the book and smile while he did it.

He wasn't some safe and easy guy. Wasn't the fucking bad boy of tech. That was just an image he'd carefully crafted.

The real man was very, very different.

The real man would not hesitate to do anything necessary in order to protect the people he cared about from harm. And in this world, he wasn't close to many folks. Antony. Winston.

*Alyssa.*

Some asshole had just made the fucking worst mistake of his life.

*If you come after her, then you'd better get ready to face me.*

# CHAPTER FOUR

"You're back!" Alyssa jumped from her chair. Her bare toes immediately curled against the hardwood floor as Sebastian's gaze lasered in on her.

He stood just inside the doorway of his home. His broad shoulders looked huge. He seemed to tower as he stood there, all tall and strong and...she needed to get a grip.

She was practically vibrating as she stared at him, but, dammit, she'd been scared. That whole phone call, the bit about missing her...

What was going on?

The guards approached Sebastian, and he spoke quietly to them. She inched closer as she tried to make out a few of their words.

"...keep watch on perimeter..."

"...all security protocols in place..."

"...her safety is top priority..."

"...I'll fucking dismember anyone who screws up and gets her hurt!"

Alyssa's eyes widened at that last part from Sebastian. Surely, she'd heard wrong. He hadn't just threatened to, ahem, dismember an employee?

The guards hurried out. He shut the door behind them, locked it, then stood there with his back to her and his hands pressed to the wood of the double entrance doors.

Silence stretched. A long, uncomfortable stretch.

She crept a little closer. "I need to get home."

His shoulders stiffened. With his back to her, Sebastian shook his head.

She nodded. Then realized he couldn't see the movement. Crap. What was wrong with her? *It's just because it's been one hell of a night.* Squaring her shoulders, Alyssa marched for him with a determined stride. When he didn't turn at her approach, her hand reached out and touched the middle of his back. "Sebastian, it's time for me to go home."

A shudder worked the length of his body. Then he turned. Her hand slid over him as he turned, moving around his body so that when he faced her, her hand lingered on his chest.

Why was her hand lingering?

Alyssa snatched the lingering hand back and balled it into a fist.

He looked at her balled hand and his expression was all extra broody and dark. "It's really late. You should just stay the night."

Her heart seemed to stop. "You want me...to spend the night...with you?"

His green gaze lifted. She swore that she saw lust burn bright and hot in his stare before he rumbled, "Yes."

Alyssa swallowed. "That's not going to happen." *But I've sure dreamed about it a time or fifty*. You couldn't control the dreams that snuck into your mind late at night. Turned out, her unconscious self was super naughty and X-rated when it came to Sebastian.

"Relax." His sensual lips quirked. "I didn't mean that as an invitation to crawl into my bed."

Her eyes turned to slits. "Of course, you didn't."

"Though, should you be interested..." He let the sentence trail away.

"Obviously, I'm not interested in joining the hordes."

His brow furrowed.

"I am interested in going home, though. You're kind of in my way. You know, literally blocking the door and all as you stand there. So if you could just move aside..." *Hint. Hint.*

He didn't move. "What hordes?"

"You're in my way." She should probably call a taxi.

His head cocked to the right. "Who told you there were hordes? Was it Antony?"

"Still in my way."

"There aren't hordes. I'm very particular about my personal life."

This was one of the worst conversations ever. "I have no interest in hearing about the women you take into your bed."

"Really? I've always been curious as hell about the lucky men who get into yours."

He had not just said that to her.

"Curious. Jealous. Pretty much in the mood to beat the shit out of them." A shrug of one shoulder. "You know how it is."

She shook her head. Alyssa had no idea how it was. She could only gape at him. Her eyes weren't slits any longer. She was sure they'd doubled in size.

"Oh." A nod from Sebastian. "Am I oversharing?"

*You are, yes.*

He scraped a hand over the stubble on his jaw. "Been a fucking long day with lots of unexpected developments. Ignore me. I'm talking bullshit."

"I..." She cleared her throat. "I figured you were just messing with me."

His hand fell. His stare slid slowly over her face. Ever so slowly. Carefully. Tenderly?

She swallowed.

"It's late," Sebastian told her.

It was. He kept mentioning that fact.

"I know it's been a rough night for you," he added in that deep, low voice of his. He eased a little closer to her.

Maybe she should have stepped back, but retreating from Sebastian had never been an option for her. Alyssa held her ground. "It was my first time to have someone shoot at me." She considered the situation. "Hopefully, my first and last time."

"The bastard called you."

Yes, about that... "How did you get his phone?" Her teeth bit into her lower lip as she waited for—

"Don't hurt yourself. It would be a fucking sin to hurt lips as sexy as yours."

She let go of her lower lip. His eyes were on her mouth. She was *definitely* seeing lust in his gaze. Lust—directed at her?

"He left the phone in my limo. Probably his idea of some taunt. I gave the phone to Winston. He's working the case, and he'll let us know what he turns up."

Winston. *Detective Lewis.* Her shoulders relaxed a bit. She liked him. As a detective, he was top notch. As a man, he was one of the real good guys out there.

"Winston said you could get police protection." His eyes were still on her mouth.

"Do I need police protection?" This was way out of her league. Things like this didn't happen to her. She lived a quiet, easy life. She designed custom jewelry pieces, and she sold them on her website. She volunteered at the local animal shelter, she went out on occasional dates, and she hung out with her friends. Drama had never been her drug of choice.

*Quiet and easy. Quiet and—*

"I told him you didn't need police protection because you have me."

*But I don't have you.*

"This place has the best security system in the world. Got my buddy Eric Wilde to wire the home for me after it was built. *And* I have guards outside. If you stay here with me tonight, you'll be safe."

"Is it..." Her stomach had just dropped. "Is it really that serious?" What was she even saying? *Bullets were fired.* God, she was in some sort of frightened denial. Time to face facts. "It wasn't random." It couldn't have been random if the shooter had *called* her. "I wanted it to be a mistake." She had to blink because her vision had just gotten a little blurry.

Sebastian's eyes weren't on her mouth. They'd snapped up to meet her own gaze. He swore and then he—he wrapped his arms around her and pulled her tightly against his body.

"What are you doing?" Alyssa's voice was muffled against him.

"Comforting you." His hold tightened.

"Why?" Again, muffled. But, damn, he smelled good. And he felt good. All warm and strong and solid. Her arms lifted. Snaked up and curled around his waist.

His body hardened even more. "Because I don't like it when tears are in your eyes."

"I didn't cry." She hadn't. She'd blinked away the tears. It was just—she squeezed her eyes shut a moment and held him. "Why would someone want to hurt me?"

"I'll stop him. Don't worry."

She *was* worried. She was also holding fiercely to Sebastian. "It doesn't make sense. What could I have done?"

"Nothing. You haven't done anything."

Her eyes opened. She pulled away and stared up at him. There had been something about his voice... "Sebastian?"

He looked down at her.

Wow. They hadn't been this close to each other since...

Well, the limo. When he'd been sprawled on top of her. And when he'd made that whole joke—

*had to be a joke*—about her kissing him as a thank you. But this was different. This was...

"Stay the night." His words were a sexy rumble that sent a shiver over her. "I'll keep you safe. Tomorrow, we can figure everything else out."

Now she was the one staring at his mouth. She'd often wondered about how he kissed. How it would feel to have his mouth on hers. She'd wondered that, you know, when she wasn't busy hating him.

*Such a liar. You've never hated him.* Even when she probably *should* have hated Sebastian.

So, no, she hadn't been lying earlier when she'd told Sebastian that she didn't hate him.

When it came to Sebastian, her emotions were far more complex than that. Hate would be easy. It was the other stuff that was hard.

"Just stay, Alyssa. You can have any guest room you want. I won't bother you at all."

*What if I want you to bother me?* Because damn if her traitorous toes hadn't just pressed into the hardwood in an effort to lift up her body and get her closer to his mouth. "It would be a mistake."

His eyes flared. "No, Alyssa, it's not safe for—"

"Kissing you would be an absolute mistake, so why am I even thinking about it?" Alyssa continued. She had an unfortunate habit of often saying what she thought. When she was stressed, the truth tended to pop out.

She felt seriously stressed.

"You're thinking about it?" If possible, his voice deepened even more. "You're thinking about what it would be like to have my mouth on yours, my tongue tasting you?"

*Yes. So much yes.*

"Welcome to my world, baby."

His world? He wanted her, too? "Then kiss me." The dare slipped out too fast for her to stop.

His mouth took hers.

Maybe she should have jerked away. Shoved him away. She didn't because the truth was that Alyssa had been wondering how Sebastian would taste for a very long time. So when his lips pressed over hers, she didn't back away. She shot even higher onto her toes and pushed *against* him.

Her mouth opened. His tongue slid past her lips.

And, God...

*Better than dreams.*

He kissed her with a hot, possessive desire that had a moan building in her throat. He tasted her like she was the best wine he'd ever had. He used his tongue and his lips, and he had her arching toward him because she wanted more. So much more. The kind of more that would make her rip off his shirt and forget who she was and why they were so wrong together. The kind that would make her forget everything but how they could feel together.

That had always been her fear.

That his kiss would be so good...she wouldn't care about anything else.

Her breasts were aching, the nipples tight and all eager. She could even feel her panties getting wet. Just from a kiss.

If she responded this way to his mouth on hers, what would happen if their clothes were gone, if he was naked and she was naked and—

"No!" Now she shoved against him. "We are not getting naked."

His breath sawed in and out. His pupils were huge, turning his eyes dark, and the handsome lines of his face seemed savage.

"We are not getting naked," Alyssa repeated as she panted.

"Didn't realize that option was on the table." His voice...*like rough sex.*

She locked her knees. "I was just..." Alyssa licked her lips and tasted him. *Oh, God. I tasted him.* "I was letting it be known that wasn't going to happen."

"Pity. Getting you naked is pretty much item one on my top ten dream list."

"What?" Shock ripped through her. He fantasized about her? Was that what he was saying?

"Fuck." His eyes squeezed shut. "Ignore me. I'm a horny bastard, and you need to go to bed with me."

"What?"

His eyes flew back open. "I mean, you need to go to bed *alone.* I said alone the first time, you just misheard me."

Her heart was about to burst out of her chest. "It's the adrenaline."

He swallowed. She saw his hands clench and release. Clench and release. "There is a whole lot of adrenaline going on," he muttered.

Adrenaline. Lust. Fear. She spun on her heel. "Fine. I will stay the night." She was practically running for the stairs. "Just because things are crazy. Because someone shot at me, and I think it's only smart to stay in a secure environment until we find out more." Her words were flying out now. She grabbed for the bannister.

"Alyssa."

The way the man said her name...She had to lock her knees again. She'd never had to deal with an adrenaline rush like this before. Normally, the wildest thing she did was ride a roller coaster every now and then. But even when she did that, she would scream her way through the ride.

Tonight...this was a thousand times more intense than a roller coaster. Her whole body was quivering. Her heart racing. Her breath heaving...

Her sex quivering.

Her breasts aching...

Wait...those last two didn't come from adrenaline rushes. They came from...

Alyssa cast a horrified glance over her shoulder.

*They came because I want him.*

"Why did you kiss me?" Sebastian asked her.

"Why did you kiss me?" Alyssa threw right back. Oh, no. She shouldn't have said that. *Take control of the situation.* "Adrenaline," she announced, hoping her voice was crisp and not sultry. Even to her own ears, though, it sounded sultry. Huge difference between crisp and sultry.

"I was riding an adrenaline high, and I acted impulsively. Didn't mean anything."

A nod. "Right. Didn't mean anything. Of course, not." His voice *was* crisp. No, it was flat. Unemotional.

Her hand slid over the bannister. "Besides, I thought you wanted a thank you kiss."

His head tilted as he studied her.

"Back in the limo, didn't you ask for one?"

"I want a hell of a lot." Now his voice was rougher than she'd ever heard it before. "If I ask for everything I want, will you give it to me?"

A shiver slid over her. She should get up the stairs. Go in the guest room that she'd hid in earlier. Lock the door. Sleep this shit off. Instead... "You didn't tell me why you kissed *me*."

He lifted one eyebrow.

"I answered the question. You didn't."

"But you lied, Alyssa. Does a lie count as an answer?"

"I most certainly did *not*—"

"I kissed you because I've wanted that sexy as hell mouth of yours beneath mine for a long time, and I doubted the opportunity would present itself again. Like I told you in the limo, I wanted to see how you'd taste."

He—

"By the way, you are one fucking fantastic kisser. That thing you did with your tongue...and then the way you sucked my lower lip...*damn*."

Her cheeks burned. "You're teasing me." Making her into a joke.

He walked toward her. Slow. Steady steps. "I'm dead serious. Your kiss was so hot that I need an ice shower."

Her breath sawed out again. *I need one, too.*

"So how about we make a deal? You feel any other adrenaline spikes, and you want to work them from your system, then you come right to me. *Only* me. Because I will be more than happy to help you out."

He wasn't serious. Obviously. Shaking her head, she climbed the stairs.

She didn't look back.

\*\*\*

He couldn't look away.

Sebastian's gaze was glued to Alyssa as she headed up the stairs. Her feet were bare, her legs were sinful perfection, and the black dress slid over her skin like silk.

He could still taste her.

Still feel her against him.

Sure, he'd wondered about kissing her before. But he'd sworn he wouldn't do it. He owed Antony far more than he could ever repay. No one knew about how their unlikely friendship had started, no one knew that Antony had changed Sebastian's life.

And he'd *promised*. He'd vowed not to put his hands on her.

*Unless she asked for them.* Tonight, she'd asked for his kiss. He'd given it to her, and his control had gone down in flames. He'd always known that Alyssa would be lethal to him. He just hadn't realized he'd enjoy the danger of her so very much.

She was at the top of the stairs now. He was still staring after her like some kind of obsessed idiot. The thick carpeting upstairs swallowed the sound of her footsteps as she strode for one of the guest rooms.

He had her in his house. She'd be safe.

Provided, of course, he could keep his hands off her. Because if he gave in to the dark desire he felt for Alyssa, *safe* was the last thing she'd be.

One kiss...and he was ready to kill for her.

One fuck...damn, who the hell knew what he'd do for her then?

Good thing they weren't going to find out. Good thing he'd given his promise to Antony.

*Unless she asks for me...*

Not like Alyssa was going to ask him to fuck her.

But if she did...

"I need the freaking ice shower," Sebastian muttered.

# CHAPTER FIVE

"Damn. You are beautiful in the morning."

She nearly spat out her orange juice when Sebastian's deep, rumbling voice sounded from right behind her. She hadn't heard him approach. Alyssa whipped around toward him.

"Oh, look at that." He smiled. Dimples flashed. "Even more beautiful from this angle."

She put her orange juice down on his gleaming, white kitchen countertop. "Did you just basically tell me that my ass was beautiful in the morning?"

His grin stretched a bit. "It was my first view."

"You're a bastard."

He shrugged one bare shoulder. Bare because he wasn't wearing a shirt. He was clad only in a pair of jogging shorts and some sneakers and sweat coated his body. She could see his rock-hard abs. So many abs. Glistening, muscled—

"Do you like your view, Alyssa?"

*Please don't let me be drooling.* She sniffed. Her gaze rose. "I like my view from home, thanks so much. It's a view that I intend to see again very soon."

His eyes narrowed.

Oh, did he not like her answer? Too bad. She motioned toward him. "Guess you've been working out." Unless you did some other activity that caused you to be half naked and sweaty, and, nope, I do not want to think about you doing that activity.

But, too late, because now she had a mental image of him, naked, arms braced on either side of her head as he stared down at her. His face would be locked into hard lines of desire as he drove in and out, in and—

"You okay? You look flushed."

Sweet hell. She grabbed her orange juice again. Drained it. "Fine. Just need to head home." Alyssa blew out a breath and put the glass back down. "Though it will totally look to my neighbors as if I'm pulling a walk of shame."

Silence.

She wiggled her brows. "You know, because I'm in this dress from last night. Coming back home the next day, still wearing the same dress that I left with on my date...it looks like—"

"I know what a walk of shame is."

"Of course, you do. You—"

"Do *not* say that I probably take a ton of them. I don't. This obsession you have with inventing lovers for me has got to stop."

Her mouth opened, but Alyssa couldn't think of something to say.

He headed around her. Opened the fridge. Took out some water and began chugging it. Her gaze slid to the strong column of his throat. Then she noticed a dot of sweat sliding down, down his chest, down, down...

What are you doing? Stop it! "I'm sorry."

He stopped chugging. Put the water back in the fridge. Shut the door. Then Sebastian frowned at her. "For what?"

"For getting into your business. For seeming judgey. For prying." Her hand fluttered back and forth between them like some kind of drunk bird. "Not my business. It is not at all my business who you sleep with."

He absorbed that. "Did you sleep with Isaac?"

"*What?* No, that was our first date. I don't sleep with guys on the first date, thank you very much for asking."

A nod. "Good to know. So, when we go out on our *second* date, will you sleep with me?"

Alyssa gaped at him.

"Is that a yes? Or a maybe?"

"You don't want to sleep with me."

He lifted an eyebrow.

"The kiss last night was a mistake. It was late. The day was crazy. Let's forget the kiss ever happened."

Sebastian glanced away. "Can't promise that," he mumbled.

She'd misunderstood. "What?"

He looked back at her. "How about I take you to your place so you can pick up a change of clothes?"

Alyssa had a better idea. "How about you just take me to my place and drop me off? Because I'll be fine there. I have a security system, too, you know."

"Not one as good as mine."

"That's because I'm not some kind of Batman-like billionaire with my own bat cave. You and I both know Isaac was not too far off with that charge."

His lips quirked. "You can always make me smile."

And his smile always made her stomach do a little flip.

"Look," she ignored the flip and plowed on, "I just need to get home. Get to my stuff. I'll stop looking like a late-night party animal—"

"You look beautiful, not like a party animal."

"I am wearing zero make-up. My hair probably appears to have squirrels living in it—"

Again, that twitch of his lips. "No, it looks more...sexy. Tousled. Like your lover ran his fingers through it last night."

She looked up at the ceiling because it felt too awkward to stare in his eyes when he was telling her things like that. "I'll call Detective Lewis—Winston. Find out what he knows about the shooting. If he offered police protection last night, then maybe I can get some patrols to sweep past my home over the next few days." She'd given this matter a whole lot of thought while she'd tossed and turned during the night. "I'll be fine."

"No."

Her gaze lowered. Met his.

He glared. "No."

"Why are you telling me no? This is my life, and my decision."

"I—" He stopped. "I want you safe."

"Trust me, I want to be safe. So I'll be careful." Something was nagging at her, though. "Last night, you told me that you got a tip that something might happen to me. That was the reason you came to get me at the theater." But she still didn't know exactly how he'd figured out that she was *at* the theater.

He nodded.

"Was it a call, like the one I received?"

His face hardened. "I got a text."

"Are the cops trying to trace it?"

Sebastian straightened. "Let me get showered and dressed, and I'll take you to pick up your clothes."

Unnecessary. "I can call a taxi."

His brows lowered. "Five minutes, that's all I need, and I'll take you to pick up your clothes," he said again.

It would take longer than five minutes for the taxi to arrive. Heck, she'd be lucky if a taxi arrived in the next thirty minutes. "Fine. I'll just eat my way through your supply of chocolate chip muffins." She grabbed a muffin as he passed her. "They're my favorite, so it won't be my fault when I eat them all."

He paused for a moment. "Of course, they're your favorite. Why do you think I had them brought in this morning? Eat every fucking one. They're all for you."

He...

He was gone.

And she was gripping a warm, soft, chocolate chip muffin. A muffin that—now that she actually looked at it and its fluffy goodness—that muffin *must* have come from her favorite bakery in town. There was no mistaking it.

But how had Sebastian known that she loved that particular bakery?

How had he known that chocolate chip muffins were her favorite?

She took a bite, moaned and wondered...*what else does he know about me?*

\*\*\*

"The first thing you need to do is stop hiding the key under your damn rock," Sebastian ordered as he bent and reached into the little flower garden near Alyssa's front door. A pudgy gnome winked at him as Sebastian picked up the rock and slid its false bottom to the side. "That is like begging for thieves to walk right in your home." He tossed the rock back into place and looked up to find Alyssa frowning at him. "What?"

"How did you know my spare key was hidden there?"

"Seriously? It's an obvious spot." He would be keeping the key. No sense leaving it for bad guys to find.

"What else do you know?"

She was being all suspicious. This was probably not the time to tell her...*A whole damn lot.*

"Sebastian?"

He freaking loved it when she said his name. He'd love it even more if she screamed it or moaned it. He exhaled slowly. "I know that your alarm code is your favorite holiday."

Her eyes widened.

He leaned in close. "Fourth of July." God, he wanted her mouth again. "Because you like the fireworks so much, and you also enjoy sweet apple pie."

"How—" Alyssa swallowed. "You seem to know a lot about me."

*You have no idea.*

From the corner of his eye, he spied her neighbor craning to get a look at them. Since he knew Alyssa hadn't been keen to the idea of people seeing her in the dress—*walk of shame, my ass, she never needs to be ashamed of anything*—Sebastian casually moved his body to block the lady's view.

Sebastian unlocked the door. Muttering, Alyssa hurried inside and typed in her security code—yep, Fourth of July—and then she kicked off her shoes.

He followed her in and, as usual when he was at Alyssa's place, some of the tension slid from his body. Her home was so damn warm. Cozy. Happy?

Her furniture was comfortable. Vivid, framed and giant photos of the area lined her walls. Photos of all the amazing waterfalls that he knew she loved. Most weekends, she slipped away to hike those falls. Her home was full of color and character. Bookshelves overflowed and a bright red throw was tossed over her couch.

"I'll be right back," Alyssa promised as she disappeared down the hallway.

He headed for the nearest bookshelf. Not like Alyssa invited him to her place often, so he liked to check for new things when he did get the chance to slip inside her home. Usually, he tagged over when Antony gave him an off-hand invite, like for an occasional game night or—

"Sebastian!"

He whipped around and ran toward the sound of Alyssa's shout. He reached her bedroom and threw open the door. He—

She spun toward him. All of the color had drained from her face, and he had never, *ever* seen Alyssa look so pale.

"I...I think he knew my security code, too," she whispered. "And I guess he knew where I kept that extra key."

Sebastian glanced over her shoulder. Saw the red spray paint on her wall. Saw the message.

*I will kill you.*

"The fuck you will," he snarled. He grabbed Alyssa's hand and pulled her close. "You're coming with me."

"But—"

"He could be watching." *He could be fucking here.* "Come with me." He stared into her terrified eyes. *Hated* her fear. Wanted to destroy the person who'd made her afraid. "Trust me. I will keep you safe."

She swallowed. "Okay."

Okay? His body shuddered as her fingers curled around his. Alyssa had just given him her trust. Her faith.

He knew precisely how precious the gift was. He would not let her down.

\*\*\*

"The neighbors didn't see anything," Winston announced as the detective paced in Sebastian's den. "I'm betting the perp came by under the cover of night. Got in, got out, and no one was the wiser."

"What if she'd been there?" The thought made Sebastian want to drive his fist into a wall.

Winston stopped pacing. "She wasn't."

"She wanted to go home last night. I was basically a dick, and I insisted she stay here. She wanted to leave—"

"Then she owes you. Consider this a solid point for *Operation*—"

"Stop," he snapped.

Winston frowned at him. "She's all right, man. Take a breath. The woman is upstairs right now. She's changing into some of the clothes I brought over. She is safe." He edged closer to Sebastian. "I've never seen you like this. Usually you're rock steady."

Sebastian yanked a hand through his hair. "Yeah, well, usually, Alyssa is safe." *I will kill you.* "He was in her house. In her bedroom. If she'd been alone—"

"Stop it," Winston ordered as his voice roughened. "There is never any good that comes from playing the 'What if' game. You will only drive yourself crazy as you imagine every bad situation that could go down."

He'd already imagined plenty. His body burned with rage. *In her home. In her bedroom.*

"Alyssa is safe," Winston repeated. "You have her."

Sebastian's head moved in a jerky nod. "Damn right I do."

"And I'm guessing you're keeping her?"

"Ahem."

He'd heard Alyssa's approach. The soft tread of her steps. But Sebastian had kept his head averted because he didn't want her to see the blazing fury on his face. But when she cleared her throat and made her very deliberate *ahem*—

His head swiveled toward her.

She'd dressed in white tennis shoes, jeans that hugged her hips, and a sexy white top that exposed part of her midriff and made him want to drop to his knees, put his mouth on that sweet skin and—

"I'm not his to keep."

*Oh, the fuck you aren't*—

Her gaze locked with Sebastian's. "I'm not yours."

*But I've always wanted you to be.*

He couldn't quite manage speech. He mostly wanted to growl and snarl and carry her back upstairs so that he could lock her in the guest room and keep her safe from whoever the hell wanted to hurt her. Maybe he could get locked in that room with her and explore every inch of her tempting body.

"So..." Winston cleared his throat. "How are you doing, Alyssa?"

"I've been better. A lot better."

On the days when someone wasn't terrorizing her.

Sebastian tried mentally counting. Maybe that would calm his ass down. He got to ten and realized, nope, not helping.

"Why is someone doing this to me?" Alyssa asked. Her voice was strained.

Winston headed toward her and gave her a comforting pat on the shoulder. "I'm not sure, but I will find out."

Sebastian didn't move, even though he wanted to be the one comforting Alyssa. He wanted to pull her into his arms and never let go.

Probably not the best plan at the moment.

"Do you have any enemies?" Winston asked her. "Anyone you can think of who might want you hurt?"

"No. I mean, I'm not a saint or anything, but I can't think of anyone I've pissed off so much that the person wants to kill me!"

"No exes who couldn't let go? No one who gave you trouble and made you feel nervous?"

Sebastian lurched forward.

"No." Alyssa shook her head. "I haven't dated anyone seriously for a while."

Winston pulled out a small notebook from his pocket. The guy liked to be old school with his little notebooks. "What about Isaac Swain? You were with him at the theater, weren't you?"

"Yes, but that was our first date."

"First and last," Sebastian clarified.

Winston frowned at him.

"What?" Sebastian demanded defensively. "She didn't like him. Guy got on her nerves. She was *glad* when I showed up. I could see the relief on Alyssa's face."

Winston's attention shifted back to Alyssa.

She rolled one shoulder. "Yes, I might have been glad. But then Sebastian told me that he'd gotten some text saying I was being targeted." She hurried toward Sebastian. "Why contact you first? That keeps bugging me. Why go to you and say that I'm in danger? I don't mean anything to you."

"You're wrong." *You mean everything.*

She wrapped her arms around her stomach as she stood less than a foot away from him. "I tried to call my brother last night. I couldn't get hold of him."

*Yeah, about that...*

Winston lifted a brow and stared knowingly at Sebastian.

*Shit. This is gonna be a hard conversation.*

"I'm worried about him," Alyssa added. "What if he's targeted, too?"

*Quite possible.*

"And my parents?" Her voice rose. "They could be in danger!"

He had to touch her. His hands curled around her shoulders. "They're okay."

"How do you know? I couldn't reach them either—"

"That's because they are in freaking Antarctica, and you know how hard phone communication is down there. Half the time, the satellite phones are on the fritz."

She swallowed.

"I made sure they were okay." Her parents were some of the most brilliant scientists that he'd ever encountered, and they were currently completing a six-week stay in a research lab at what he'd heard Alyssa accurately describe as "the ends of the earth" a few times. "I checked in via email earlier. They are good. They'll take extra precautions, but, seriously, sweet—um, Alyssa..."

Her gaze sharpened.

"No one can get to them. It's not like you can just take a train to where they are."

"Did you tell them about the shooting?"

Now he hedged a bit. "I told them that there was some trouble here and that I was looking after you."

Beneath his hands, he felt her shoulders tense, but she said, "Good. I don't want them worrying. It's not like they can do a lot to help when they're so far away."

He rubbed her shoulders.

And caught a knowing glance from Winston.

Sebastian snatched his hands away from her. He shoved them behind his back.

Alyssa turned to face Winston, and as she did, she moved her body a bit closer to Sebastian's. Her arm brushed against his. "What happens next?"

"I have a team still gathering evidence from your home. I'm sorry, but it's a crime scene right now. I brought some clothing and essentials to you because the place is going to be off-limits for a while."

"Thank you." She fiddled with the edge of her shirt. "I appreciated getting out of my date dress." Her hands dropped. "If my home is off-limits, then maybe I should move into Antony's condo for a while. He's got good security there."

Sebastian eased a step back, moving out of Alyssa's line of vision, and he gave several hard, negative shakes of his head. *Bad plan,* he mouthed to Winston.

"About that..." Winston pursed his lips as if he were thinking over the matter. "Why not stay here? If you're with Sebastian, then you won't be alone. We both know he has top-of-the-line security at this place."

Sebastian nodded.

Alyssa's head whipped toward him.

He kept nodding. "Excellent idea, Winston. Great suggestion."

He could see the suspicion on Alyssa's face. He also saw—

Her refusal even before Alyssa said, "That can't happen."

*Yeah, it can.*

"I don't want to be a burden to Sebastian."

"You never would be," he denied immediately. It was the truth.

Her lips parted.

"I have plenty of room here. I've got great security. Hell, I've got great security *guards*, too. While Winston is investigating the case, it makes perfect sense for you to stay with me. Total done deal."

"It's *not* a done deal."

Winston coughed.

Their gazes flew to him. He smiled. "Hi, there."

*Come on, buddy, back me up.*

"Alyssa, I can offer you police protection, if you'd like. We even have a number of safe houses in the area. I can see about getting you set up in one of those."

*Oh, man, seriously? You're going to do me like this? Fine.* Voice hard, Sebastian demanded, "Would you truly feel safer with a stranger guarding you in some dank safe house, Alyssa?"

Winston stiffened. "Dank?"

Sebastian kept this focus on Alyssa. "I told your brother I would look after you, and that's exactly what I intend to do."

"Wait—you talked to my brother?"

*Whoops.* But, shit, she needed to know the truth. Or, as much of it as he could provide to her. Otherwise, she'd be running for a safe house with Winston, and then how was he supposed to keep watch over her? "Yes," Sebastian drew out the word. "But I'm afraid he's now out of contact."

A furrow appeared between her brows. "What did he say?"

*Cover blown. Protect my sister. Do anything necessary.* "You know, the usual. That he was glad I was around to take care of you."

Her brow crinkled.

"That he appreciated my efforts. That he'd get back to the US as soon as he could."

"He's still working on that gaming distribution in Russia?"

"Um..." That *had* been the cover story they'd circulated about Antony's trip. "Look, I'll tell you everything in a little bit, okay? But first, give the good detective your assurance that you're safe, and he can be on his way. He has lots of things to investigate."

"Lots," Winston agreed, deadpan. "Like that extra house key of yours, Alyssa. I need to give it to my crime scene team. Though since Sebastian apparently likes to touch all kinds of evidence, I'm sure I'll be turning up his prints on it."

That was just insulting. He didn't like to touch *all* kinds of evidence. Just some. "I didn't know it was fucking evidence at the time."

Winston smirked at him. "First the phone. Then the key. What's next?"

*Next, I want to get my hands on the bastard who is doing this. I want to beat the hell out of him.*

Winston turned his attention to Alyssa, and his smirk morphed to real concern. "What's next?" he said again. "The choice is yours, Alyssa."

Alyssa hesitated. She sucked on her lower lip. Her gaze met Sebastian's. Lingered.

Sebastian's cock shoved hard at the front of his jeans. He was such a bastard.

"Are you sure I won't inconvenience you?" Her voice was very careful.

"Not even a little bit." He didn't look away. "If you're not here, I'd just worry myself to death, anyway. So you're helping me out."

"You'd really worry about me that much?"

"Absolutely."

She glanced toward Winston.

"He *does* have good security," Winston allowed.

*Thank you for finally backing me up!*

"Though our safe houses are hardly what you'd call dank."

*Agree to disagree.* When he'd been a punk-ass teen, Sebastian had spent far too much time being shuttled around in those pits.

"I'm sure the investigation will be wrapped up quickly," Alyssa continued. Sebastian wondered if she was trying to reassure herself with that line. Probably. "Okay." She nodded decisively. "I'll stay with Sebastian, but we are going to establish rules. Firm rules."

He sighed. "Why? They just suck the fun out of everything."

For a moment, her eyes seemed to gleam. He stopped breathing. He liked it so much when her eyes lit up and a faint smile would tease the corners of her mouth and—

Winston waved his hand near Sebastian's face. "Yo. I'm leaving. Walk me out."

Dammit. He'd been caught gaping at her. Sebastian shoved back his shoulders and inclined his head to Alyssa. "Start mentally making your rules. We'll go over the list when I come back." He marched out, keeping his stride all strong and aggressive, but as soon as they were outside—

"Oh, man, you are so in over your head," Winston said, voice almost pitying.

Sebastian wasn't in the mood for pity. "I've got this."

"You were practically drooling over her. There is no way you'll keep your hands off that woman if she is sleeping in your house."

He didn't disagree.

"Can you keep her safe when you're so tangled up in her? Serious question. I need to know because if you can't—"

"No one is going to hurt her. I would kill before that happened."

Winston blinked. "You're not supposed to tell a detective that you're ready to kill people."

"I didn't tell a detective. I told my friend."

"You are always pulling this shit with me."

He was. "I'll try to be better."

"You are lying."

Maybe. "I have to tell her."

"Good. It's about time." A firm nod from Winston. "Just begin by saying that it's not some fleeting emotion, that you've felt this way for years and—"

"Not that." He grabbed Winston's arm and hauled him away from the house. "And, Jesus, lower your voice, would you? I have to tell her about the side business I do with Antony."

Winston whistled. "That will not go well."

"Yeah, well, she's in the middle of this mess." *His* mess. "She needs to know what she's dealing with and why cops might not be the best choice to keep her safe." A pause. "No offense because you are definitely not an ordinary cop."

"Damn straight, I'm not. I'm the best there is." Winston released a long breath. "Your big reveal is going to blow up in your face. Probably going to make her super angry with you."

"Yes, and that's why I'm not telling her until you're gone. I don't want her changing her mind and trying to leave with you as she hitches a ride to your safe house."

"My *dank* safe house."

Winston wasn't going to let that one go. "You know some of those places the PD uses are holes in the wall."

"Because they are *hidden*. They are supposed to be low profile." He gestured toward Sebastian's house. "Not like it's supposed to be lifestyles of the rich and assholey."

"I love you, too, man."

Winston laughed. "Watch your ass. Watch her ass."

"Always."

"But, listen, if you get intel I can use—not your classified BS, but real, usable intel—you call me, got it? Because this is my city, and I don't care if you are playing spy, you tell me when things threaten my people."

He wasn't playing spy. He'd never played. "Got it."

Sebastian watched Winston hurry to his waiting car. Guards were on the perimeter of the property, and he nodded to them. Then he turned and headed back into the house.

*Your big reveal is going to blow up in your face. Probably going to make her super angry with you.*

Super angry? Nah. More like enraged.

And maybe...hurt?

Damn, he didn't want Alyssa to be hurt. But when she learned the truth, when she learned that he and her brother had been lying to her for years, Sebastian knew she'd probably explode with fury *and* be hurt.

He squared his shoulders. There was no escaping this reveal. Time to face the music. He headed for the den, but Alyssa wasn't in there. A quick search showed him that she was in the kitchen. She stood in the middle of the gourmet setup, and her short, unpainted nails tapped on the granite top of the island he'd recently had installed.

For a moment, he just stared at her. *My favorite view.* She had been since the first moment he'd seen her. Sebastian's hands sank into the back pockets of his jeans as he rocked forward onto the balls of his feet.

He could stare at her for hours and be a happy man.

Then her head turned. Her gaze lifted and met his. That dark stare of hers hit him with the force of a punch and stole his breath.

He'd had the same reaction the first time he'd seen her.

"I want to know what's happening," Alyssa told him. "Tell me everything."

A slow sigh slipped from his lips. "Have you ever heard the expression...you should be careful what you wish for?"

"I'm not wishing for anything. I'm asking for the truth. *Tell me.*"

"Fine. But when I'm done, promise that you won't run from me, okay?"

"Run?"

"Um, yes, promise you won't run." Though if you did, baby, I'd chase you. I think I'd follow you anywhere.

# CHAPTER SIX

He wanted her to promise not to run? Alyssa blinked. Then she laughed. A nervous, shaky laugh. Mostly because she felt extremely nervous and shaky. "It's not a time for jokes."

Sebastian didn't flash his dimples at her. "I wasn't joking." He strode toward her, all tall, muscled and lethal. He'd always moved with a silent, almost scary grace. You didn't hear his steps, didn't even know he was there, not until he wanted you to know.

Her shoulders stiffened as he approached. She was on one side of the kitchen island. He stopped on the other. Stared at her.

The tension stretched, and it made her even more nervous. "I think we can stop drawing the moment out," she muttered. "Just tell me already because I am imagining a thousand things in my head right now, and every single thing I think of is very, very bad—"

"I'm a spy."

Her eyebrows shot up.

"So is your brother."

She shook her head.

"And his cover has been blown. His enemies know about you, and I have to keep you safe until we can get the situation contained." Sebastian nodded. Expelled a rough breath. "Okay. I think that's done." He started to turn away.

She half-leapt over the island, shoving her body across the granite top, and grabbed his arm. "That's not funny."

Sebastian turned back toward her.

She let go of his arm. Eased back onto her side of the island. "I want a *real* explanation. Not some bullshit." Anger churned inside of her. "Why the hell can't you be serious about this? Someone shot at me. Someone broke into my home. Someone—"

"I assure you," there was still no sign of the dimples and she didn't think she'd ever seen his green gaze be so flat and hard, "I'm dead serious. When it comes to your safety, I don't play."

"You're telling me some bunch of BS about my brother being a spy."

A nod.

"About *you* being a spy—"

Another nod.

She growled. The sound was animalistic and angry. Exactly how she felt. Her hands fisted. "My brother is a gaming designer. He spends every free moment working on his tech. *You* are a gaming designer. Yes, you've made spy games for folks to play, but this isn't a game. This is real life, this is—"

His hand flew over the island. Caught one of her fists. "I'm not playing anything. I'm telling you...your brother is a spy. So am I."

"This is ridiculous! I should have left with Winston—"

"I've been working for the government since I was barely eighteen years old. It was either work for them or get my ass tossed in a cell. I'm not a big fan of prison jumpsuits and being locked behind bars, so I played ball with them. Put my shady talents to good use, so to speak."

Her heart raced in her chest.

"I was a hacker as a kid. It was the only way I could..." His gaze jerked away as Sebastian seemed to try and collect his thoughts. "I could do anything with a computer. Much like your brother." Now his stare slowly swept back to her. "I recruited him. I'm sorry about that. Didn't even know what it would do to us both..."

She shook her head.

His fingers slid along her inner wrist. "It's true, all right? The government recruits all the time from college campuses. Young, smart, eager...shit, it's like a perfect checklist for them. I knew what they were looking for—and I found the ideal recruit in Antony. I brought him in. He and I worked cases together. When we studied abroad our junior year, hell, that was just a cover, it was—"

"Stop."

He stopped talking. His fingers didn't stop caressing her wrist. Soft. Careful.

Her breath hitched. "You own a gaming business with my brother. You have Shark Gaming and Design. You...you're gonna take a bite—"

"Out of the industry," he finished their motto softly. "The business is real. Everything we've created there is real. All our designs are legit. But Shark is also a cover. It allows us to travel around the world anytime we want under the ruse of marketing or development, when the truth is that we're sometimes going in for some up-close and personal intel collection for Uncle Sam."

She couldn't believe this. Expected it to be a joke. "The government has people." That was a thing, right? A whole cyber tech team someplace? "Why would they need you two? Why—"

"We *are* the people they have. Part of their team. And they need us because sometimes, you can't do the job remotely. Sometimes, you need boots on the ground, you need a body in the fucking room, and you need someone *on site* with the knowledge to get the job done in twenty seconds flat."

Her heartbeat echoed in her ears.

"That someone is me." A roll of his shoulder. "And sometimes, it's your brother."

He was still holding her hand. Her skin felt warm where he touched her. Every other part of her body? *Ice cold.* "Tell me that you're lying."

His gaze glittered.

"Tell me that you're messing with me. Tell me that this is some horrible prank and you don't mean—"

"I mean every word that I've said." Sebastian swallowed. "You weren't supposed to know. Not ever. And you can't tell anyone else, Alyssa. Not even your parents. Swear to me that you won't tell."

Her lips parted, but she didn't promise. Instead, she shook her head. "If Antony's cover is blown, I don't have to tell anyone. People already know!" People who'd come after her?

"I don't know how big this situation is yet. I called Antony's handler—our handler—and he's working on things."

Her brother had a handler?

"If we can eliminate the threat, then Antony may be able to continue the work he's—"

"I need a drink."

Sebastian blinked.

She pulled her hand from his. Stepped back from the island as she put some much needed space between them. "You're a spy."

"Yes."

"My brother is a spy."

"Yes."

"I'm just supposed to take your word for it?"

His head cocked. "Yes?" This time, he made the answer seem like a question.

Alyssa crossed her arms over her chest. "You're a playboy."

"That's hurtful."

"You are in the news constantly."

"I do tend to get my share of headlines," Sebastian modestly confessed.

"That's not low key."

"Hardly." His right hand flattened on the granite top.

"Spies are low key. They don't try to get their faces flashed everywhere—"

"They do if that's their cover. If you're pretending that all you are is some bastard with too much money who likes to party and play hard. If that's what you want the world to see so that your enemies will never know the real man, then that's exactly what a good spy would do."

*The real man.* Oh, God. If he was serious...if everything he was telling her was the truth, if her brother was a spy...

*I don't know Antony at all.*

And...

*I don't know Sebastian at all.*

"Don't," he rasped.

Her breath caught as she stared into his suddenly glittering—and angry—gaze.

"Don't look at me like I'm a stranger."

But... "Aren't you?" *If* she believed this...and, it was crazy. Sebastian, a spy? Her brother, a spy? Antony seemed to stumble around most days, his mind occupied with whatever new tech he was developing. She was supposed to buy that her brother was some kick-ass, super agent who could fight off bad guys?

"I couldn't tell you. Knowing the truth would have just put you at risk."

"I'm sure that's the line Superman gave to Lois back in the day, but it's BS." Her chin notched up.

His nostrils flared.

"You're a spy."

A curt nod.

"And my brother...he's a spy."

"I told you—"

"Where is he? Right now? You talked to him, and I want to talk to—"

"He's gone dark, Alyssa. I tried to reach him, but I can't. He probably ditched his phone right after he texted me. It's standard procedure when your cover is blown. He may not know if he can trust others in the organization. He has to figure out who turned on him."

"But...he contacted you."

"He sent me a text. Told me his cover was blown. Asked me to protect you." He raked a hand through his hair. "And the next thing I knew, someone was shooting at you."

Yes, someone had shot at her. In the next instant, Sebastian had swooped in. Picked her up. Tossed her into the limo and gotten her the hell out of there. "So bad guys want to kill me in order to hurt my brother?"

"Looks that way." He stalked toward her, moving to her side of the island and walking with that silent stealth of his. "But I'm going to keep you safe."

"Because you're a super spy."

He kept heading toward her. "Yes."

"Prove it."

He stopped right in front of her. "Excuse me?"

"Prove that you're a super spy."

"It's not like I carry super spy ID on me, sweet—um, Alyssa."

She stared up into his eyes. "How do I know you're not lying to me?"

"Because the bullets were real. The message at your home was real. The bastard after you is *real*."

"Okay." She swallowed the lump in her throat. "You make some excellent points."

His hand lifted. His knuckles brushed over her cheek.

Alyssa stiffened.

"Don't," he seemed to bite off the word. "Please, don't be afraid of me."

What? "I'm not." Was she supposed to be?

"Then why do you always tense when I touch you?"

"Because I like it too much."

Oh, sweet hell. She had not just told him that embarrassing truth.

But, yes, judging by the way his eyes had widened, she had. "I'd like to take those words back now."

Sebastian shook his head. "That's not going to happen."

"Then I'd like for you to forget I said them."

"That's not going to happen, either."

"Then what is going to happen?"

"You're going to ask me to kiss you."

She laughed. "No, that's—"

"You're going to ask me for *anything* that you want." His gaze was on her mouth. "And I'm going to give it to you."

Why was she breathing hard? Why was she leaning toward him? Why was she thinking way too much about the one kiss they'd already shared? "I'm not your type," Alyssa blurted.

Shit! She had to stop that. Worst habit ever. When stressed...blurt.

"You are exactly my type." He was still staring at her mouth.

"Oh, sure. And that's why you've kept your distance from me all these years."

Now his gaze lifted.

*Lust.*

Need. A consuming desire.

Her heart slammed into her chest with one very powerful *thud*. He'd never looked at her that way. No man had ever looked at her with such wild hunger in his eyes.

"Sometimes, if you don't keep a distance, then you don't keep control." His voice was rough. "With you, I've kept control."

This was some seriously uncharted territory.

"You don't know the real me. You saw the image. The same one everybody else saw. But that image is falling away. Because of what's happening, it has to vanish with you. So now you're going to see me for exactly who I am."

"Why does that sound like an ominous warning?" Her voice was husky, and, oh, jeez, sensual. She wet her lips.

He growled.

She liked that sound far too much. It had a primitive power that sent heat surging through her.

"It's a warning. Because you want the truth about me? The full truth?"

"It *is* what I've been asking for." In case he'd missed that part.

"I want to strip you naked."

What?

"I want to lift you up and drive into you right now. I want to fuck you for hours. No, days. And that would only be the start. Because I've wanted you for so long, the need is almost savage. I'd have to take you over and over again, and, I know that every time I have you, I'll only want you more."

She couldn't breathe. Alyssa was also pretty sure that she'd imagined his words. Instinctively, she shook her head.

His hand fell away. "Right." He backed up a step. "Forgot. I'm in this shit alone. You never felt the same way. Should have kept my mouth shut." A rough laugh. "Chalk it up to some oversharing madness. Don't worry, I know how to keep my hands to myself. Just—you asked for the truth, so I gave it to you." His gaze scorched her. "Or maybe I was just tired of holding back with you." His jaw locked. "I can keep you safe *and* stay away from—"

"How do you know I never felt the same way?" Her heartbeat was so loud. Surely, he heard it.

Sebastian shook his head. "You don't."

"So you're telling me how I feel?"

He winced. "Your brother told me that most days, you hate my guts. On good days, you tolerate me. On bad days—"

"Even on bad days, I fantasize about having sex with you."

His jaw dropped.

"No!" Alyssa slapped a hand over her mouth.

"Say it again."

She was *not* saying anything again. She side-stepped around him. Hurried to get out of the kitchen.

"Because I fantasize about you all of the time, Alyssa. You're in my head. Have been since the day we met, and I can't get you out."

She stopped. Her legs felt absolutely rooted to the spot. His words rushed through her. They pretty much splintered everything that Alyssa had *thought* that she'd known but...

She glanced over her shoulder at him. "You're a spy."

"Yes."

She sucked in a deep breath. "That means you've been lying to me for years."

Did she want a denial? She didn't get one. He simply stared back at her.

"Right." She squared her shoulders. "You lied to me before. You could be lying to me now. How am I supposed to trust anything that you say to me?"

"You think I'm lying about wanting you?"

"I..." God, she was so confused! And scared. And a thousand other things.

"Ask me to kiss you," Sebastian said.

"What?" She whirled to fully face him.

"Ask me to kiss you. Then I'll kiss you, and you'll know exactly how I feel." His hands clenched at his sides.

"This is an insane conversation. Everything that is happening is insane!" She needed some space. She'd go upstairs and have a meltdown in peace, thank you very much. Once more, she spun away.

And once more...

"I've wanted you since the first time I saw you, and that is not a lie."

Her hand rose and pressed to her heart. For some reason, it ached. "Liar." Barely a whisper. So she said it again. Louder. Harder. "Liar."

He didn't make a sound behind her, but she could feel him closing in. "That's not a lie."

*Don't look back at him.* "I'm not some super genius like my brother. Not like my parents," Alyssa spoke the words flatly. "Or even like you." She'd been the one who didn't fit in her super over-achieving family. The wild one who ran barefoot whenever she had a chance and colored on all the walls because she'd wanted to make things look pretty. Not gifted with a sky-high IQ like Antony and her scientist parents. *So different from them.* When she'd been a kid, that knowledge had hurt. No, it had devastated her. She'd always felt lost. Or, worse, like she didn't belong.

"Alyssa—"

"But I'm not a fool. And you know what? I have one very good memory." Certain words in particular had haunted her. Her voice roughened as she added, "'I swear that I will never, ever put my hands on your sister.' Such a fun birthday gift to me. You...announcing your plans."

Behind her, he cursed. Low, savage, and very inventively.

"I'm going upstairs. I need to be alone for a while." Her spine was so straight and stiff that it hurt as she marched forward.

"You forgot the last part."

She hadn't forgotten anything.

"Or maybe," he added softly. "You just walked away before you could hear the rest."

She shouldn't stop.

Why had she stopped?

"Antony said I was wrong for you. He didn't want me—or my hands—anywhere near you. Protective older brother in full effect."

Her brother was protective of her. He also had a tendency to butt in where he didn't belong when it came to her personal life.

"So I told him that I'd keep my hands off…"

Right. An agreement so quickly and easily given. A humiliation that still haunted—

"Unless you asked for my hands to be on you."

Shock rolled through her.

"Because if you ever ask for my hands, for my mouth, for *anything* from me—you'll get it. When you want me, I'm yours."

She didn't move.

"I'm tired of having the woman I want most in the world so close and not doing a damn thing about that desire."

No, no, he was not saying—

"I told you how I feel," he growled. "Now you get to decide what happens next."

What would happen next? Slowly, she turned to face him once more. His eyes seemed to burn with green fire. His jaw was locked tight. His face appeared almost savage with his emotions. He looked wild and rough, and so very different from the man she usually saw. The guy who flashed his dimples and got everything he wanted.

Only he's telling me that I'm what he wants. "You've never said anything before."

"No, I pretty much just watched and wanted in silence." A pause. "And I wanted to kick the asses of the jerks you dated. Hell, when I thought you were going to marry that ER doctor, I nearly lost my shit."

"I wasn't going to marry him. We were just dating. He wanted to move faster. Wanted more than I was ready to give. Didn't feel right." Because...

Because even back then, she'd been fantasizing about Sebastian. Even when she'd known he was wrong for her.

Wrong in so many ways.

And maybe that was why she was so drawn to him. Alyssa nodded. "It's because you can't have what you want."

A faint line appeared between his brows. "I don't understand."

It was a basic psychology thing. People wanted what they couldn't have. Forbid someone from having something? You instantly make the person crave that object more. "You only want me because my brother told you to stay away. It's the whole appeal of forbidden fruit thing. If I was one of the long line of women who surround you so eagerly, you wouldn't care about me. I'm different because you think I'm a challenge. Once the challenge is over, you'll walk away."

His eyes gleamed. "Wanna bet?"

"Is everything a joke to you?" she whispered.

"No. Not everything. You're not. You're also not fucking forbidden fruit. You're the woman I've dreamed about for years, and getting you into bed isn't a challenge. It's more like the freaking end game. Because *you're—*"

An alarm sounded. The ear-piercing shrieks had her flinching as her gaze flew frantically around    the    room.    "Sebastian?    What's happening?"

"Rear of the property. Sensor just caught motion."

Her head jerked back toward him. He'd pulled out his phone and was staring at the screen.

"Some fucking asshole is out there." He tapped a button on his phone and barked, "Close in, now! Get the sonofabitch!" Then he lunged toward the back of the house.

She rushed after him and grabbed his arm. "Stop!"

He frowned back at her.

"You can't run out there! Let your guards handle it! You're not—um, you're not—"

"This is the kind of shit I handle." His voice was grim. "He comes here, thinking he'll get you? The bastard will be dealing with *me*."

Because Sebastian wasn't some spoiled playboy like she'd thought.

*He's a freaking spy.*

# CHAPTER SEVEN

"I didn't know I was trespassing!" The guy lifted his hands. "I was...hiking. Taking nature pictures." He glanced at the burly guard and then at Sebastian. The fellow's eyelids flickered. "I must have gotten lost."

"Do I look like a dumbass?" Sebastian asked him conversationally.

"Uh..."

"The correct answer is...'No, you don't look like a dumbass.'" His eyes narrowed on the trespasser. "I know you."

"No, I don't think we've met—"

"I don't forget faces. Ever. I know your face." He mentally ran through the list in his head and... "Fuck, you're a reporter. Gavin Hall. You joined up with the *Asheville Sun* a few months back."

The sunlight glinted off Gavin's blond hair and the bright light easily let Sebastian see the uneasiness on the other man's face. "I'm a reporter, yes," Gavin responded cautiously. "But I was out here doing a nature piece and—"

"Bullshit." He didn't have time for this crap. "You want me to get your ass fired? Because I can do that with one phone call."

Gavin's Adam's apple bobbed.

"Let's cut the crap. Why are you on my property?"

"Because you're the story." A miserable shrug from Gavin. "I was at the theater last night...uh, doing a report on the new show. I happened to be outside when all the action went down, and I saw those shots nearly hit your lady."

*My lady?*

"You got her in the limo and out of there fast as lightning, and then the cops swarmed. They weren't sharing info, so I thought I'd come out here and see what I could find..."

His words trailed away. He seemed to waver and pale a bit more. He should go pale. He should be freaking terrified.

Sebastian lunged toward him. "You were out there when the shots were fired." He grabbed the reporter's shirt front.

"I don't—I don't think you should be—"

"You took pictures of the scene, didn't you?" He could see the truth in Gavin's eyes. "Pictures of me and my lady."

"When you get a story like that, you have to act. I mean, I only had my phone with me, but it's top of the line and the camera on it was good enough for me to—"

"I want the pictures," Sebastian cut through his words. "And I want them now."

Gavin's gaze darted away.

"Oh, hell, no." Sebastian shook his head. "Do *not* tell me—"

"They're already up on the website. It was a big story, man. My boss was thrilled. He knew other news outlets would want to pick up the details and link back to us so—"

Sebastian let Gavin go. Disgusted, he snarled, "You put her picture up on your site."

A miserable nod. "It's the news..."

"You know who she is. You recognized her, didn't you?"

Gavin licked his lower lip. "Hard not to recognize Antony Kyle's little sister. Just didn't know the two of you were an item. That part right there was news, you know, it was—"

"Take the photos down. Delete any copies you have."

Gavin gaped. "Dude, that's like shutting the barn door after—"

"Come on my property again, and I'll have your ass thrown in jail for trespassing. I've got cops on speed dial." Well, one cop. "Don't push me." He motioned to the silent, watchful guard. "Escort his ass out of here."

As Gavin brushed by him, mumbling some half-ass apology, Sebastian let his hand slip into the reporter's coat pocket. And as easy as one, two, three...

Gavin walked out, not even realizing that he'd left his phone behind. Or rather, not even realizing that his phone had been taken.

By the time Sebastian walked back in his house, he had unlocked the phone, and he was scrolling through the pictures Gavin had taken. *Like I'd really trust the guy to delete them on his own.*

Sure enough, there was Sebastian, grabbing Alyssa. Scooping her into his arms. He zoomed in on the picture a bit, and Sebastian swore when he saw the expression on his own face—

"Did you catch him?"

He glanced up. Way up. Alyssa was on the second floor. Her hands were spread along the wooden railing.

"Was it the guy who shot at me?"

"No." Sebastian tightened his hold on the phone. "Just a jerk reporter after a story. I've taken care of him." He'd make sure all of the photos vanished from the website, too. But...shit, they'd already been recirculated on the internet.

Good thing he was talented at making certain things vanish.

"I have to do some quick work in my office." He turned away from her. "Why don't you try to rest a bit? We can talk again later." He had to get those photos taken care of *now*. He hurried into his office. Sebastian fired up the computer, and his fingers flew over the keyboard as he went after his target and—

"You don't want me to know something."

His head whipped up.

Alyssa stood in the doorway.

He frowned at her. "You got down the stairs fast." Like ninja fast.

"What are you doing?" She bit her lower lip. "Better question...what are you hiding from me?"

"The reporter who just got his ass tossed off my property? He took pictures of us outside the theater. The pictures are circulating on the web, and I'm making them vanish."

Silence. Then... "Why?"

His fingers were poised over the keyboard. "What do you mean?"

"Why are you making them vanish? Is there something in the pictures that people shouldn't see?"

"They—"

"You know what? *I* want to see them." She strode forward. Moved behind the desk. Leaned in close to him and—

"Lavender," Sebastian mumbled as he inhaled.

"What?"

He pulled in more of that scent. "When we first met, I didn't know the scent you wore was lavender. Didn't know shit about stuff like that. I could do anything with a computer, but hell, beyond that, I was pretty much clueless. Antony had to teach me how the world worked. Had to teach me what damn fork to use when I was at a fancy dinner. See, Uncle Sam skipped those bits of instruction."

Uncle Sam had taught him how to defend himself. How to fight like a beast. How to shoot. How to attack all of his enemy's weak spots.

When you wanted to take someone down, you always went after what made that person weak.

His gaze slid to the computer screen. To the large picture of him holding Alyssa tightly against his chest.

"*The Bad Boy of Tech rushes his girlfriend to safety...*" She leaned closer. "I swear, you always get good press. And was I just reduced to the status of random girlfriend? Did they not even put my name in this piece?"

"Nothing random about you," he immediately replied. *Not a damn thing.* "And Gavin names you, specifically, later in the article." Because he'd already scanned it. "The jerk reporter glosses over the shooting and focuses on the fact that I'm romantically involved with my business partner's sister. Talk about having his priorities screwed up."

"I think he knew exactly what he was doing."

She was so close to him. And that lavender scent...*fuck me.* She smelled so good.

"You attract attention. I'm sure the story will get tons of clicks." She waved her hand toward the screen. "It already has. Don't see the point in you deleting it now."

He'd clenched his back teeth. With an effort, he gritted out, "Everyone will think we're sleeping together. The reporter came here. He's going to spread the word that you spent the night at my place. You're going to be gossiped about and dragged through the mud, and I know you like to stay quiet. You're private, and I didn't think you wanted—"

"To be linked to you? To have people think we're sleeping together?" A pause. "But I thought that was what you did want. I thought you wanted us sleeping together."

He turned his chair so that he faced her. They should be clear. "I don't care a whole lot about sleeping. Truth be told, I usually only get four hours of sleep or so a night."

Her brow scrunched. "That doesn't seem like enough."

It was all he needed. Speaking of things he needed... "I care about fucking you. About touching and kissing every single inch of your body and sinking my dick into you over and over again."

Her lips parted.

"But I didn't think you'd want the reporter spreading *that,* either." And she wasn't like the women who wanted to be photographed at his side because they enjoyed the fame. For as long as he'd known Alyssa, she'd avoided the spotlight that came from Shark Gaming and Design. "I was trying to protect you." Simple. "Kind of like I always have." He lifted one eyebrow. "So, if you'll let me get back to work, I'll make this vanish—"

"I thought things on the internet were there forever."

"Not when you have my skills."

He turned away. Reached for the keyboard.

"Don't." Her hands settled on top of his.

Her touch sent fire right through him. His dick had already been up because he found her lavender scent sexy as hell. No, he found *her* sexy as hell, and when she'd gotten all close to him, he'd responded the way he normally did.

*All freaking in.*

He inhaled and swore he tasted her. "You want the world to think we're screwing?" His head turned. His gaze met hers. "You want them to believe a lie? How very unlike you, Alyssa." Because he'd always thought of her as the good girl.

While he'd been...

Just the bastard. The asshole. The man who would never be good enough to touch her.

Except she was touching him right then.

Touching him and staring straight into his eyes as she said, "If I'm staying with you, if I'm here for any length of time, people are going to wonder why. I mean, it's not like I get to just go home tomorrow."

Hell, no, she didn't.

"We were involved in a shooting. Other reporters will ask questions. We can't just hide from this."

*Technically, I can do any damn thing I want.*

"It can be a cover story," she continued doggedly. "Let the world think we're together romantically. It's much easier to say that lie because it's not like I can reveal my brother is a spy, and I'm in danger because of that fact."

No, they couldn't reveal that part.

"I'm sure you use cover stories all the time." Her gaze searched his. "How is this any different?"

It was different because she was involved.

"When it's over," her voice lowered, "we'll just say that we broke up. End of the big story. The press can move on to catching pictures of you with other women. I'll be forgotten in no time." She eased back.

"No, you damn well won't."

Her eyes widened.

"I've never been able to forget you. Trust me, I tried. That shit doesn't work."

He heard the faint catch in her breath. "You weren't lying...you've really wanted me..." Her voice trailed away.

"Since the day we met."

"But you didn't do a thing about it."

He forced a shrug. "You seemed to hate me, so what was there to do?"

"Hate is a strong word. And like I said before, I don't hate you."

She was right in front of him. Close enough to touch.

*But I'm not supposed to put my hands on her.* Because if he put his hands on her, he'd never let her go.

"If you want the truth, I often think you're an arrogant ass."

He nodded. "Most days, I am."

"I also think you have a wild streak. That you believe most rules don't apply to you."

"Rules are made to be broken." He flashed her a smile.

She didn't smile back. "You know your dimples don't work on me."

A crying shame.

"You break most rules...but my brother asked you to stay away from me, and you did. You followed that rule."

He looked away.

"Why?"

"Like I told you, I just added a stipulation. I said I'd stay back until you wanted me. Since you didn't seem to want me—"

She caught his chin in her hand.

*She touched me.*

Alyssa carefully turned his head toward her. She stared down at him. "You make me crazy."

Her fingers felt so soft. "Only fair. You've been driving me insane since I saw you blowing out birthday candles."

Her lush lips parted. "What do you think is going to happen? That you announce you want me, and I'll suddenly be jumping into bed with you?"

"A guy can dream," he muttered. Her mouth was close. He wanted it.

*I want her.*

"We haven't even had a first date yet, and I told you that I never sleep with guys on the first date."

*"Ahem. Sorry to interrupt..."* The voice came from the doorway, and no, the guy speaking didn't sound particularly sorry at all.

Alyssa gasped and jerked back even as Sebastian shot to his feet and jumped in front of her. He narrowed his eyes on the bastard who stood there, with one shoulder propped against the doorway.

"I would have said something sooner," the man continued, "but I was really curious about where the conversation was going. Engrossed, if you will. All invested in the ending. But then I realized it was probably rude to watch you. Voyeur-like, you know."

*"Dex,"* Sebastian growled.

Alyssa's fingers locked around Sebastian's shoulder. "I thought your home was secure."

"It is secure. Don't worry."

Her hold tightened on him. "It's not secure. There's a man *standing right there.* He got past your guards, he got past your security, he got in here without us even catching the sound of his footsteps—"

"Because I am that good," Dex bragged. "What can I say? I have mad skills."

Sebastian turned to glance back at Alyssa. They'd been having a freaking moment. *A moment.* Trust Dex to screw things up for him. "It's okay. I called him." And he'd given orders for the guards to let Dex pass when he arrived. Those were actually standing orders—Dex always could get to Sebastian.

*Because he's my handler.*

"You called him?" Alyssa's dark eyebrows rose. "Why? Is he another bodyguard or something?"

"Or something," Dex drawled.

Sebastian shot him a killing glance.

"What?" Dex blinked. "Come on, buddy, you know I'm here to help." He smiled. "Why don't you introduce me to the lovely lady? Though I have heard so much about her that I feel like we're already besties."

Sebastian shifted his position so that Alyssa could get a full look at Dex—and so that he could stand at her side. They were still behind his desk. Dex was still lounging against the doorframe. He didn't look particularly intimidating—he never did. His blond hair was messy and a little too long. His arms were crossed over his chest, and his body seemed ever so casual.

The casual pose was a lie, though. Sebastian knew nothing about Dex was casual.

"Alyssa, this is Dex." Sebastian waved vaguely between them.

Dex roused from the doorway and headed across the room.

Sebastian stiffened.

Dex offered his hand to Alyssa. "I'm a friend of your brother's and of Sebastian's."

Alyssa took his hand.

His fingers closed around hers. "You definitely got the looks in the family," Dex added. His head tilted. "You are gorgeous. Are those flecks of gold in your eyes?" He leaned closer. "Yes, they are. Beautiful."

Alyssa's head turned toward Sebastian.

Dex kept her hand.

"Can't imagine why Sebastian didn't tell me how gorgeous you are," Dex continued. "He mentioned plenty of other little details, but he skipped that particular part. Oh, wait, now I know. I bet it was because he didn't want the competition since he was trying to get in your—"

Sebastian shoved a hand against Dex's chest. "Drop your act."

"I'm not acting," Dex fired back, seemingly offended. "Friends don't keep friends from—"

"You're not my fucking friend." And Dex wasn't touching Alyssa any longer. Good. "Antony is my friend. Winston is my friend. You? You're my pain in the ass handler."

Dex's face tightened. "I think you'll want to stop now."

Because he wasn't supposed to tell Alyssa about Dex's real identity. Because Sebastian wasn't supposed to tell her who he really was, either. "Screw that. Alyssa already knows. From here on out, she knows everything."

Dex's gray eyes glittered. "Do you know what the hell you're doing? Do you really want to fuck Antony's sister so much that you would risk destroying everything else?"

He could hear a fast drumming in his ears. Sebastian smiled at Alyssa. "Would you scoot back just a little bit?"

She blinked at him.

"Please?" Sebastian added.

She scooted.

"Thank you." Another smile for her. One with his dimples.

Then he turned, drew back his hand, and plowed his fist right into Dex's jaw.

# CHAPTER EIGHT

Well, that had certainly accelerated quickly.

One minute, the blond-haired guy with the torn jeans had been all smirky and insulting with his whole, "Do you know what the hell you're doing? Do you really want to fuck Antony's sister so much that you would risk destroying everything else?"

And in the next moment, Sebastian's blow had sent the man—Dex?—stumbling back.

"Lucky punch," Dex snapped.

His lower lip seemed to be bleeding.

"Let's see if I can get lucky again," Sebastian fired back as he lunged for the other man once more.

Were they seriously about to have a fist fight? Right there?

"Stop! Sebastian!" The sharp cry exploded from her before she could give it a second thought.

Sebastian stopped. He turned to look at her.

And Dex shoved his fist into Sebastian's side.

Her eyes widened in horror.

"Sonofabitch," Sebastian breathed. "You'll pay for that."

"Yeah? Will I?" Dex taunted. "Did you see what just happened? Your crush over there called out your name and your fool self got distracted. You get distracted in this business, and you get killed. *That's* why I'm taking her away from you."

She'd misheard. Obviously. Or he was just insane. "I'm not going anywhere with you."

"Damn straight, she's not." Sebastian straightened. His body moved protectively closer to hers. She could practically feel the tension pouring from him as he dared, "Try to take her and let's see how fast I can kick your ass."

If this Dex person was his handler, were they really supposed to be fighting? Because the air was so thick that she could barely breathe. "I think we all need to take a moment and calm down."

Dex quirked a brow. "I am super calm. Folks say I have ice in my veins." He motioned toward Sebastian. "Everyone knows he's the crazy one."

"Try to take her from me, and I will show you just how crazy I can be."

"Sebastian." She put her hand on his chest. "I'm not leaving you."

Some of the stiffness left his shoulders.

"He's not taking me away. He...he can't do that." *Can he?*

"With the power of the government behind me, I can do lots of things," Dex assured her. "So don't go making assumptions over there."

"Let me kick his ass," Sebastian muttered. "It will be fast, I promise."

"He's your *handler*."

"He's a douche."

"I heard that," Dex said.

"You were supposed to. There's a reason I said it *loudly*."

Alyssa stared into Sebastian's eyes. "I'm scared."

His whole expression immediately changed. "You do not have to be. I will never let anything happen to you."

Behind her, Dex coughed. "He's not Superman. Or, if he is, then you're his kryptonite. So, yes, shit can happen. We should talk about it. Get it all out in the open."

"I'm his kryptonite?" Now she did glance back at Dex. "What are you even talking about?"

He smiled at her. He didn't have Sebastian's perfect dimples, but she supposed he was an attractive guy. Good bone structure. Slightly hawkish nose. Hard jaw. Tanned skin.

But...

He was scaring her and pissing her off so she didn't like him. At all.

"You." Dex waved vaguely toward her and ignored his swelling lower lip. "He's distracted by you. Normally, Sebastian knows when I'm close, but I walked my ass right into his study, and he was so busy trying to get in your pants that he didn't even hear me—"

Sebastian tried to surge past her again.

She pushed her hand against his chest. "Don't. I get that it's tempting—"

"He shouldn't talk about you that way." His hard glare was on Dex. "Just going to teach him manners. You don't say shit like that to a lady."

Now Dex laughed. "Since when do you care about manners?"

"Since Alyssa."

She could feel the frantic beat of Sebastian's heart beneath her hand. Alyssa nibbled a second on her lower lip, then asked, "Won't you get in trouble for, um, kicking his ass?"

A shrug. "Like I care about trouble."

"Yeah, that's what I'm *saying,*" Dex pointed out. "You don't typically care about anything. Except maybe hitting up your next adrenaline rush. So why you are trying to pretend to be some kind of knight in shining armor for her is beyond me. I mean, I clearly heard her tell you that she didn't have sex on the first date and that you two hadn't been on a date so..."

Alyssa turned toward him. "I don't like you. You're rude and insulting."

He blinked. "You're direct."

"I'm also terrified. Someone shot at me. Sebastian is helping me, and you bust in here, eavesdrop on our private conversation, and then start insulting us both. You know what?" She nodded decisively. "Maybe he should kick your ass."

Dex's lips twitched. "I think I see why he likes you."

"And I definitely see why he wants to kick your ass so much." She puffed out her cheeks and blew out a breath.

Sebastian surged past her.

Dex held up his hands. "Hold on, man. Just hold on."

It didn't look as if Sebastian wanted to hold on. She was also no longer in the mood to hold him back.

"You called me, remember?" Dex's words rapped out. "You called me *late*. As in, I should have been the first person on your speed dial, but instead, I had to catch your big story on social media and only then did you give me a ring. Probably because you knew I was already heading your way." His gaze flickered to Alyssa. "By the way, you photograph beautifully. Probably those cheekbones of yours. Did I mention you are gorgeous and that I'm available?"

Her hands flew to her hips. "And did I mention I'm not interested?"

"Fair enough." He straightened. "Let's start over. My name's Dexter Ryan, and I'm the man you want on your side when the world goes to hell."

She wasn't so sure about that.

Dex slid his gaze to Sebastian. "You should have called me first." His voice was lower, rougher. "As soon as you received the text from Antony, you should have reached out to me. I could have collected Alyssa and moved her to a safe location. You didn't have to get involved."

Nothing Dex said made her like him more. "I'm not a thing to be collected."

Sebastian stood toe-to-toe with the guy. "I don't trust anyone else with Alyssa's protection."

A sigh escaped from Dex. "Yes, I was afraid you'd say that." His shoulders hunched. "Just how much have you told her?"

"Everything."

And at first, she hadn't believed him. It had seemed so crazy. But...

Someone was trying to kill her.

Now Sebastian's handler was there. Though she didn't even understand exactly what a handler was.

*It's all true.*

"Everything," Dex repeated with a wince. "That's going to be a problem." When he looked at her again, he wasn't smiling. His eyes were cold and hard. "Just how much do you trust her, Sebastian?"

"I trust her completely." An instant response. One that surprised her.

"Do you trust her with your life? Because by revealing the truth about yourself to her, that's what you're doing, you know. Putting your life in her hands. In the hands of a woman who I've been told doesn't even like you very much."

Who had told him that?

"I've done research on you," Dex continued with an incline of his head toward Alyssa. "Had to do it, of course, considering my working relationship with your brother. And, of course, Sebastian here. It's important to look for any threats that might exist."

"You think I'm a threat?" Why did it suddenly feel so cold in that room?

"That's ridiculous," Sebastian snarled. "She's hardly dangerous!"

"That depends on your definition of dangerous." Dex's eyes were on her. "I see her as quite a very serious threat."

Sebastian swore. "I didn't call you over so that you'd insult her."

"No, you called me over to protect her."

"*I* can protect her," Sebastian thundered right back. "I wanted you to find out where the hell Antony is. I wanted you to tell me what mission he was working on that blew up in his face."

She flinched.

"Sorry," Sebastian murmured.

"I'll be happy to tell you everything I know about Antony Kyle," Dex responded, suddenly seeming all genial.

She was instantly suspicious.

"As soon as Alyssa leaves the room," he finished, voice all smooth like cream.

The man was such a jerk. "It's my brother's life you're talking about! I think I have a right to hear what you have to say."

"Yes, well, you don't have the security clearance to hear what I know, so I'm afraid this is a non-negotiable point. I can't discuss this with a civilian."

"Seriously?"

"Dead serious."

Her stomach twisted. "Is my brother alive?" Oh, God, was he holding that terrible truth from her? Someone had shot at her, and what if someone had shot at Antony, too? What if Antony—

"As far as I know, yes, your brother is alive." A flicker of sympathy appeared—then almost instantly disappeared—from Dex's face. "But I truly can't say more. Not with you in the room."

He was kicking her out. "I don't like you."

"You mentioned that before. Thanks for noting it again. And it may surprise you to hear this, but I actually get that line quite a bit."

"This is some bullshit." She turned to Sebastian. "Tell him it's bullshit."

"It's bullshit," he said.

But...

His gaze slid carefully over her face. "Government red tape is a freaking bitch. I'm sorry, Alyssa."

So he was shutting her out, too. Her brother's life was on the line, her life was on the line, and Sebastian pulled spy rank. Her stare jerked between the two men. "Fine. Don't worry, I know how to find the guest room. Have your spy talk. See if you come up with a way to help my brother." She marched for the door.

"Alyssa!"

She stilled at Sebastian's call.

Then she glanced back.

"We *will* finish our discussion from earlier. We aren't done."

Oh, they definitely weren't done. Did he truly think she was just walking away with her tail tucked between her legs? He'd said she didn't know the real man that he was. Perhaps he had no clue who she truly was, either.

Because she would get him to tell her every single thing that he learned from Dex. Screw government clearance. Her brother could be in danger. Most likely *was* in serious danger. She'd do whatever was necessary to help him.

Alyssa stormed up the stairs and headed for her guest room. As soon as she shoved open the door, she heard her cell phone ringing.

Her heart lurched because the last time she'd gotten a call, it had been from the jerk trying to kill her. She rushed across the room and grabbed the phone.

*Isaac Swain.*

What? Why was he calling her? She almost ignored his call, but then wondered if perhaps he'd seen something at the theater, something that could help with this whole mess. She answered the call and put the phone to her ear. "Isaac?"

"Alyssa! I've been so worried! Are you okay?"

"I'm fine." As fine as she could be with someone trying to kill her.

"I went by your house, but there were cops there!"

Wait, he'd gone by her house? "Why did you go by my place?"

"Because I was worried. You were shot at! I'm sure the attack was meant for Sebastian but—"

"It wasn't. It was meant for me."

"Holy shit! Does Antony know? What does your brother—"

*I can't find him.* "Look, I appreciate you calling, but I've got protection, and I'm good."

Silence. "What kind of protection?"

The kind of protection that a secret spy offered.

"You're with him, aren't you? You're with Sebastian right now!"

Seriously? Had that been an edge of jealousy in Isaac's voice? "I have to go. Again, thanks for checking, but you don't need to worry about me. I'm secure."

"You're not safe if you're with Sebastian! He won't keep you safe! You need to go to the police! Their job is to literally keep people safe!"

"Good-bye, Isaac."

"You just want to stay with him! Here I was, all worried about you, but you're happy to be with him! You're happy—"

Her spine snapped straight. *Enough.* "Happy I was shot at? Is that what you think? Hate to disillusion you, but the gunshots didn't thrill me. Being terrified didn't thrill me. But having Sebastian being willing to risk himself and rush me to safety? Yes, I *did* appreciate that, and I appreciate him. So, for the final time, good-bye, Isaac."

She hung up the phone.

Why the hell did everyone want to keep painting Sebastian as the bad guy?

\*\*\*

When the study door slammed behind Alyssa, Dex let out a long exhale. "She is pissed."

Sebastian shot him a look of utter disgust.

"And she's sexy as hell. I'm sure you noticed that part, though, since when I interrupted, I found you trying to seduce her."

"What we were doing was not your concern."

Dex shrugged. "I don't know. Some would say that ensuring a positive working environment between my two top agents—that would be you and Antony—some would say that was absolutely my job. My main priority. If I saw something that would screw up that working relationship—you know, like you trying to get his sister into bed—then perhaps I should intervene. Perhaps it *is* my job to intervene."

They needed to be clear on something. He stood right in front of Dex. "You don't come between me and Alyssa."

"Or what? You going to take another swing at me?"

He didn't speak. He'd already said plenty. Either Dex would take the warning or he wouldn't.

Dex glanced away. "Look, I get that things are stressful, but you need to chill out, man. I'm not the enemy."

*You sure about that?* "Where the hell did you send Antony?"

Dex licked his lips. "The mission was low risk. Should have been a walk in the park."

"I know he used a cover story of going to Russia in order to work on gaming distribution, but *where—*"

"He's not in Russia." Dex tugged on his t-shirt. "Or at least, he's not any longer."

"Where is he?"

"Like I said, that mission was low risk. Should have been a walk in the park, and all indications are that it *was* an easy mission. He completed the job. Sent in his intel. Then he flew back here to the US. Landed in Atlanta three days ago."

That didn't make sense. "So where the hell is he?" And why hadn't Antony contacted him as soon as the guy arrived back in the states?

"I don't know." Dex swallowed. "Because the last time anyone saw your buddy, he was slipping into the back of a limo at the Atlanta airport. After that, he vanished."

"What about his phone? He texted me—"

"We can't locate the phone. If Antony didn't want it found, you know it wouldn't be."

Yes, he knew that. Antony could have completely dismantled the phone right after he'd sent the text.

"But there's another possibility that we have to look at here," Dex continued. "It's possible that, seeing as how he said his cover was blown, that Antony has been taken."

That was not the news Sebastian wanted to hear. He'd feared it, but he'd damn well not wanted to have Dex confirm that worry.

"If he's being held, then whoever has him will try to get Antony to turn. To reveal every secret he knows." Dex's voice was grim.

"Antony wouldn't do that."

Dex cocked his head. "Not even if his sister's life is on the line?"

*Fuck.*

"Tell me, because, you know, I'm a curious kind of guy...just what would you do if someone had a knife to the lovely Alyssa's throat? If someone told you that in order for her to live, you had to turn on your country? You had to turn over all the secrets that you'd learned. What would you do?"

He knew it was a test. Dex always thought he was so clever. The thing was, though, that Sebastian didn't like tests. He turned away. Headed toward his desk. Pulled open the top drawer there.

"I have an idea about what I think you'd do," Dex revealed. "And it worries me. Worries me so much that I think I have to get involved and pull rank with you. I believe it would be in everyone's best interest if you put some distance between yourself and Alyssa Kyle."

Sebastian shut the drawer. Kept his hand near his side as he returned to face Dex.

"Well?" Dex lifted his brows. "Don't you have a response?"

"Absolutely." Sebastian moved in a flash. He flew forward, lifted up the knife he'd palmed from his drawer, and he pressed that blade right to Dex's throat. "Here's my response," he gritted out. "Some bastard puts a knife to her throat? Someone threatens her?"

Dex didn't seem to be breathing.

"I will kill the bastard."

The door flew open. "Look, this is my brother's life and I want to know—*ohmyGod.*"

Sebastian's head whipped toward her.

Alyssa stared at him in absolute horror.

In fear.

"And I was just thinking you weren't the bad guy!" She shook her head, as if she couldn't believe what she was seeing.

"Good luck getting her in bed now," Dex muttered. "That ship has sailed, sailor."

# CHAPTER NINE

Alyssa stood outside of Sebastian's bedroom. Her toes curled into the lush carpeting. Her hands rubbed against the front of her jogging pants— mostly because her palms were crazy sweaty. It was the middle of the night. Thunder was rumbling outside. Lightning kept crashing.

And she'd finally hauled herself to his door.

*Just knock. Do it.*

After Dex had left earlier that evening, things had been...tense. Way tense. Scary tense.

Because Sebastian had looked scary.

She'd never seen him quite that way before. He'd had a knife to Dex's throat. An actual knife. His face had been etched into cold, furious lines, and when he'd turned his head toward her, she'd never seen his gaze appear so lethal.

She'd been staring at a stranger.

And...yes, he'd frightened her.

But they needed to talk. He'd been avoiding her ever since that scene, and they couldn't go on like this. So, in the middle of the night, when she hadn't been able to sleep, she'd decided to go to him.

Her hand lifted. She balled up her sweaty fingers and rapped on the door.

No answer.

She rapped again.

Still no answer.

Maybe she should go back to bed.

Or maybe he was just a super sound sleeper who needed another rap.

She rapped again. Harder. And—

The door swung open. "You don't give up easily, do you?"

He wasn't a sound sleeper. He *was* way, way too sexy.

Every bit of moisture dried up in her mouth. Sebastian was wearing a pair of what appeared to be silk boxers. His chest was bare. The man's muscles were a thing of beauty. Light spilled from somewhere behind him, and it outlined the awesome width of his shoulders. His hair was mussed, his body tight, and when her gaze *may* have darted down...

"Oh, sure, now you look at me like you want to eat me alive."

Her gaze snapped right back up to his. She felt heat singe her cheeks.

He lifted a glass. Sipped whatever liquid was in there. "But before, you stared at me like I was the friggin' devil." He didn't sip again. He drained the glass. Then turned away. "Go to bed, Alyssa."

She didn't move. He'd left the door open. Sure, he'd told her to go to bed, which completely sounded like a dismissal—because it was—but she couldn't give up. Since he'd left the door open, she decided to count it as an invitation, and she stepped over the threshold.

He immediately whipped back around toward her. "What in the hell are you doing?"

"Trying to talk to you." She eyed the empty glass that he clutched. "But, first, are you drunk?"

Bitter laughter slipped from him. "I wish."

"That's not exactly a yes or no answer."

"No, I'm not drunk. If I were drunk, things would be a whole lot easier." A pause. "But they're never easy with you, are they? I get close to what I want, then it's snatched away. Story of my life. Don't know why I thought things would suddenly be different."

"You've never told me much about your life." She inched a bit closer to him.

"Why bore you with gory details?"

"I don't think there is much about you that is gory."

More of the bitter laughter that she didn't particularly like. "That's because you don't know me. Okay, fine, is that why you came in here in your sexy outfit? Because you wanted to learn all my secrets?"

She glanced down at the jogging pants and the white t-shirt she wore. "Um, I think we should discuss what you believe is a sexy outfit."

"That's easy." He plunked the glass down on his nightstand. "Anything you wear."

Oh, that was rather sweet. Wasn't it? Why couldn't she get a handle on him? "Is that one of your lines?" Alyssa asked suspiciously. "Do you tell that to lots of women?"

"So, let's get something straight here. Usually, women are eager to hop in bed with me. Might shock you to discover that I don't have to feed them lines." He pointed at her. "You're an exception. Instead of running to me, you run away." He raked his gaze over her. "Would it kill you to try running *to* me for once?"

"I don't know..." Alyssa's tongue swiped across her lower lip. "Do you have a knife hidden on you right now?"

"You would go back to that." He blew out a breath. "I wasn't gonna cut the bastard's throat. Is that what you wanted to hear?"

*It is nice to hear, yes.* "If you weren't going to cut him, then why have the knife ready? I thought you were working with him—"

"I do work with him. Doesn't mean I always like him."

"Got that." Another few inches forward. Her gaze darted to the bed. Such a massive bed. She immediately had a visual of him in the bed. And— *no. Stop it. Do not go there.* "So, um, why did you pull a knife on him?"

"Dex asked me a question, and I answered it for him. I'm the kind of person who likes to use a visual aid in order to get my point across."

"It was a very strong visual." Her toes wiggled against the carpet. "And now I have to wonder, just what question did he ask you?"

His hands fisted. "You should go back to bed."

"You should answer my question."

"Why? You've already made up your mind about me." He advanced, moved with his lethal grace, and eliminated the distance between them.

The move was so sudden that she sucked in a quick breath even as he said, "You think I'm dangerous."

"Aren't you?"

"Not to you. Not *ever* to you."

"Why did you have that knife?"

"Because he wanted to know what I would do if someone threatened you. If I had to choose between keeping the secrets I've learned as a spy or saving you...what would I do?"

Oh, damn. Alyssa's heart lurched in her chest. "And your answer was the visual aid?"

"My answer," he rumbled and that rumble sent goosebumps flying over her body, "is that if someone is threatening to kill you, if some bastard has a knife and plans to use it, I'll kill the fool before he so much as scratches you."

That was intense. No, intense wasn't the right word.

"You're scared to death of me." Sebastian's voice was still a deep, dark rumble. So rough. "You're standing here, practically shaking."

"It's cold in here."

"No, it's not. You're just afraid. You go from almost kissing me to being terrified of me. That's a major one-eighty. Should have known it would happen. Like I said, my whole life, the things I wanted were always out of reach."

"But I'm not out of reach. I'm right here." Oh, jeez. She'd done it again. Why could her mouth not stay closed sometimes?

His eyes narrowed on her. "Are you playing with me?"

"I don't really play well with others."

"That's a thing we have in common." His green gaze burned. "Tell me that you're not afraid."

"I'd be lying if I did that."

He flinched. Turned away. "Go back to—"

"Not until you tell me what Dex said about my brother."

She saw his back tense.

"That's why you're here, huh?" Sebastian's voice rasped. "You come in and expect me to spill classified secrets."

"Is he alive?" Her voice broke. "Surely, telling me whether or not Antony is alive isn't classified."

"As far as we know, yes, we believe he's alive."

She waited for more. He said nothing. Dammit. She grabbed Sebastian's arm and spun him back toward her. "You can tell me more than that."

"Another test, huh?" Sebastian muttered. She had zero clue what he was talking about, but he continued, "Only this time, it's how much do I want you? If you give me what I need, will I spill all my secrets to you?"

"I'm not asking you to betray your country for me. I'm just asking about Antony! I don't want to know specifics about cases that you worked. I only want to know—"

"He's gone dark, Alyssa. I told you that much before, and there's nothing else I can tell you now." He looked down at her hand on his arm. "You should walk away. Go back to bed. You don't have to promise me anything in order to learn what I know. What I've said is all you'll get. So take your fear and go."

"You're in a mood," she accused.

His brows shot up. "Excuse me?"

"You had a *knife* at Dex's throat! And, yes, he is a jerk, but that doesn't mean it's okay to pull a knife on him. First you punched him—"

"Because he needed to watch his fucking mouth with you—"

"And then you pulled a knife! I've never even seen you get rough with someone before. You just had your crazy PR persona, but now, all of a sudden, you're threatening to cut a man's throat, so, yes, excuse the hell out of me, but that scared me. *You* scared me."

Silence.

She was squeezing his arm.

"I don't know you." The truth hurt her to say.

"You don't *want* to know who I really am."

Alyssa looked down at the floor.

"The real me would terrify you even more. If you realized how fucking much I want you, then you would be scared out of your skin." He laughed. "Coming in here was a mistake. You don't wave a red flag right in front of a bull's face, not unless you want him to charge."

"So I'm a flag now."

"You're the woman I want most, and you're scared to death of me. Hardly good for the self-esteem."

Her gaze rose to lock with his. "Like you have a problem with self-esteem."

A muscle jerked along his jaw. "I told you about your brother. You didn't have to trade kisses or promises or anything else for the news I gave you."

"Is that what you thought I was going to do?" Her hair slid over her shoulders as her head cocked back. The better to stare up at him. "Make some kind of sexual deal with you?"

"A guy can dream."

"And you dream about me?" She sounded doubting because, no, he didn't.

"Only when I'm lucky."

She didn't know what to say.

"But I'm guessing you'll have nightmares about me tonight, won't you, Alyssa?" He gazed down at her hand. "You should stop touching me. When you touch me, it makes me want you more."

Slowly, she pulled her hand away. Alyssa took a step back. One. Another. Then she stopped retreating. "Have you ever killed anyone?" The question came out as a hushed whisper.

His mocking laughter came again. "You shouldn't ask questions when you don't actually want to know the answers."

Her stomach was doing crazy flips. "I do want to know the answer." She wanted to know who he truly was.

"If I say yes, will that make you run back to your room faster?"

"I'm not running. I'm standing right here, in front of you."

"For the moment." Sebastian raked a hand over his face. "No, I haven't ever killed anyone. You good now? I haven't been in a situation where it was necessary. I've broken laws, though. Plenty of them. Back in the day, I got my ass thrown behind bars more times than I could count. That's how Uncle Sam found me. Turned out the government didn't like it too much when a punk kid hacked past a supposedly secure server." His hand fell. "I'm not like Antony. I didn't grow up in a fancy house with a mom and dad who doted on my every move. I didn't even know my parents. I bounced around the foster care system, and I caused trouble because that was what I was good at doing. Even when I landed with good people, I fucked it up. That's what I do. I fuck things up."

There was pain in his voice, and it made her heart ache. "Not always. You've made a super successful company. You're one of the richest—"

"Money isn't every fucking thing. Back when I didn't have it, I thought it was. But I learned it doesn't buy you what you want most."

*Don't ask. Don't ask. Don't ask.* "What do you want most?" And, of course, she asked.

He stared straight at her. The green of his eyes blazed with lust. With a dark desire that had her breaths coming even faster. She should leave. Right then. Absolutely. She should go back to the guest room. Climb into the bed. Try to sleep.

She didn't move. But she did ask, again, "What do you want most?"

"Not what. Who." And he said, "You."

Alyssa shook her head.

A grim smile curled his lips. "Most days, I think I'd kill to have you."

Her drumming heartbeat filled her ears.

She turned, slowly, on her heel. Took a few steps toward the door.

"Knew you'd run." His low voice followed her. Rough. Ragged.

And...

*Why am I running?*

Because she was moving blindly. Because her whole world had just flipped upside down. Because... *Tell him.* "I want you so much that it scares me, too." For once, she didn't blurt out the truth. Alyssa had to force out that painful confession.

She heard Sebastian suck in a sharp breath behind her.

*Stop being afraid.*

She whirled around to face him.

"Screw it," Alyssa mumbled. She ran toward him. She grabbed his shoulders and yanked him down toward her. Her mouth crashed into his.

# CHAPTER TEN

Alyssa was kissing him. Alyssa had run to him. For once, just like in his fantasies, she'd rushed toward him.

For a moment, Sebastian was absolutely stunned. So stunned that he didn't move. Her mouth was on his, her sweet tongue sliding past his open lips. Her hands were on him. And—

*She said she wants me.*

She'd grabbed him. She'd kissed him. Her hands were on him, her mouth was on his, and as she'd just said...

*Screw it.*

He wasn't backing off any longer. Alyssa had just proven that she wanted him, and if she was giving him this chance...

*I will take her.*

His hands curved around her hips. He lifted her up, holding her easily, and he whirled to pin her against the wall. His tongue met hers. God, she was so sweet. So delicious. He could kiss her for hours. Forever.

He wasn't restrained or controlled. Wasn't trying to seduce. He was way past the point of seduction. He was wild with his need. Desperate for her, and when she released a little moan, it made his whole body shudder.

Her breasts pushed against the thin t-shirt she wore. When she'd first come into his bedroom, he'd been able to see the outline of her nipples. He wanted those nipples in his mouth. Wanted his mouth on every single part of her body.

He kissed her, deep and hard, and then he started working his mouth down her throat. Licking her skin. Lightly using the edge of his teeth. He felt her pulse racing beneath his mouth. Such a fast, frantic beat.

He hoisted her higher. Moved her body easily. Bent his head and took one nipple into his mouth. The shirt was between him and her flesh, but she still arched toward him and gasped out his name.

The clothes needed to go.

He wanted *her*.

Every single inch of her.

Her hips were rocking against him. Pushing against him in a hungry rhythm. His cock shoved against the front of his boxers. They were doing nothing to hold him in check. His cock wanted her open and spread. Sebastian wanted to sink into her as far as he could go.

He wanted her to scream and come.

All night long.

*Her clothes had to go*.

"Why are we against the wall..." Her words were husky and sensual and made his cock twitch even more. "When the bed is right there?"

"Because..." He lifted his head. Stared into her eyes so she would get the message completely. "If I get you in my bed, I'll fuck you."

She licked her lips.

He had to kiss her again. Had to sink his tongue into her mouth. Had to taste and take and—

He tore his mouth away. Held her pinned against the wall. Realized her legs were wrapped around him. Her core shoving against his cock.

*I want in.*

His control was razor thin. He needed to get his ass in check. Five minutes ago, she'd been terrified of him.

A kiss was one thing. The wild fucking he had in mind was something else entirely.

"I need to touch you," he rumbled. "Can I touch you?"

"You are touching me," Alyssa pointed out breathlessly.

"Clothes are in the way." He wanted to rip them off her. He wanted—

His jaw locked. He caught her legs. Slowly lowered them. Took them away from his waist and eased her so that she was standing in front of the wall.

*Because if she keeps those sexy legs around my hips...*

He should move back. Step away. Instead, his hands slammed into the wall on either side of her head.

He sucked in a breath. One. Two. Three. The breaths were supposed to help calm him down.

Instead, with every breath, he pulled in more of her sweet scent.

Lavender.

His mouth was watering.

"Maybe I should be more clear...since you seem caught up on this." Her breathless voice was sexy as hell. "I want your hands on me. See what I'm doing here? I'm saying...*I want your hands on me.*"

He'd squeezed his eyes shut, but at her words—those very, very deliberate words—his eyes flew open.

He stared into her dark gaze. Saw her need. The wild need that matched his own. The flecks of gold in her eyes had gone molten. Her lips were red and swollen from his mouth.

"Touch me," Alyssa whispered as she held his gaze. "Where I need you most."

He was about to come. He wanted her *that* badly. Her words were making him shudder.

And...

His right hand fell down to her waist. He shoved down her jogging pants. They pooled on the floor. She wore the smallest scrap of white underwear he'd ever seen.

Every bit of moisture dried up from his mouth.

His hand slid down to the front of her panties.

She parted her legs a little more.

*For me.*

His finger worked under the edge of those panties. Slid between her silken folds. She was wet.

*For me.*

His heartbeat pounded. Sounded like thunder as his fingers—first one, then another—worked up inside of her. She was so tight. Tight and hot, and she tipped back her head and moaned his name.

His thumb brushed over her clit. His fingers thrust into her.

The panties were in his way.

With a savage snarl, he bent to his knees. He ripped the panties out of the damn way.

"Sebastian!"

He was almost feral in his need now. Wet for me. Moaning for me. Calling for me.

He caught her hips. Hauled her toward him. Spread her legs more. Lifted her and put his mouth on her. He licked and he sucked and he took what he'd wanted for so long.

Her hands flew to his shoulders. But she didn't push him away. She pulled him closer, and she was moaning and arching against him. Her sex was bare, shaven and so smooth, and he could lap her up for hours.

She tasted so good. He licked and thrust his tongue into her, only to withdraw and lick her again, a swipe of his tongue over her clit, and—

"Sebastian!"

She was coming. Calling out his name and shuddering before him. He could swear he tasted her pleasure on his tongue, and it just made him greedy for more. Greedy for every single inch of her.

*Greedy. Possessive.*

*Mine. I want her to be mine. Always mine.*

He could hear the panting of her breath. His breath. He licked her again because he had to do it, then he rose, staring at her.

*I could eat her alive.*

Pink bloomed on her cheeks. Her eyes were wide. Dazed. Sated.

He'd done that. He'd made Alyssa come. He'd put his mouth on her. *Finally.*

He wanted his dick in her. He wanted her to be his, forever.

Because he wanted that so fucking badly...

Sebastian stepped back.

"Wh-what are you doing?"

A rough, savage laugh broke from him. "Making you come?"

"Yes." A fast response, followed by a nod. "You did that. But now you're...backing away?"

"Because you're scared of me. Because I can't have you then watch you turn away." His dick was like frigging steel and all he wanted was to sink into her. "Go back to bed. You can walk away right now. A taste...that's what we had."

A taste that had him hungry for more. For everything.

Her chest rose and fell. "You ripped off my panties."

"Sweetheart, for the record, I pretty much want to rip off your panties every time I see you."

Her eyes widened.

His laugh was low, with a dangerous edge. "You don't get how badly I want you. You think we can fuck, and you can walk away." He kept the distance between them because if he touched her again—

*I still taste her. I want to own her.*

She'd owned him from day freaking one.

"I will ruin you for other men. I will fuck you so long and so hard and give you so much pleasure that any other bastard out there will just disappoint you."

She blinked. "Awfully c-confident there..."

"And you will absolutely destroy me for other women." She already had. He'd never get over how sweet she tasted. "I will want you, only you, because I can't take you and forget. It won't work that way."

She might think this was just a fuck. A hookup in the dark when times were crazy but it wasn't.

"I take you, and I'll want you to be mine."

"What does that mean?"

"It means..." Step back. More space. Put more space between you and her. "I'm a greedy bastard."

"I know that."

"Selfish to my core."

"So...I've, ah, heard."

"I take you once, and I will want you over and over again. It's not a one-time thing." He was warning her because...*she matters too much*. You didn't give a man his biggest wish and then rip that shit away. Not without expecting hell to follow in its wake. "I'll want to fuck you until you forget anyone before me."

Her chin angled up. "And you'll forget everyone before me?"

She didn't get it. He'd done too good of a job at turning away from her before. Too good of a job at hiding how he felt. "Baby, I already have."

Her eyes widened.

He moved to the side. Cleared a path to the door for her. "Your brother is missing. Your life is in danger. You are—"

"I know what I am. Don't stand there..." Her words came faster. "Don't stand there and tell me I'm confused. Don't tell me—"

"You were afraid of me five minutes ago!"

"I still am. Afraid of who I saw with the knife. Afraid of the way you make me feel." She grabbed *him*. Lunged forward. "And I'm also afraid that I will miss this chance with you. I've wanted you for years. I've fantasized about you for years. I'm not turning away. You say you'll ruin me? That I'll ruin you? Then let's do it. Right now. Let's just see what being ruined feels like because something tells me it is going to be phenomenal—"

He'd tried to warn her. Tried to do what was the *good* thing because Alyssa was good. Alyssa was—

"I will ruin you so hard," she breathed. Then she shot up onto her toes, pressed her mouth to his throat, and licked him.

Yeah, oh, yeah, she was going to ruin him.

He locked his arms around her, and they fell on the bed. He'd tried to do the right thing.

Now he'd do what he wanted. And what he wanted? *Her*.

He yanked the shirt off her. Finally saw those perfect breasts with the tight nipples that needed to be in his mouth. He bent over her and took one tip into his mouth. He sucked and kissed and—

She shoved his boxers out of the way. His cock sprang into her hot little hands. She stroked him, squeezed him, and his eyes damn near rolled back into his head.

He lunged away from her so he could grab a condom out of the nightstand. He tore the packet open. Kicked away his boxers—they'd somehow tangled around his legs—and he had the condom on in the next instant.

Her legs were parted. She was on his bed. Spread out for him.

Wanting *him*.

"This had better not be a dream." His voice was guttural.

He crawled over her. Put his cock at the entrance to her body.

Then he slammed home.

*Hot. Tight. Heaven.*

He was lost. His control shredded, and he let go. His thrusts were wild and uncontrolled, but Alyssa was with him every single moment. Her nails bit into his arms. Her hips shoved eagerly up against his. He knew he should slow down.

He didn't.

He knew he should be using more care.

He couldn't.

Her lips parted and her body shuddered and she moaned his name as she came again. He felt the contractions of her sex around him, and he exploded. The orgasm ripped through him, damn near incinerated him, and all he could do was take and take and take the pleasure that consumed every inch of his body.

When it was over, when his heartbeat stopped thundering and his body stopped shuddering—and still thrusting eagerly into her—his eyes opened. His hands had fisted around the covers. He was over her, and as he stared down at her beautiful face...

*Too rough. Too hard. Too—*

Her eyes opened. She smiled at him. "That was worth waiting for."

Oh, damn. He blinked. The world seemed to shift. Everything tilted and then...re-centered.

Right there.

On her.

*Hello, fucking center of my universe.*

He shook his head. Because, no, no way could he be thinking that—

Uncertainly flashed on her face. "It...wasn't? I mean, it wasn't as good for you?" Her voice turned hushed. "I-I—"

He was always such a colossal ass with her. "Good doesn't begin to describe it. More like fucking fantastic." He kissed her. "Earth shattering."

"Now you're just trying to make me feel better."

Another kiss. "So good that I want you again, right now."

Her lips parted.

He knew she felt him getting harder and harder inside of her. "And I do mean...right now." Only he had to ditch the condom. Dammit. "Give me a second." He withdrew from her and *hated* that. His new favorite place was right there, buried deep in Alyssa.

She licked her lips as he stood beside the bed. Her gaze drifted over him, and he liked the way she looked at him.

*Like she wants more. Just as badly as I do.*
"Hold the thought," he urged her. Sebastian turned and hurried for the bathroom. He threw away the condom and he—

An alarm was beeping. What in the hell? Another intruder? It had better not be that asshole reporter Gavin back for a second round.

But, no, that alarm wasn't the sound for his home security system.

"Sebastian?" Alyssa called. "Your phone is making a funny sound."

He rushed back into the bedroom. Grabbed his phone from the nightstand. Stared at the screen in disbelief. "Not happening."

She tugged the covers up to her chin. "What's not happening?"

Sebastian's gaze darted over her. "You should never be covered up. You're gorgeous."

Her brows climbed.

"I have to go to Shark Gaming and Design." Because the message he'd just received...*no damn way.*

"Now? You have to go right *now?*"

Unfortunately, dammit, yes. "Someone's on my computer." He started grabbing clothes.

"Uh, shouldn't you just alert security at the company? That's what the security guards are there for—"

"No, baby, you don't understand. The person is *in* my system. As in, some bastard managed to get past my safeguards. He's searching *my* computer. Right the fuck now." He fired off a quick text because the guards at the company did need to be alerted. "I'm telling the guards to form a perimeter around my office, but no one is to go in there until I arrive."

She jumped out of the bed. "I'm coming with you."

"That's a bad idea, that's—"

"I thought the safest place for me was with you."

Hell, yes, it was. But... "I don't know what I'll be facing in there."

"How many guards will you have surrounding your office when we arrive?"

"At least a dozen."

"That sounds safe to me." She stared up at him. "What if this is some trick? Some way of luring you away from me, separating us to make me vulnerable?"

It could very well be.

"I'm coming with you."

She had been, a few minutes ago. And if he'd had his way, she would have been on the way to coming again and again.

But some jackass had interrupted his plans.

The same jackass who'd been targeting Alyssa? He didn't buy that this attack on *his* system was random. No way, no day.

And leaving her at his house while he drove all the way across town...

Possibly leaving her open to whoever might be out there?

"Get dressed," he told her. "We leave in five."

And Sebastian put in a call to the man he trusted to have his back. Just in case this scene didn't go as planned, he always believed in having a contingency plan in place.

Alyssa hurried for the bedroom door.

"Stop."

She stilled.

He sucked in a deep breath. Fury and adrenaline burned through him.

*Some asshole is trying to hack my files.*

But... "I'll have you again."

She looked back at him. Her hair trailed over shoulders. Her eyes seemed extra dark and mysterious.

"And again," he added gruffly. "This is just beginning for us. You get that, don't you?" Once wasn't going to be enough. He'd warned her.

There would be no going back.

# CHAPTER ELEVEN

"Is there video footage of the guy going in my office? Is there footage of him getting into the building? Getting off the elevator and onto my freaking floor?"

Alyssa tensed when Sebastian asked his rapid-fire questions. They'd made it to Shark Gaming and Design, and Sebastian had immediately been greeted by the head of security, Ella Webb. She'd ridden up on the elevator with them and given status updates to Sebastian. Now they stood just beyond the elevator, in the small lobby on Sebastian's floor. It was the top floor of the building, and three different corridors stretched out from the lobby. One corridor led to Research and Development, one led to HR, and the final corridor led to Antony and Sebastian's offices.

Alyssa had known Ella for a while and always found the other woman to be no-nonsense and more than capable of handling any situation that arose. Ella sort of oozed quiet confidence, a trait that Alyssa had often envied. The two women had even gone out for a few ladies' nights. Ella had some mean dance moves, and she knew how to stop annoying, would-be suitors dead in their tracks.

At Sebastian's questions, Ella shook her head. "Negative." Unease flickered over her face.

It was the first time Alyssa had ever seen Ella appear uncertain.

Then Ella continued, and Alyssa understood the reason behind the uncertainty as Ella revealed, "I reviewed the footage, and the feeds went out for a few moments. So brief it wasn't detected by our system. The guy knows what he's doing."

"No, he doesn't. If he knew exactly what he was doing," Sebastian retorted, "he wouldn't have set off my fail-safe."

Alyssa had no idea what his fail-safe was, but she was certainly grateful for it, especially if they were about to catch the bad guy and end this nightmare.

"Our guards have maintained their positions as ordered. No one has gone in your office, and no one has come out."

"Then unless he's pulled a serious Houdini on us, I'm about to catch my prey." Sebastian nodded. "Good job, Ella."

She shook her head. "No, it's a crap job, and we both know it. He got in *your* office. On my watch. I apologize, and please know, this will not happen again." Her spine straightened. "I also don't think you should be the one going in there to confront him. You don't have experience dealing with perps like this, and I do. You know I worked for five years as a cop. I should handle this, not you. You're in way over your head. And, ah, of course, I mean that with respect."

*You're in way over your head.* Ella didn't know about Sebastian's side jobs. No one did.

*Well, now I do.*

Ella's gaze flickered to Alyssa. "Tell him to stand down. He'll listen to you."

"Excuse me?"

Ella sighed. "He always listens to you."

"No, no, he doesn't—"

"You told him to put in the exercise room on the third floor, and he did it a week after you mentioned it would help staff deal with stress. You told him that it would be great if we had a coffee shop closer to the building, and he put in one downstairs so I think that—"

"Ella," Sebastian cut through her words.

Her brows rose.

"I got this," he assured her. "But I want *you* sticking to Alyssa like glue while I'm inside with the perp. She doesn't leave your line of sight, not even for a moment, got me?"

Ella immediately nodded.

"Good." He turned to Alyssa. "I'll be back before you know it."

Her gaze darted around the lobby area. Down the corridor that led to Sebastian's office, she could see the guards as they waited.

Sebastian took a step toward that corridor.

Alyssa grabbed his arm. "Do you have a weapon?"

He looked back at her.

Ella cleared her throat but didn't speak.

"I'm good," Sebastian assured her.

This scene didn't feel good to her. "Why don't you let the guards go in first? There are a lot of them."

His face hardened. "Because this bastard broke into *my* office. He is trying to hack into *my* computer, and I will be the one that the SOB deals with. I'm not risking my people in a confrontation with him." He lowered his head, bringing his mouth close to her ear, and he whispered, "If this is about my work for Uncle Sam, my guards might not be equipped for the kind of trouble he could bring them. I've got this." When he pulled back, his lips skimmed over her cheek. "Trust me."

It wasn't about trust. It was about her wanting to keep Sebastian safe.

He squeezed her hand.

And walked away.

Ella sidled closer. "You two are an item now?"

"I don't know what you're talking about." She knew exactly what Ella was talking about. Because *maybe* when she and Ella went out, they shared over the occasional glass of wine and talked about their men troubles. And the men they'd like to have trouble with.

"You are such a dirty liar," Ella whispered. "Tell me the truth. I saw him holding your hand when you walked into the building. Security footage caught that part."

Of course, it had.

Alyssa was still staring after Sebastian's back.

"So, was one time enough?" Ella asked, voice barely more than a breath. "Because I think you once told me that a hate fuck would be good for the soul."

Jeez. She had said that. After too many glasses of wine. "It wasn't about hate," she muttered.

Ella sucked in a quick breath.

And Alyssa realized what she'd confessed.

"Antony will lose his overprotective mind," Ella warned.

*First, we have to find him.* They had to make sure he was safe. They had to help him.

After that, they could deal with the fallout.

\*\*\*

Sebastian didn't go into his office via the main door. That would have been too obvious, and Sebastian tried not to be an obvious man.

So he entered Antony's office, instead. Fun little fact, he and his buddy had secretly installed a passageway that connected the two offices. A passageway that could double as a safe room when shit hit the fan. Because, unfortunately, they'd been in several situations when the shit had blown sky high.

The passageway would open to the left of Sebastian's desk. When he stepped out, he'd be right on the bastard who thought he could hack Sebastian's system.

He had his gun ready. He'd taken the liberty of bringing a few weapons with him. He hadn't shown them to Alyssa because, hell, seeing him with the knife earlier had seemed like more than enough show-and-tell business for one night.

Before he left the passageway, he checked the weapon once more. When the panel soundlessly slid open, he stepped out. "Give me a fucking reason not to shoot you." His voice was low and lethal, and he had his gun aimed at the shadowy figure who sat behind his desk.

The glow from Sebastian's dual screens fell onto the man. His fingers were poised over the keyboard. His whole body stiffened.

After a tense moment, his head turned slightly toward Sebastian. "A reason? Well, how about the fact that if you shoot me, then you lose the best—and only—partner that you've ever had," Antony Kyle responded.

*Antony Kyle.*

Sebastian didn't lower his weapon. "You went dark."

"Well, yeah." Antony shrugged. "Trying to get some alone time, if you know what I mean. I had Dex breathing down my neck and pressuring me to take other assignments, and I wasn't even sure I wanted to stay in the business longer and—"

"How did they find out about Alyssa? How did your cover get blown?"

Now Antony jerked, as if his body had just been surged with electricity. "My cover has not been blown." He rose and put his body right in front of Sebastian—and Sebastian's gun. "I've been friendly so far because, you know, we're friends, but want to tell me why you're pointing your gun at me?"

"Want to tell me why you broke into *my* office?"

"Uh, I just did." Antony's gaze was hard behind the lenses of his glasses. "I told you, I was trying to get alone time. Didn't know if Dex was tracking my online activity—you know that jerk does that sometimes when he's keeping tabs on me—so I figured if I came here, to your office, it would just look as if you were the one in Shark doing some late-night work." His hands were loose at his sides. "Now what the hell did you mean about Alyssa?"

"You know exactly what I meant! *You* sent me the text asking me to protect her!" This was some bull—

"I didn't send you any text," Antony responded slowly. "I told you, I went dark. As in, dark from everyone. I haven't used my phone in days. Hell, I didn't even take it with me on the mission. I left it here in my office. I did not text you."

"You told me your cover was blown."

Antony shook his head.

"You told me to protect her."

Once more, a negative shake of Antony's head.

"To do anything necessary."

Antony's Adam's apple bobbed. "I never contacted you about Alyssa."

Tension poured through Sebastian's body. *If Antony didn't contact me, who did?* "You didn't see any of the media reports? You haven't heard what's happened?" Sebastian demanded.

"I've been staying off-line, like I said. This is my first time to be at a computer. Got some big damn decisions to make. I went off-grid for a reason. Now tell me what is up with my sister!"

Sebastian lowered his gun. "Someone shot at Alyssa. The same person later trashed her house."

Antony's eyes widened. "Someone *shot* at my sister? Is she hurt? OhmyGod, was Alyssa hit?"

"I got her." He should say more. Sebastian cleared his throat. "She's safe. I've been taking care of her."

Antony's grabbed him and pulled him in for a hug. "Thank you. God, you know how important she is to me! If something happened to her…"

Sebastian was stiff. Too tense. "Nothing will happen to her." Not on his watch.

Antony pulled back. Frowned. "Where is my sister right now?"

Sebastian backed away and stalked for the door. "Waiting with the guards."

Antony rushed up behind him just as Sebastian hauled open the door. "Stand down," Sebastian immediately snapped to the assembled guards.

"Wow." Antony's voice was low. "They were out here the whole time? How'd you even know I was in your office? 'Cause, man, I was careful. Made sure no one saw me entering this building."

That would explain the mysterious tech glitches. Figured they'd come from one of the guys who knew the system inside and out. "I knew you were in here because no one touches my tech without my knowledge." No one could get to the secrets he had.

No one.

He hurried forward. "Go back to your stations," he ordered the guards. He flashed his smile at them and gave a rough laugh. "The situation is contained. One of your bosses just forgot to follow protocol and decided to scare us all to death."

"Low key," Antony muttered. "I was trying to be—"

"*Antony!*" Alyssa's shocked voice. And then she was rushing forward. Her whole face lit up as she ran forward.

*She's not running to me.* Sebastian wanted that. He wanted Alyssa to light up and run to him.

Sebastian stepped to the side. He got out of the way.

Alyssa ran into her brother's arms and hugged him tightly. Antony buried his face in her hair.

"Everything okay?" Ella asked. Her voice seemed oddly cautious—even for Ella—as she sidled closer.

Sebastian nodded. "Sorry for the false alarm. Didn't realize Antony was in tonight." *Because the bastard had gone dark.*

And...

*Antony didn't contact me.* Sebastian was keeping his mask in place and trying not to show just how unnerved he was. If Antony hadn't contacted him about Alyssa that first time, then it meant the perp they were after had done it.

The perp had deliberately contacted Sebastian right in the middle of a giant press conference. He'd deliberately chosen *that* moment to reveal that Alyssa was being threatened.

Why?

Only one answer came to mind for Sebastian, and it wasn't good.

*He was testing me.* The guy had caught Sebastian in the spotlight, and he'd forced him to choose...

*I chose her.*

"If you don't need me, I want to talk with the guards," Ella said. "Unless there is something else I need to know about?"

He gave a flash of his dimples. "We're good."

Ella nodded briskly, then strode away. As she hurried off, her gaze darted toward Antony.

"I'm so glad you're okay," Alyssa said as she eased away from her brother. "I was afraid something had happened to you, and when Sebastian told me—" She stopped. Pressed her lips together.

*I told her everything. I thought there was no choice, and I told her.*

Antony didn't know that part, not yet.

Actually...

There was a whole lot that Antony didn't know.

Alyssa glanced over at Sebastian.

"We need to go back into my office," he said. "Talk privately." Without anyone else overhearing what was sure to be one hell of a conversation. He maneuvered toward Alyssa and Antony. When he was near her, Sebastian's hand immediately lowered and curled around Alyssa's side. He wanted her close because he wanted to protect her.

He also just wanted her.

Antony's gaze flickered at the movement. Then his eyes narrowed. "Uh..." Antony began.

Sebastian strode toward his office with Alyssa. What they had to say could wait until two more minutes until they were away from the lingering guards.

Alyssa slid inside before him. Sebastian held the door open for Antony.

His friend passed him, but sent Sebastian a hard, warning glance. "I was only gone a few days."

Sebastian inclined his head. "A whole lot can happen in a few days." In fact, a man's entire world could change in just a few days. Sebastian followed them into his office and shut the door behind him.

He pulled in a deep breath as he considered where to start. How to start. How to be tactful.

But...screw tactful. Tact had never been his strong suit, anyway.

Alyssa stood uncertainly near his desk, and Antony was already crowding in around her.

"You were shot at?" Antony's face showed his worry.

She bit her lower lip. Cast a glance at Sebastian. "He saved me. Literally carried me away from the scene, threw me in his limo, and rushed me back to his place."

Sebastian saw Antony's shoulders tense. But he turned his head toward Sebastian and said, "Thank you. I owe you."

Yeah...about that... "You really don't." He strode forward. Deliberately put his body right next to Alyssa's. His shoulder brushed hers.

The move was to show that he was aligning himself with Alyssa.

Or...to show...*she's mine.*

"I can't believe someone went after her." Antony hauled a shaking hand through his hair. "I mean, that's crazy. There's no reason for anyone to ever try and hurt—"

"I know, Antony," Alyssa cut in. Her voice was flat.

"Uh, know what?" He took off his glasses. Polished them on his shirt. A typical move that he used to buy time in uncomfortable situations. Sebastian had seen him pull that move over and over again.

*Sorry, bro. This situation is about to get a whole lot more uncomfortable for us all.*

"I know about your side business."

Antony kept polishing his glasses.

"About the work that you do for the government?"

Antony popped the glasses back on. "I have no idea what you're talking about."

She surged toward him. "I had no idea you were such a good liar."

Antony's mouth opened.

Sebastian cleared his throat. He seemed to be doing that a lot lately. "I told her."

Antony gaped at him as if Sebastian had lost his mind. "Excuse me?"

"I told her," he repeated. "Her life was on the line. Alyssa deserved the truth."

"Alyssa..." Antony began, his voice halting and careful. "Look, it's not what you must be thinking—"

"I'm thinking that you're a spy," she responded crisply. Her thumb jerked toward

Sebastian. "So is he. I'm thinking that you've both been keeping secrets from me for years, but it's time for all the secrets to end."

"Okay," Antony mumbled. "So maybe the situation is what you're thinking." He blew out a breath. "There was no need to pull you into that world. It was too dangerous for you. You couldn't handle—"

"Don't tell me what I can handle," she cut through his words. "I'm not some kid any longer, and you don't get to decide what happens in my life."

Antony's gaze swept over her. "No, you're definitely not the kid who used to tail after me." He nodded. "Okay, I'm a spy. But you can't tell anyone, understand? You can't blow my cover and I—"

"It's not like I'm going to broadcast it on the evening news," she huffed. "And, besides, I'm pretty sure your cover is blown. At least, that's...wait, isn't that what you told Sebastian? That's what started this whole mess. Your cover was blown so you told him to protect me."

Antony gave a grim shake of his head. "I didn't contact him. My cover wasn't blown. That's what I was saying to Sebastian a few minutes ago. I never sent him a text. I never warned him that you were in danger. I *never* asked him to protect you." He advanced toward Sebastian. Gave him a weary smile. "But, damn, man I am grateful to you. I am so glad that you were there for my sister. So glad that I can always count on you to do the right thing with her."

Oh, yeah, this was going to turn bad very, very soon. "About that..." Sebastian began.

Antony clapped a hand on his shoulder. "You carried her to safety? You brought her into your house?"

"He's been giving me twenty-four, seven protection," Alyssa murmured. Did her cheeks pinken? It looked as if they did.

Antony smiled at him. "Above and beyond. That's what you do. Go above and beyond. You are the best friend I've ever had, and you have no idea how grateful I am to you. Thank you for everything that you did for Alyssa. I'm sure she appreciated all that you did."

Her cheeks didn't just pinken. They went pure red.

"I think she liked some parts more than others."

Her head whipped toward Sebastian. Her eyes flared.

"I'm sure of it," Sebastian added softly. "The highpoints are burned in my memory." A highpoint...his mouth between her legs and her coming for him.

"That's great," her brother said.

Um, probably not so great for him.

Antony backed away. "But you don't have to worry any longer. I'm here. I'll take care of her." Another nod. "Alyssa, until we can figure this out, you can stay with me. I've got security to match the setup at Sebastian's place. I'll contact my handler, and we'll figure this out in no time." He seemed utterly confident.

Alyssa frowned at him. "Dex has no idea what's going on."

Antony blinked. "You've already met Dex?"

"Yes, and he doesn't know who is after me, either."

Sebastian rolled back his shoulders. "He's working on it."

"Working on it?" A furrow appeared between Antony's brows. "Hell, if he thought my cover was blown, I'm surprised I didn't find him camped out in this office with you."

Sebastian was a bit surprised by that, too. "I'm sure he's watching things." Dex always did.

But he didn't think Dex was the only one watching. The perp had played him, all along. This had never been about Antony.

*It was about me.*

*Me and Alyssa.*

"If I'd had any idea this was going on, I would have come back sooner," Antony told Alyssa. "You know that, don't you? I'd never leave you in danger."

"You haven't heard anything?" She tilted her head to the right and studied him. "Haven't seen anything on social media? Didn't catch any of the news stories?"

"I had some soul-searching to do. When I go dark, I go dark."

"The timing of that is too coincidental." Sebastian's body was tense. This couldn't be overlooked. "In order for this to all work, our bad guy had to know that you were going to be out of touch."

Antony stiffened. "I didn't tell anyone what I was planning."

"He used your phone. How the hell did he get your phone?"

Antony's brows furrowed. "Told you, I left it in my office. But...when I got here tonight, I looked for it. It wasn't in my desk. Someone took it. At the time, I thought maybe you had snagged it, but, hell, guess not, huh?"

"Definitely not." Every red flag was flying. "He *knew* you were dark. He counted on that to work this whole situation. He wanted me with Alyssa. He wanted me close to her." Maybe that shooting outside of the theater...hell, he'd thought that they'd gotten lucky and the shooter had missed her but... "What if he intended to miss?" Sebastian demanded as he thought this scenario through to its end point.

Antony's brows rose. "You need to back up because I am not following where you're leading right now."

"Alyssa was shot at outside the Langley Theater. I thought he missed her. Maybe he didn't. Maybe the guy hit exactly where he wanted to hit."

Alyssa shifted closer to him. "And my house? When he left that message on my wall?"

"Whoa!" Antony threw up a hand. "What message? Could you please catch me up all the way?"

Sebastian considered the message that had been left. "I thought he'd missed you. That he'd gone to your house in an attempt to get to you, but he could have left that message just to scare you and to make sure that you stayed with me."

"Why?" Alyssa's confusion was clear to see. "Why would he want me with you?"

Because when I'm with you, when I'm focused on you, I'm distracted. I make mistakes. Shit. Like when he'd immediately rushed out of the press conference.

When he freaking showed the world what mattered most to him.

He was the one who was screwed.

"Why is he trying to distract me?" Sebastian mumbled, half to himself. "What does he want?"

"We'll figure this out," Antony assured him. "And you won't be distracted again." He reached for Alyssa's hand and tugged her toward him. "I'll be taking over Alyssa's security until this mess is sorted out. You don't have to worry. I've got her now." He turned for the door and pulled Alyssa with him. "Let's get out of here. I don't like the idea that someone could be watching us. We'll sleep on things tonight and start fresh tomorrow."

Sebastian stared at Antony's back. The guy thought he was just going to take Alyssa away from him? "That's not happening."

Antony looked back at him. "Excuse me? Sorry?"

"You're not taking Alyssa." *Not when I just got her.*

"Uh, sure I am." Antony laughed. "She's my sister, man. Thanks for looking after her, but I've got her now."

Alyssa stared at Sebastian. He couldn't read the expression in her eyes, and he damn well wished that he could.

"Come on," Antony urged her. "Let's go, Alyssa."

*Over my dead body.* Sebastian lunged forward even as—

"No," Alyssa said. Her voice was firm and clear, and it seemed to cut through the room like a knife.

Antony swung toward her. "What?"

"You're both acting like this isn't my decision." She lifted their joined hands. "You're literally trying to pull me after you."

"I'm trying to keep you safe and—"

"Sebastian has been doing a stellar job of that so far."

"But he doesn't have to do it anymore! You don't have to be a burden to him and—"

"She is *never* a burden," Sebastian barked.

Antony's gaze suddenly narrowed on him.

Sebastian caught the flash of suspicion in his friend's gaze.

"*She,*" Alyssa fired pointedly, "can also make decisions for herself. And I'm going to spend the night with Sebastian. That's my choice."

*I'm going to spend the night with Sebastian.*

"I'm staying with him," she added simply.

Antony laughed. "But he has a life to get back to living! I'm sure the ladies in his life don't appreciate having to share space with you over at his place."

Alyssa's expression tightened.

"Alyssa doesn't share me with anyone." *Keep it up, Antony. You're about to piss me off. I'll only be grateful to see that you're alive for so long.* "I'm living my life just fine with her. Alyssa's choice." That was what it came down to for him. "You heard her. She wants me."

And there it was. He saw it. The flicker of Antony's lashes. The flash of realization.

Antony never forgot anything. He was much like Sebastian in that regard. Every word he'd ever read, every conversation he'd ever heard...

All on constant replay in his mind.

So Sebastian knew that Antony would remember their long ago conversation about Alyssa and the one stipulation that Sebastian had made.

"You sonofabitch," Antony breathed.

Alyssa pulled her hand from his. "Why are you calling him names? Sebastian saved me!"

"No." Antony's hands fisted. "He just took what *he* wanted." He lunged toward Sebastian.

Alyssa stepped into his path and shoved against her brother's chest. "What are you doing? Are you crazy?" Her voice rose.

Antony's face darkened as he glowered over her shoulder at Sebastian. "I told you! It was the *one* condition, and you knew it!" His voice was loud. Too loud.

"You need to calm down," Alyssa snapped back. "Take a breath. Take twenty of them!"

Footsteps rushed outside of the office.

"*I am calm!*" Antony bellowed.

"Doesn't sound that way to me," Sebastian said. He crossed his arms over his chest. Propped his hip on the desk. Waited.

He figured that he had a swing or two coming his way. He'd take them.

*For her, I'd take just about anything.*

"Do not tell me," Antony blasted, "that this jerk brought you in his home, saying he'd protect you—"

A fist pounded against the door. "Everything okay in there?" Ella called.

"Only to seduce you!" Antony shouted.

The door flew open. Ella gaped in the doorway.

Alyssa put her hands on her hips. "Don't be ridiculous."

Antony released a ragged breath. His shoulders sagged. "Thank Christ." He waved his hand toward Sebastian. "Sorry, really, *sorry,* but this night has been crazy, and I don't know what I was—"

"I seduced him," Alyssa clarified. "Obviously."

Antony surged for Sebastian with his fist swinging.

Sebastian waited for the blow.

But...

Alyssa tripped her brother. Antony went down, hard.

She put her hands on her hips. Glared at Sebastian. "Really? You were just going to sit there? Let him punch you?"

He could not drag his eyes off her. "Seemed like a plan at the time."

Antony groaned. He pushed himself up.

"Why the hell would you do that?" Alyssa asked Sebastian.

"Because I figure you're worth a broken nose or a busted lip." He shrugged. "Actually, I think you might be worth just about anything."

She didn't respond.

"Ahem." Ella's voice was strained. "Everyone's okay here, yes? I think you are. I'll just back away."

Antony made it to his feet. He pointed at Sebastian. "We had an agreement."

"And that's some BS." Alyssa kept her body positioned between Sebastian and Antony.

*She's protecting me?* He'd noticed that she seemed to do that a lot. Put herself between him and others. Hmm.

"Antony, you don't get to make decisions about the men I see. About the men I might want to be involved with. If I want to be with Sebastian, I'm going to be with him."

Sebastian straightened. A smile pulled at his lips. She wanted to be with him?

"If I want to be with a dozen men," Alyssa blazed on, "I'll be with them."

He lost his smile. *A dozen men?* Sebastian's eyes narrowed. "The hell you will."

She ignored him and jabbed her brother in the chest. "You don't run my life. I love you, but you don't dictate who I sleep with, just like I don't tell you who to see." She removed her hand as her shoulders heaved. "Got it?"

Antony rubbed his chest, right on the spot where she'd jabbed him. "Got it."

"Good. Now, it's late, and I'm going to bed."
She marched for the door. Angry, fast steps.
Alyssa wrenched open the door and fired a fast
glance over her shoulder. "Coming?" Alyssa
locked eyes with Sebastian.

He rose. "No way you're leaving without me."

"Good." A firm nod.

He moved to follow her.

Antony slid into his path. "This isn't over."

Sebastian flashed his dimples at the other
man. "Of course, it's not. As I told your sister just
a little while ago, things are just beginning."

Antony's face flushed.

Sebastian lowered his voice and warned, "Try
to get between me and Alyssa again, and it will be
your worst mistake." He was done playing. "She
came to me. She wants me. And like I said
before..."

"She's my sister!"

"I will take care of her."

"No. You don't take care of things. You amuse
yourself with them, and then you toss them
away." Antony's voice was low, rough. "I've seen
you do it, time and time again. You like
challenges, but when the challenge is over, you get
bored. *You can't get bored with her.* Don't you
see? You can't hurt her!" Fury flashed on his face.
"But you didn't think about the consequences, did
you? You took what you wanted, and now it's too
late."

Sebastian stared into his friend's eyes.
"You're right. Now it is too late." Because he'd
finally gotten what he wanted.

But Antony was wrong. Sebastian wasn't going to get bored. He wasn't going to hurt Alyssa.

And he had no plans to ever toss her away.

He wasn't a damn fool.

# CHAPTER TWELVE

"That went well." Alyssa rode the elevator down with Sebastian. Her brother had tried to lunge onto the elevator with them, but she'd shut the doors just in time. She needed some privacy with Sebastian, STAT.

"You think?" He lifted his brows.

"Oh, definitely." Rage poured through her. "You know, especially that part where you just stood there and waited for Antony to punch you. Great moment. Highlight reel material."

His lips twitched.

He thought this was funny? Her hand flew out, and she slammed the emergency stop button.

His lips stopped twitching. "Why did you do that?"

"So that I can scream at you in privacy. So that Ella won't rush in when she hears me yelling...*What were you thinking? You don't just stand there and let someone punch you!*"

His gaze swept over her face. "I knew your brother would be pissed."

"Because I seduced you."

He shook his head. "That's not what happened. That's not—"

"Let's recap, shall we?" She rubbed her palms over her jeans. Before they'd left his home, she'd thrown on jeans, a black blouse, and her trusty sneakers. "I was the one who went to your bedroom. I was the one who kissed you. I was the one—"

"*I* was the one who went down on you because I've spent too many years wondering how you'd taste."

Okay. When he said things like that, he made her whole body heat. "How did I taste?" She almost slapped her hand over her mouth after that question burst out.

He stepped toward her. "Delicious."

The elevator sure was small. Tight.

Or maybe he was just big.

"I'm not fucking bored."

She side-eyed him. "Don't remember saying you were."

"I don't toss away things that matter."

"That's good to know, but, again, I don't remember saying that you did."

His lips thinned. "I'm not tossing you away."

"Great. Because I'm not a *thing* to be tossed away. Look, I think you and Antony have the wrong idea here."

He came even closer.

She didn't back up. Was the elevator shrinking? "I'm staying with you because you saved my life. I trust you to keep me safe."

"Your brother can keep you safe, too," he said. He sure sounded grudging with that admission.

Did she have to spell it out for him? "I'm sure the cops can keep me safe, too. I'm sure Winston has a great safe house."

His lips parted—

"I'm even sure that Dex could set me up with protection. Or I could hire my own bodyguards. I have lots of options." Had he gotten that last part? *"I,"* she emphasized, "have plenty of choices, but I want to stay with you." She forced a shrug. "Antony can deal with it."

"Why?"

Her head tilted back. He was right over her. Their mouths were only inches apart. They'd made love less than two hours before. Her body was still hypersensitive and too tuned to him. The pleasure had blasted through her. Everything with him had been so much stronger and more intense than it had ever been with anyone else.

"Alyssa, you're not answering me."

No, she wasn't. She leaned onto her toes. Her hand reached toward his side—

His eyes blazed.

She touched the emergency button and got the elevator moving again. Still on her toes, she brought her mouth even closer to his. So close that she knew her breath would whisper over his lips as she said, "You're a smart guy." *Maybe* she let her tongue lick over his sensual lower lip. "I'm sure you can figure out the reason why."

His hands flew up and locked around her upper arms. "Don't play with me." A hard warning.

"I'm not playing." Again, she let her tongue lick over his lip.

Then his mouth took hers. Her lips were parted and ready, and she met him eagerly. In the back of her mind, she was thinking...*Maybe* this kiss won't be as good. Maybe we've been together once and now we have that whole wild lust situation out of our system, maybe...

Desire ignited within her. Her tongue stroked his. Need churned through her. The kiss was hot and frantic and passionate. Her nails bit through his shirt as she angled to get closer and closer. She moaned and her body rubbed against his.

The man's mouth...

The way he used his mouth...

His tongue...

He backed her up. Her shoulders hit the wall of the elevator. Sebastian's hand slid down to her—

*Ding.* The doors opened.

"If I were a bad guy, I could shoot you right now. You'd hardly be able to put up much of a fight."

In a flash, Sebastian had lunged away from her, *and* he'd pulled out a gun. He had it aimed right at the man who stood just beyond the open elevator doors.

Dex.

"If you were a bad guy," Sebastian threw right back, "you'd be dead right now so a fight wouldn't be necessary."

Her breath heaved in and out.

Dex laughed. "I'm not bad, so why don't you lower the gun?"

"I'm supposed to have guards down here. Why the hell are they not meeting me?"

"Because I sent them away. Waved my magical government ID and powers at them, and I overrode your orders. But don't worry, I've got you covered. The lady, too." He craned to look around Sebastian at Alyssa. "Hi, there."

The doors started to slide closed again.

Dex leaned forward and stopped them. "You can't hide in the elevator all night."

"Hardly hiding," Sebastian drawled right back.

"No, you seemed to be busy with, uh, other things. And I think that's an issue."

Sebastian hadn't lowered his gun yet. She touched his shoulder. "Why don't we listen to what the government handler has to say, hmm?"

Another ding sounded.

"Ah." Dex leaned back. Glanced to the left. "That'll probably be Antony. Wonder if he will be making out with someone when the doors open? If so, I am curious about who his partner will be."

Sebastian's body tightened.

"*Don't,*" Alyssa urged him.

He looked at her. "Fine. For you." He tucked the gun into the back waistband of his jeans. He pulled his shirt down and covered the gun. His fingers curled with hers, and they walked out of the elevator together.

"Thought you'd beat us down," Sebastian said as he eyed Antony.

"Especially since they paused for a pit stop." Dex was all smug. She was becoming convinced that he was always smug.

"Had to stop and check some other files." Antony's voice was wooden, but his eyes were dark and turbulent.

They stood in the building's lobby, and, Sebastian had been right, the guards were gone. Well, one guard remained. A lone security guard hunched behind his desk.

The marble gleamed under their feet as they stood there. A tight, uncomfortable group.

"Are you tailing me, Dex?" Sebastian asked mildly.

"I was looking for Antony. Finding him was a priority, of course. Had to make sure that the agency hadn't been compromised."

"I *wasn't* compromised," Antony growled right back. His voice didn't carry beyond their circle. "That text was a lie. I never asked Sebastian to protect Alyssa and—"

"I know," Dex said smoothly.

He...knew? Her focus sharpened on him.

Dex turned his attention to her. He put a genial smile on his face as he said, "I've come for you."

Sebastian stiffened. "I don't think so."

"I very much think so." Dex's stare didn't leave her. "You're being taken into protective custody. Your safety will be my priority."

"I didn't ask to be taken into protective custody." What was going on? Her gaze darted to the glass entrance doors and the darkness that waited outside. She could see Sebastian's limo. The driver stood near the side of the vehicle. Two men in Shark Gaming and Design security uniforms flanked him.

"You didn't have to ask. Consider it a gift."

Alyssa shook her head. "Then it's a gift I don't want."

"I'm afraid you don't get to refuse." Dex offered his hand to her. "I assure you, when the danger has passed, you can go right back to living your life normally."

She didn't take his hand. "I'm good exactly where I am."

"You mean you're good with Sebastian. But you're not. In fact, I think you being with him puts Sebastian in considerable danger."

Her heart squeezed in her chest.

Dex's expression hardened. "Now you can take my hand or I can cuff you to me and we'll walk out of here that way. All very prisoner-like. Either way, make no mistake, you will be leaving with me."

"The hell she is," Sebastian snapped. "You're *not* cuffing her!"

Even Antony was frowning at Dex. "Did you just threaten to cuff my sister?"

"I'll do whatever must be done." Dex waited with his hand extended. "Now, shall we go, Alyssa?"

"No." She was adamant. "We absolutely will not—"

Why was there a red dot on Antony's chest? But even as that thought ran through her mind, Alyssa was lunging toward her brother because she watched plenty of TV shows. She loved crime shows in particular, and a red dot on someone's chest always meant trouble.

She screamed and threw her body against his even as she heard the sound of shattering glass.

They hit the floor as shards of glass rained all over the lobby.

"OhmyGod." Antony stared up at her in shock. "Someone just shot at me."

"And I saved your life," she told him quickly. "So how about a thank—*you!*" Her voice rose in alarm as she was grabbed from behind. Grabbed and carried fast only to be basically thrown behind the main check-in counter in the lobby.

Sebastian had been the one grabbing her. He was also the one now glowering at her. "What the hell? *Why* did you do that?"

"Because there was a red dot on Antony's chest." Her arm was hurting. A hot, fast throb in her upper, right arm. "I saw one like that last week on a *CSI* re-run. Someone on that show was using a scope to get a lock on his target."

"This isn't freaking *CSI!*"

Antony and Dex had crowded behind the counter, too. The security guard who'd been at the counter was taking cover with them and calling for backup on his phone.

Sebastian had his gun in his hand. "I'm going after the bastard."

She grabbed him and held tight. Pain throbbed in a hard, burning burst in her arm. Damn but that pain was weird. "You just said this wasn't *CSI!* You can't go chasing after bad guys!"

"Yeah, sweetheart, I can, because it's what I do." He jerked his head to Antony. "If your sister gets so much as a scratch, I will kick your ass."

She'd just gotten a good look at her arm. And the blood there. "Little late for that," she mumbled. Oh, crap. The sight of blood—particularly her own—had always caused her to feel more than a bit...

Like fainting.

*Do not faint now. Do not lose your shit now.*

"What do you mean it's too late?" Sebastian rumbled.

"The bad guy is probably escaping," Dex pointed out. "I'm going after him." He leapt away.

"I think I've already got a scratch." She angled her body so Sebastian could see her arm. "Or...maybe it's a...bullet wound?" Her eyes widened. "Oh, God, I think I was shot!"

# CHAPTER THIRTEEN

"You weren't shot." Antony was in the hospital exam room with her. Family only, per the doctor's order. "That's a good thing."

She frowned down at the bandage on her arm. No, she hadn't been shot. But she did now sport six stitches because when the front door window had shattered, a clunk of glass had flown into her arm.

It had actually still been in her arm when Sebastian had realized that she was injured. When he'd first gotten a good look at her arm, all of the color had left his face, and his gaze had become downright scary. He'd stayed with her. Kept her body protected and covered until the cavalry arrived.

She'd wanted to immediately yank the glass out of her arm, but Sebastian had stopped her. He'd mumbled something about damage and blood loss and told her they had to wait for the EMTs.

She hadn't passed out.

A win.

She'd sat there, bleeding and shocked, as the minutes ticked by.

They hadn't caught the bad guy.

Not so much a win.

Dex had returned empty-handed. And pissed.

"Alyssa, are you listening to me?" Antony asked, even though the tone of his voice told her that he already knew the answer, and, no, she wasn't listening.

"I want to see Sebastian."

"Of course, you do." He put his hands on his hips. "I am going to have to fight him."

"You're an adult. He's your best friend. You don't have to fight anyone." She frowned down at the white bandage that covered her stitches. The nurse had numbed the area before the stitches had been carefully inserted. The doctor had told Alyssa that she was lucky. The glass hadn't penetrated deep enough to damage her muscle.

"He's sleeping with you."

She twisted her arm a bit to see if the stitches pulled. "We didn't actually get around to sleeping."

"Oh, sweet Jesus. Don't say stuff like that to your brother!"

Her head turned back toward him. "You made an incorrect statement. I was just helping out by correcting you."

"You were not."

"I was helping, the same way I helped when I saved your life in the Shark lobby." She sat on the side of the exam table, and her legs swung before her. The room was icy, and she just wanted to get out and go home.

With Sebastian.

"Never do it again."

She squinted at him. "Never save you again? Sorry, I can't promise that. You are my brother, even when you drive me crazy."

"Never risk your life that way again. You could have easily been shot. What would I have done then?"

"Rush me to a hospital?" she guessed.

"Not funny."

"I think she's fucking hilarious."

The door had opened. She hadn't heard it open. But now Sebastian stood in the entranceway. She was pretty sure she saw a blood stain on his jeans. Her blood. Another red smear slid across the side of his shirt.

He'd carried her to the ambulance when it finally arrived.

His pose was relaxed, but his expression—and his eyes—told a whole other story. In fact, Alyssa was pretty sure that she'd never seen his eyes look so enraged before. They seemed to burn with fury.

"I mean, she has to be making a joke," Sebastian continued in a voice that made her want to shiver. Both because it was so low and sexy and also because there was a dangerous edge to the words. *To him.* "Because there is no way Alyssa will *ever* jump in front of a bullet again, am I right?"

Delicately, she cleared her throat. "No, I'm afraid you're wrong."

"The fuck I am." His eyes glittered even more.

She nodded. "The fuck you are."

He stalked toward her. She knew exactly how prey felt in that moment but she just lifted her chin and kept swinging her legs as she sat on that exam table. "I do have a question, though," Alyssa announced. "Why do spies keep sneaking into rooms? I've noticed it's happening a lot."

He stepped between her swinging legs. He put his hands on either side of her hips and flattened them on the white paper thing that hospitals always had on their exam tables. Sebastian leaned in close.

"You are not risking yourself again," he growled.

"Uh, Sebastian, you need to back up," Antony told him. He clapped a hand on Sebastian's shoulder. "You're crowding my sister."

Her breath was coming in shallow pants. She couldn't look away from Sebastian's eyes. This was such a different guy. No flashing dimples. No drawling, mocking words. Just a lethal intensity that had her stomach knotting.

"I'm going to do a whole lot more than crowd her." His eyes turned to slits, and he didn't back away. "You don't ever try to—"

"So, you're sexy when you're all intense and dangerous, I have to give you that." She saw the flash of surprise on his face. A flash that was very quickly masked. "But here's the thing." She wet her lips.

His eyes dropped to her lips.

*Wow.* That stare of his heated even more.

She swallowed. "There was a red dot on my brother's chest. I've seen enough TV shows to know what that dot meant. There was no way—let me repeat, *no way*—I was just going to stand there and let Antony get shot."

"Thanks," Antony muttered. His hand had fallen from Sebastian's shoulder. "Appreciate that."

She didn't look at him. It was too hard to look away from Sebastian. His gaze had risen from her mouth and locked with hers again. "And if that dot had been on *your* chest," she told Sebastian, aware that her voice had gone all husky, "I would have done the same thing. I'm not going to stand there when I can help. I get that I'm not some super spy. It's not like I'm going to be signing up to go on secret missions with you, but I can still do what's right. I will protect you both whenever I can." There. She waited for Sebastian's response. Would it kill the man to say that she'd done a good job? She had saved Antony, after all.

But Sebastian's face didn't exactly show wonderment at her bravery. Nope, his expression was still all hard and dark and stormy.

"You think you're going to do the same thing again?" he finally rumbled. "You think you'll risk yourself for him?"

"He's my brother," she answered. "What else would I do?"

Antony sidled closer to her. "You know, Sebastian, I don't like the way you're glaring at my sister—"

Sebastian's glare whipped to him.

Antony winced. "And I don't like the way you're glaring at me. See? This whole thing you have going on?" He pointed at Sebastian. "The way you turn things off and you run on fury? That's why you should have always stayed the hell away from Alyssa. I told you before, you're my best friend, but Alyssa can't handle the kind of danger that you like—"

"Get the hell out," Sebastian snarled.

Antony's eyes widened. "Excuse me?"

"I need to talk to Alyssa alone. So get the hell out."

But Antony's shoulders straightened. "I don't think so. Like I said, I don't like the way you're glaring. I don't like this whole looming thing you're doing with her, and I don't like—"

"I would damn well cut out my own heart before I hurt her, so just step outside and give us a minute."

Alyssa's heart surged in her chest.

Antony frowned. "Well, of course, you wouldn't physically hurt her. I've always known that. But there are all kinds of pain in this world, and I don't want Alyssa—"

"You don't want—what? For her to get shot? For her to get her arm sliced open when she tries to save your ass? Or mine? Because guess what? I want the same thing, and that's why I need to make sure that Alyssa understands me very, very well."

Okay. Now he was pissing her off. "I understand the situation extremely well, thanks so much." He was still...looming over her. Trapping her. His hands were on either side of her hips, his body between her legs. His face was inches from hers. She frowned at his hard profile as he stared at her brother. "And what *you* need to understand..." Her hand rose. She jabbed him in the shoulder.

His head turned toward her.

"I *will* risk myself if it means protecting Antony. He's my brother. I love him. And I'll risk my life in order to protect you, too. I would do it because—" Alyssa broke off.

Just in time.

Or, no, maybe it had been too late. Maybe Sebastian had caught her slip. He was watching her now with what felt like the predatory gaze of a snake that was about to strike, super fast.

"Antony," Sebastian snapped, only he didn't glance at her brother again. "Get the hell out before I throw you out."

"Hey!" Antony's voice rose. "I don't like the way you're—"

"You want her to risk herself for me? Or you want me to fix this shit?"

A pause. "Fix this shit." Antony's steps shuffled for the door. "Fix it and let's go back to normal."

The door shut behind him.

When that door shut, her shoulders stiffened even more. "You're looming over me."

"Damn straight, I am." His gaze searched hers. "Why aren't you shaking in your sneakers? We both know I scare the hell out of you."

"No."

He blinked. Waited.

She pressed her lips together.

"Don't." A hard shake of his head. "One of the things I like best about you is when you say things and you let your real truth slip out. You don't filter or try to bullshit me. You tell me what you think, and I love that about you."

He'd just used the word *love*, but it didn't mean anything. "I have an issue with oversharing. Antony's always telling me that I shouldn't say everything I think. That I need to filter more."

"You don't say everything. You say the important things."

"I blurt—"

"I like it. Don't stop. Screw what Antony says."

She could feel the warmth from his body. She could feel *him*. He surrounded her. And if he wanted to know what she was thinking? Fine. "You're trying to intimidate me."

"What makes you say that?"

"Because..." She'd still been poking him with her finger. She let her hand fall. "You're trapping me here. Hands on both sides of me. Body between my legs."

"I want to fuck you, not intimidate you."

Her jaw dropped.

"But since your brother is on the other side of the door and a doctor will probably be walking in any moment, that's not going to happen right now."

He wanted to have sex with her? "I thought you were mad at me. You look mad."

"Oh, yes, I'm pissed as all hell." His mouth brushed over hers. A slow, drugging kiss that she hadn't expected. "But I also want you. I had you once, and I'll want you over and over again." Another kiss. One that tasted and tempted.

She had seen the fury in his eyes, but he kissed her with tender care, and the whole situation and his behavior made zero sense to her.

This time, both of her hands flew up and clamped around his shoulders. "I don't understand you."

Another kiss. Slow and sensual. His tongue slid into her mouth. Caressed hers. Had her moaning and tightening her hands around his shoulders.

"*Alyssa!*" Antony's voice. His hand pounded on the door. "You okay? It sounds like you're in pain!"

Sebastian lifted his head. Their eyes met.

"She'd better not be in pain, Sebastian!" Antony blasted.

"She's not," he called back. "Don't even think of coming in here."

"You are such a bossy bastard," Antony groused. A loud grouse.

"You are bossy," Alyssa told him.

"I'm also a bastard. Don't forget that. I will do anything necessary to get what I want in this world. I waited for you, I gave you time, but you chose me, and that means all bets are off."

"I didn't realize we were betting on anything. Are we playing some kind of game?"

A slow shake of his head. "Hell, no. And that's why you will not...*ever*...risk yourself again."

She wasn't going to make that promise. "Life's about risk. If you aren't taking some risks, then I think you're missing out."

"*You were bleeding.*" His voice was different. Almost guttural. "Your blood was on me."

"It was only a scratch," she whispered.

"What if it hadn't been? What if you'd been hit in the heart because you were trying to save Antony?"

"We *are* playing a game. The 'What If' game. I don't like that. I'd prefer not to play it."

"So the hell would I. But the problem is that I can't. I can't stop thinking about what I would do if I lost you."

"You'd be fine." An instant response. "I mean, you slept with me once, it hardly—"

He kissed her again. Rougher this time. Deeper. Harder. "Fine," he growled against her lips, "doesn't even begin to describe what I'd be. *I can't risk you.*"

"Doctor's coming!" Antony called out.

Sebastian slowly backed away.

A moment later, the doctor entered, and he was tailed by a watchful Antony. The doctor went over a few instructions—mostly about trying to keep her stitches dry and not doing any heavy lifting—and she listened to him, she *did,* but her attention also kept slipping to Sebastian.

He stood near the doorway. His arms were crossed over his chest. He appeared tense and hard, and his gaze was still as dangerous as before.

Only now, she knew he wasn't just pissed.

*"I want to fuck you, not intimidate you."* His words played through her mind once more. Her body ached, and she realized that as soon as they were alone...

The control that he was holding onto—the control she could see now—would vanish.

"Any questions?" the doctor asked.

She shook her head. She just wanted to leave.

"I'm assuming you'll have someone to take you home?" the doctor pushed. He glanced over at Antony. "Your brother?"

"*I'll* be taking her home," Sebastian responded.

Antony threw him a hard glance. "I think we need to talk. Outside."

The doctor's brow furrowed. "Is there a transportation issue?"

"Oh, there's an issue." Antony's smile was grim. "But we'll work it out, don't you worry." He inclined his head toward Sebastian. "I gave you time to talk with her alone, but now, you'll want to talk with me. You *owe* me that."

She held her breath as the two men filed out.

The doctor frowned at them.

"It's okay," she assured him. "Like my brother said, they'll work this out."

He nodded. Went back to studying her file.

And Alyssa tried to ignore the sinking in her stomach, the rough feeling that told her...no, they might *not* work things out.

\*\*\*

"You think I'm just going to let you take my sister home?" Antony stared at him as if Sebastian had gone crazy. "After what has already happened between the two of you—"

"I'm keeping her safe."

"Yeah, well, you're also trying to get her into your bed!"

*Not trying. I already had her there.* But he did want her in his bed again. And again. "I get that I owe you some hits, but that shit is going to have to wait."

"This isn't a joke!"

"That's why I'm not laughing." He stared solemnly at his friend. "I understand you're furious. She's your sister, you want what's best for her, and we damn well know that I'm not it."

"Look, that's—"

"On *most* days," Sebastian corrected, "I'm not it. On this freaking day, with this mess that's going down, I'm exactly what she needs. I can keep her safe."

"So can I! You think I wouldn't risk everything for her?"

He surged forward. "And you think I wouldn't?"

Antony blinked. "She's my family. I love her."

"She certainly proved she loved you when she jumped in front of you and that bullet."

Antony's nostrils flared. "She'd do the same to save you. That's who Alyssa is. You get that, don't you? Her heart has always been too big. She wants to help everyone. Thinks everyone deserves a chance, that good is just out there waiting in the world. She's a freaking Mary Poppins. I spent my teenage years shielding her because while Alyssa might think the world is sunshine and roses, it's not."

"She knows that." Anger hummed in his voice. "She's not a kid any longer. Stop treating her like one."

"I *love* her," Antony said again, voice thickening. "Can you say the same?"

Just over Antony's shoulder, Sebastian caught a flash of movement. His head cocked a little as he strained to get a better look at the fellow who'd just entered the corridor.

A nurse moved to the side, and Sebastian saw Winston hurrying forward. The detective didn't look happy.

*Yeah, buddy, join the club.*

"That's what I thought," Antony snapped. "And if you don't love her, then you need to stop this crap before she gets hurt. Hell, hurt more than she already has been."

The hospital exam door opened.

Sebastian's head immediately whipped toward the door—and Alyssa. Her eyes seemed extra dark. Extra deep.

And...sad?

Shit. What the hell had Antony been saying?

Sebastian had been distracted by Winston's appearance, but he did a quick mental replay of the conversation with Antony. He'd heard the words even if he hadn't processed them at the time, so it was mostly a matter of hitting a mental replay button in his mind.

*"I love her. Can you say the same?"*

Only Sebastian hadn't said anything because he'd been distracted by Winston's appearance.

"That's what I thought. And if you don't love her, then you need to stop this crap before she gets hurt. Hell, hurt more than she already has been."

How much had Alyssa heard?

"I didn't see him," Winston announced grimly as he closed in on Sebastian. "I'm sorry, man. I was looking for threats, I was watching the building, but the bastard was good."

Antony frowned. "What are you talking about?"

The doctor exited the exam room. He glanced expectantly at Sebastian. "Did you work out her transportation home?"

He reached for Alyssa's hand. "She's with me."

But Alyssa tried to pull her hand back.

"*Trust me,*" he told her softly.

She stilled.

The doctor was called away by a nurse. His coat flapped behind him as he rushed off.

"You okay, Alyssa?" Winston asked her.

She nodded. "Just a scratch." She gave Winston a weak smile.

Antony's expression darkened. "It could have been a lot more than a scratch! We've got to stop this bastard!"

"Lower your voice," Sebastian ordered. For a spy, Antony was sure as hell loud lately. "Look, we were trying to catch him tonight. That's why I had Winston there."

Winston nodded. "I was backup, in case there was trouble."

"There was trouble," Antony instantly said. "A lot of it. Only I didn't see you when the bullets were flying."

"Bullet," Alyssa corrected. "I think there was only one bullet. Not multiple bullets."

Winston straightened his spine and pinned Antony with a hard glare. "You didn't see me because I was trying to locate the shooter. As soon as the shot was fired, I was racing to where I thought he would be." He shook his head. "But he was gone before I arrived, then I had to deal with some government jerk named Dexter Ryan who tried to pull rank on me."

Sebastian released a low sigh. "I am familiar with the jerk in question."

"Yeah," Winston pursed his lips. "Figured you would be. He wouldn't let me or my men anywhere near the scene to investigate. He kicked our asses out."

"Can he do that?" Alyssa asked. Her voice was husky and soft, and Sebastian just had to slide a little closer to her. "Can he kick out police officers?"

Sebastian's hold tightened on her hand. "Dex thinks he can do anything."

"He usually *does* anything. Anything he wants, that is." Antony glowered. "Can you believe that guy wanted to take Alyssa away?"

Sebastian's stare met hers. "Not happening." He wouldn't be separated from her.

"Yeah..." Winston looked extremely uncomfortable. He even released a little cough. "About that..."

Sebastian didn't like this. Didn't like this situation at all.

"I'm sorry," Winston said. "I saw them in the parking lot, and he has already given orders that passed through my department. There isn't anything I can do."

Sebastian saw the team in the corridor. The men in bad suits who were coming toward him. Men who were walking with Dex.

Dex's gaze wasn't on him.

It was on Alyssa.

"They're going to take her," Winston added softly. "But this isn't over. I have people I trust pulling traffic cams from around Shark Gaming and Design. We'll find the perp. We'll stop him, and then they'll let her go."

Dex was almost on top of them.

"Sebastian?" Alyssa's voice trembled. "What's happening?"

Winston glanced back at the approaching men. His shoulders slumped a bit as he stepped to the side. To *Sebastian's* side. "Don't fight, not here. Because if you make a scene...look, I don't know how that guy has the power he possesses, but he's got some serious connections...and if you make a scene, I'm supposed to lock your ass up."

"Then you'd better get ready to put cuffs on me," Sebastian told him. "Because if he thinks he's taking Alyssa away, I will sure as hell be making a scene."

Dex stopped just a few steps away. The men behind him immediately stopped, too.

"Alyssa." He inclined his head toward her. "I believe we were interrupted before."

Interrupted by a bullet.

"But I'm here now to take you into custody."

"No," Sebastian snapped.

"You're not taking my sister anyplace," Antony announced at the same time.

Dex's brows rose. "This isn't a negotiable situation, as I'm sure the detective has told you." He motioned vaguely to Winston. "He has his orders, just as I have mine." A small hesitation. "And, Sebastian, Antony—you have orders, too. In this case, your orders are to *stand down*."

He got it. He was being given a direct order from his handler. The problem? Sebastian didn't fucking care. "You should have brought more men."

The men in cheap suits stiffened.

"I mean, seriously, is it amateur hour?" Sebastian asked.

Dex's jaw tightened. "Do you want your friend to arrest you?"

Want it? Not at the top of his wish list but... "See, I don't think he will. At least, not until after I kick your ass. And if you think you're taking Alyssa anywhere, then you will most definitely get your ass—"

"Stop," Alyssa demanded.

He stopped. Turned to her.

Her face was far too pale. "You think I'm going to let you get locked up because of me?"

Oh, no. *No.* He did not like where this was—

"Antony was almost shot tonight. You could be shot next time."

"I'll accept the risk." *Any* risk for her.

"I don't think the situation that we're in is about your brother, Alyssa," Dex said. Figured the dick would interrupt. "I don't think it's about Sebastian or Antony. I think it's always been about you."

Now he was playing a very, very dangerous game.

"So if you come with me, the threats to them will be eliminated," Dex added smoothly. "And you can keep your boyfriend out of jail. It's a win, win situation."

"He's a prick, isn't he?" Winston muttered.

Sebastian nodded. But to Alyssa, he said, "Don't believe him. Dex is one of the best liars I've ever met."

"That's high praise, coming from you." Dex didn't look amused. "Now, I'm not exactly keen on standing in the hospital corridor all night, so let's move this along, shall we?" And, just as he'd done at Shark Gaming and Design, he offered his hand to Alyssa. "Willingly or in cuffs?"

Antony swore.

So did Winston.

Sebastian didn't say a word. He just moved his body so that he was standing between Dex and Alyssa. He thought the movement expressed his intentions perfectly. In order to get her, Dex would have to go through him.

Except...

Alyssa brushed past Sebastian. He immediately curled his fingers around her wrist. "Baby?"

Her gaze met his. Shit. Were those tears in her eyes?

He hadn't ever seen her cry.

Normally, he didn't like tears. He didn't like to see *any* woman cry. But when Alyssa had tears in her eyes, when she stared at him and he could see them glistening...

*Hell, no.* He hated them. He wanted to haul her into his arms, then destroy the person who'd made her cry.

In this case, that person was Dex, and it would be Sebastian's pleasure to—

"There is no need for you to jeopardize so much for me, and I'm certainly not letting you go to jail for me."

"Alyssa..."

"I can't let you do this."

It wasn't about letting him. He *was* doing this.

A tear slid down her cheek. "You don't want me taking risks. Don't you get that I don't want you in danger, either? And if I can stop this mess, if I can do something to keep you and Antony safe, then I *have* to leave with Dex."

"I don't care about danger."

"No, you might not. But I do. I care about you." Alyssa blinked, as if she'd just said something she hadn't intended to reveal.

He'd been dead serious before when he said that he loved her confessions. Even before he'd ever met Alyssa, Antony had once laughed and told him about his sister's tendency to blurt out exactly what she was thinking.

Sebastian had met her, seen her in action for himself, but hadn't found the trait humorous.

He'd found it fucking adorable.

"I'm asking you to let me go right now," she told him. "Because if you're in jail, you can't help me. If I'm gone with Dex, then you don't have to look out for me every moment. You and Winston and Antony—you can try finding this guy. You can work together and find him."

Sebastian shook his head. She didn't understand Dex the way he did. "No."

"Please."

Shit. She'd just said *please* to him? Didn't the woman get it? She didn't have to beg him, not for anything. Not when he'd give her everything.

"You can't go to jail for me. Winston can't get in trouble for me. And Antony—he can't get shot at because of me." Her breath released in a low rush. "I'll see you soon. This isn't forever. It's just for now."

The hell it would be.

Her hand pressed to his chest. "I don't want to be in cuffs, and I don't want you in cuffs, either."

"Listen to the lady," Dex quietly ordered him. "She's offering you some good life advice here."

Sebastian's gaze cut to Dex. *Fuck you,* he mouthed.

Dex smiled at him. "I'll keep her safe. I know how to do my job, and I'm not so obsessed by her that I can't see the threats around me."

Sebastian lurched for him, but Alyssa pushed her hand back against his chest. Winston grabbed his arm.

"Get yourself in check," Winston urged him. "Because if you go for him and I don't arrest you, then I'll be sharing a cell with you. That doesn't help either of us."

"Sebastian."

His gaze flew to Alyssa's face. She didn't say his name enough. He loved to hear it on her lips.

She smiled at him. "It's okay. I know what I'm doing."

"You don't. You don't know him."

She swallowed. "But I know you. And Antony. And Winston. And this is what's right for all of us."

She was basically trading herself—going into Dex's custody—in order to protect them.

His stare whipped to Dex. "You were supposed to help her."

Dex raised his chin. "I am."

The hell he was.

"I'm also helping you. You'll thank me later."

He would rip out the man's heart later.

"Goodbye, Sebastian."

His name again, slipping from Alyssa's lips, only she wasn't supposed to be saying good-bye to him. He wasn't supposed to be losing her. He *wasn't* going to lose her.

She stepped back from him. Turned toward Dex and the bastard's stupid outstretched hand.

"No!" The word burst from Sebastian. "I don't care what I have to do, he's not taking you from me!" Once more, he surged forward.

This time, Winston caught one of his arms. Antony caught the other.

"Play the game," Antony rasped to him. "Do it *your* way."

"Don't make me haul your ass to jail," Winston muttered. "Shit, you know I won't do it, so I'll wind up losing my damn badge."

Alyssa took Dex's offered hand.

"We can get her back," Antony added quickly. "Just not here. Not when he has a whole team in the hallway and nurses are gawking at us. Pick the time. Pick the place."

The time was now. The place was now. It was—

"He's got media waiting outside," Winston revealed in a grim voice. "If you do this, you'll take us all down in a blaze of glory that no one will forget anytime soon. The media won't know you're a spy. They'll just think you're a dumbass rich boy who picked a fight in a hospital, and your detective buddy and your business partner backed your ass up, and we will all lose everything."

Alyssa glanced back at him.

*Please.* She mouthed the word again. Asking him to stand down. Asking him to let her go.

Asking him to let her sacrifice herself for him.

"*Dex!*" Antony shouted.

Dex stiffened. Slowly glanced back.

"I thought we were on the same side," Sebastian said.

"We are. You'll realize that soon enough. Once you're thinking clearly again."

"My mind is crystal clear." He smiled at Dex. A deliberate flash of his dimples. "See you soon, my friend."

Dex frowned.

"Very, very soon." It was a promise.

Dex hurried away with Alyssa. The goons he'd brought along closed in around them.

Antony and Winston didn't let Sebastian go. If anything, their grips tightened on him, as if they expected him to make a last-minute lunging attack.

He wasn't. Because Alyssa had asked him not to attack. So he wouldn't.

Or, at least, he wouldn't attack *there*.

He watched the group until they vanished.

"That was a close call." Winston still didn't let him go. "I thought you were going to fight for her."

"I am," Sebastian promised. But he wasn't doing it in the freaking hospital. And he wasn't going to take his friends down with him.

Besides, Alyssa asked him to stand down, and for the moment, he would.

He would just take the fight to a different location. And I'll make sure that my friends aren't pulled into the battle between me and Dex.

"Hell." Antony sounded worried. "What are you planning?"

"Let go so I don't have to hurt either of you."

They slowly let him go.

He marched forward.

They followed quickly.

His mind spun as he considered possibilities. "Winston, get your connections to work on those street cams. You see our perp, you call me immediately."

"On it."

The elevator was up ahead. The doors were open.

He could see Alyssa. For an instant, their eyes met.

The doors shut.

"He's not going to let her go." Antony stared at the closed doors. "Not until the threat is gone. You and I both know why."

Yes, they did. Because Dex had put the pieces together, too. Because Dex had realized that Alyssa was the key in this mess. The tool that the perp planned to use against Antony...because she was his sister, and he loved her.

And the tool that the perp planned to use against Sebastian.

*Because even Dex knows I'm obsessed with her.* After the way he'd run out of the Shark Gaming and Design press conference and gone straight to her, the perp damn well had gotten the message about Sebastian's feelings, too.

"Maybe it's safer to let her stay with him. Until we catch the SOB out there," Antony amended. "I mean, you heard her. It's not forever. It just...for now."

A set of elevator doors opened to the right. Sebastian headed inside. "I made her a promise."

The others strode into the elevator. "What was it?" Winston asked.

"I said I wouldn't let her go."

Antony hesitated. "But...she left to protect us. You get that, don't you?"

Oh, he damn well did. But what Antony wasn't getting... "I don't break promises to Alyssa."

Antony and Winston shared a long, worried look.

"She's not going to be taken from me." He knew how Dex operated. He knew exactly the type of shit that the man would pull.

And how he would use Alyssa to get what he wanted.

*Not happening.*

"I'll get her back."

# CHAPTER FOURTEEN

"I know it's not exactly the Ritz." Dex rolled one shoulder in a shrug. "But we don't all have Sebastian's limitless budget. Uncle Sam does the best that he can."

She stood in the middle of the apartment with her arms loose at her sides. He'd rushed her through a maze in downtown Asheville and set her up in what had *looked* like an old warehouse. Once inside, though, she'd quickly discovered the warehouse had been converted into apartment units. The other units had still been under construction, but this one—it was finished. Finished, furnished, and, apparently, her new safe house.

"Didn't think he was going to let you go." Only Dex had entered the apartment with her. The men in suits—silent guards—had stayed beyond the door. "Rather expected Sebastian to put up a fight. Thought you'd matter more to him."

That was just insulting. Her spine stiffened. "I asked Sebastian to stand down."

Dex's brows lifted as he made his way toward a stocked bar on the right. "And he always does what you ask?"

*Do not answer that.* But...now that she thought about it...

Usually, yes. Hmm. How about that?

"You know, you slipped under my radar." Dex poured a drink into a shot glass. Downed the liquid in a fast gulp. "That doesn't happen often. I usually am pretty good—great even—at seeing threats."

"I'm not a threat."

"Of course, you are." He put down the shot glass. Turned toward her. Propped his elbows on the bar. "It's the threats you never see coming that are the most dangerous."

"Okay, you are obviously under the wrong impression. I'm not a threat, and I'm not dangerous. I'm a law-abiding citizen who happens to find herself in the middle of a nightmare." She huffed out a rough breath. "Could totally happen to anyone."

He laughed. "I don't think so. This situation is very unique to...you."

Her stare sharpened on him. "What does that mean?"

"It means you're an important piece in the puzzle." He smiled. It was an enigmatic, Sphinx-like smile.

She was done. "Playtime is over."

"I rather think it's just getting started." His smile widened.

She crossed her arms over her chest. "I know your game."

"I highly doubt that you know—"

"I may not have my brother's IQ, but, trust me on this, I can spot a player like you from a mile away."

His smile slipped a little. "Excuse me?"

Now it was her turn to laugh. Mockingly. "You don't care about keeping me safe."

"I'm a government agent. My job is to—"

"It's to be a spy. Or to handle the spies or something like that." She waved the specifics away with a negligent flick of her fingers. "Your job is not to put women into protective custody because you secretly want to be a hero."

He didn't argue.

"So let's circle back to that point, shall we?" She began to pace. She often did that when she was stressed. Walking was good for the soul. And for a person's stress level. "You handle spies. That means that you look after Sebastian's and Antony's best interests."

"That is one of the things I'm supposed to do."

She could feel his eyes on her. "Antony didn't tell Sebastian to watch me."

"So it would seem."

She turned and paced back toward him. Her hands slid to her sides. "You think I'm a threat to them."

"I do not think that you would ever physically hurt either of those men. Not your brother. Not your boyfriend."

Her eyes raked over Dex. "We're not talking about physical pain here, are we? At least, not pain that I would personally inflict."

His lips pursed. "I don't know. You're the one doing all the talking."

"Because you're the one doing all the bullshitting." She stopped in front of him. Tilted back her head and stared into his eyes. "You think someone is trying to use me against them."

His eyelashes flickered. "Do I?"

"It's obvious that Sebastian was sent after me."

"And he went running, didn't he? Tore you away from your date and whisked you to his home."

"Then my brother appeared at my side, and someone immediately took a shot at him."

"I did notice that shot at Shark Gaming and Design."

She swallowed. "I'm the bait, right?"

His brow furrowed. "I'm sure I don't know what you mean."

He was such a jerk. "Do you lie all the time? Or only when you're risking someone's life?"

What could have been appreciation flashed in his eyes. "I took you into custody in order to protect you *and* the two men you care so much about. Because, yes, it does seem that a particularly dark brand of trouble is following you. People close to you appear to be in danger."

Now they were getting somewhere, but all the cards still weren't on the table. Time to expose his hand. "You took me because you want to draw the attention of the man who is after me. You're pretending to keep me safe, but, really, you'll leak my location. Then you and your guards will stay in the shadows while he closes in on me. You want to find out who is threatening your agents because, after all, you *handle* them, so I'm sure this compromise in security reflects badly on you."

"It could."

"This isn't a safe house." She looked around. Sighed. "It's a trap. One that you'll be springing at any time. So let's not insult each other by pretending this setup is anything other than what it truly is." Her gaze slid back to him.

Now he cocked his head and studied her. "If you knew that, why come with me?"

Her lips pressed together.

"Why?"

"Because you're right. Danger is following me. And I didn't want to put Antony and Sebastian in jeopardy."

He laughed. "They're spies. Don't you think they are far more equipped to handle this situation than you are?"

He was deliberately taunting her. "You keep pissing me off. You need to stop."

His laughter died away.

"Yes, they are spies." She'd accepted that. "But you obviously think my presence puts them in danger. You think they're at greater risk when I'm with them. And if you have that worry, seeing as how you've worked with them for so long, then so do I." Tension tightened her muscles. "You were also threatening to have Sebastian arrested *by one of his best friends*. I couldn't let Sebastian be tossed in jail, not if I could stop that crap from happening. You were obviously trying to drive a wedge between Sebastian and Winston by making Winston choose between his job and his friend, and that kind of manipulation makes me crazy."

"Now I'm a master manipulator? I'll consider that as a compliment." His eyebrows lifted. "You see a whole lot more than I thought."

"It goes with hanging in the background. When you watch others, you can see some of the things they give away." She licked her lower lip. "Why is it that you think they're at greater risk when I'm close?"

"Because you have Sebastian..." He reached for her left hand.

His fingers were callused, rough, but his touch was gentle.

He wiggled her pinky. "You have him wrapped around this finger. You say jump, and Sebastian does everything you ask."

Her shoulders stiffened.

"You know why he does that?"

"Because he's my friend."

Laughter exploded from Dex.

She was not amused.

"And here I thought you said..." More laughter, but softer now. "I thought you said that you saw things that others gave away." His eyes gleamed. "Or are you just blind..." His voice lowered and his head dipped toward her. "When it comes to Sebastian?"

"What is that supposed to mean?"

"You're dangerous to him because Sebastian would risk everything for you. He wouldn't hesitate. He'd trade every secret he knows if it meant keeping you safe. So would your brother. I can't have that. Those are *my* secrets. By taking you, and, yes, by planning to *use* you, I changed the equation for us all. If everything goes according to my plans, this will be over in a few days—hell it might be over in the next few hours—and you can get your life back."

"You believe both Antony and Sebastian would trade government secrets for my safety?" That was crazy. They wouldn't. Would they?

"Yes." Dex's answer was immediate and absolute. "I think the perp we're after has realized that, too. At first, perhaps he thought he could only use you against Antony. But now he's seen Sebastian with you. Seen how he reacts when you're in danger. I guess that...*friendship*...of yours cuts pretty deeply."

Her heart thudded into her chest. "But we're going to catch the bad guy."

One eyebrow quirked. "Oh, *we* are?"

"Yes, *we* are. I came willingly because I want this to stop. I don't want Sebastian or Antony having to risk anything for me."

He was still holding her hand. Frowning at it. "So delicate."

"I'm stronger than I look."

His gaze met hers. "I'm starting to think that you are."

"Well, this shit sure is cozy."

Her shoulders stiffened. Sebastian? She glanced over her shoulder. Yep, that was him. Standing a few feet away. Hands on his hips. Eyes hard with fury. No dimples. And a whole lot of hard intensity on his face.

And he had orchestrated another spy entrance that made no sound. At this rate, she was just going to have to start assuming spies were standing behind her. Or at least, one spy in particular.

"You take her away, saying you're going to protect her." Sebastian advanced with a slow, languid grace. "You toss out a song and dance about keeping her safe. Threaten her with cuffs. Threaten to have one of my closest friends lock me in jail if I put up a fight..." His nostrils flared. "Then I find you here, holding her freaking hand?"

She snatched her hand away from Dex. "It's not what it looks like."

"Oh, baby, I trust you completely. I'm sure you weren't planning to flirt with Dex and get the guy in your bed."

She couldn't quite read his mood other than realizing that it was...*dangerous*. "Good." She stepped to the side. Faced him. "Because I had no intention of trying to get Dex into my bed." *I'm still adjusting to having you there*. One spy in her bed was more than enough.

Sebastian kept advancing.

"I think we all need to take a breath here," Dex announced. "I wasn't trying to get your lady in my bed—"

"You won't try. Ever. And you will not put your hands on her again."

Dex threw up his hands. "Listen, man, I don't know how you found this place, but you need to calm the hell down. Then you need to get out. You're going to compromise the location!"

Now Sebastian smiled. Who would have thought dimples could be so lethal? "Do you think I'm buying your bullshit?"

"Uh...yes?" Dex asked.

Sebastian shook his head. "I know what you're doing." His gaze dipped to Alyssa. Sharpened. "But I don't know why *you* went along with him."

Her mouth had gone dry. Sebastian in this particular mood was a whole new beast for her.

"What is it that you think I'm doing?" Dex demanded.

"Using her."

Oh, well, Sebastian was right.

"You wanted Alyssa away from me because you were afraid of what I'd do in order to protect her."

Sebastian was still staring at Alyssa. She couldn't look anywhere else. Did the green of his eyes always burn so brightly when he was furious?

"Was I wrong?" Dex's voice was low. Guarded.

A muscle flexed in Sebastian's jaw. "Why did you go along with him, Alyssa?"

"Because he would have made Winston arrest you. Because that would have created more trouble for you and Winston and—"

"Why?"

"Because I want this to stop. I knew that Dex was planning to use me, and if using me meant that you would be safe, then fine, I'd be used."

"*The fuck you will.*" He reached for her.

Dex shot between them. "You need to go."

"I'm not going anywhere without her." Sebastian's voice was crazy hard and intense. She scooted around Dex to get a better look at

Sebastian's face. Yep, crazy hard and intense. A perfect match for his voice.

"You're compromising this location," Dex accused. "You—"

"The place is a friggin' trap. You were planning to compromise the location yourself. That's why it was child's play to track you both here. You're waiting for the perp to come in, and you think your team will swarm and take him down." He nodded. "Fine. Do that shit. Commence the swarm, but I'm not leaving her alone."

"You...you let her go at the hospital, though." Dex's chin jutted up. "You let her walk away!"

"No, I let anyone watching see her leave. I stopped Winston from having to lose the job he loves because you were screwing around with him, and I even managed to get Antony off my back." A shrug. "Then I made sure to get right to Alyssa, only to find you holding her damn hand. Want to tell me what that was about?"

"Well, sure," Dex began. "I think she's got you wrapped around—"

"It wasn't about anything," Alyssa hurried to say. The last thing she wanted Dex to do was say that he thought Sebastian was wrapped around her finger. Obviously, Dex was wrong. A million times wrong on that score.

"Maybe for you, it wasn't," Sebastian growled to Alyssa. His gaze pinned Dex. "Something you want to add?"

"Sure."

Why would Dex not shut up?

"Alyssa knew I planned to use her, too. She thought by coming here, she was helping to keep you and her brother safe. She made the choice, she made the sacrifice, and I think it was brave of her to do that." Dex's jaw was locked just as tightly as Sebastian's. "I hope you know how important she is. I hope you don't dick this up."

"I've got Alyssa."

"I'm standing right here," she snapped. She *had* herself.

Sebastian's blazing stare immediately shot to her. "Oh, baby, I see you. I have always seen you."

She'd always seen him, too. She was just seeing new sides of him now.

"Ahem." Dex's throat clearing was ridiculously loud.

Sebastian glanced back at him. "No one saw me get in the building. As far as your perp is concerned, she's up here with you and your guards."

Dex nodded. "So you are fine with me continuing my plans. Fine with me setting the stage to see if our bad guy takes the bait."

"It's not his choice," Alyssa fired. "It's mine."

Oh, yes, Sebastian's expression *could* get darker. His stare flew back to her.

She would not be intimidated. "My choice, and I'm fine with the plan. Let's see what happens. I've got a whole group of guards."

"I got past them," Sebastian pointed out. "Hardly what I'd call top-of-the-line security."

Yes, that was...um, true. Not exactly reassuring.

"And that's why I'll be staying at her side," Sebastian added grimly. "If the perp gets up here, I'll be waiting."

Dex frowned at him. "I don't remember offering an invitation to join our party."

Sebastian just looked at him.

Dex turned to her. "What do you say, Alyssa? Does he stay or does he go? Because I have this theory that I am dying to test..."

"What theory is that?" Sebastian rumbled.

"Why, it's simple, really. I think you do anything she wants." Dex's expression was expectant. "Does he stay or go, Alyssa?"

"You've got to stop playing your games," she warned him. "One day, they're going to get you in serious trouble."

He didn't look concerned.

Her attention slid back to Sebastian. Yeah, one look at the wildness in his eyes, and it should be clear to anyone that this man only did what he wanted. "I was trying to protect you."

"Noted."

"You don't want me taking risks."

"Risks like jumping between your brother and a bullet? Nope. Can't say I like that."

"And I can't say I like you being risked, either. So I was trying to catch the bad guy."

Sebastian's head inclined toward her. "We'll catch him together. Because—just so we are clear—I am staying."

She nodded. "Just to be clear, I figured you'd show up sooner or later."

His gaze sharpened.

"I mean, you are a super spy. If anyone could find me, it would be you. I thought you might track my phone or something and then pop up in the bedroom when Dex wasn't looking." She slanted a quick glance at Dex.

Dex blinked a few times, almost as if he had to do some kind of mental reset. "Back up. You knew he'd come after you?"

"Of course. Didn't you?" She was so on to Dex and his manipulations now. "Isn't that why you left orders for the guards to let him come up when they saw him approaching the building? Because, I mean, if they really slipped up and let him get this close to us, I think you need to consider retraining them. *Unless* you gave orders for him to be allowed entrance."

Dex smiled at her. "You got me."

She *almost* smiled back. "I know I do."

"I told the guards that *if* Sebastian appeared, they weren't to interfere. No need to shoot to kill...or even shoot to maim," he murmured. "They could let him slip right up." He cut a glance toward Sebastian. "Sorry to break it to you, but you didn't slide past them based on your superior skills."

"If that's what you need to tell yourself." Sebastian didn't seem concerned. "But maybe you should go check in with them and see if they really *did* notice me. And when you check with them, tell them that they'd better be paying a hell of a lot more attention to the west side of the building."

Dex frowned.

"Go," Sebastian urged, voice roughening. "Have an up close and personal chat with your crew because I want to be alone with Alyssa, and I want to be alone with her now."

Dex took a step toward the door. Then stopped. "You're going to play nicely with her, aren't you?"

"When it comes to Alyssa," Sebastian's voice roughened even more, going almost savage, "I never play."

"No." Dex coughed. "I'm realizing that you don't." Then he left.

The apartment door shut behind him. She heard the click of the lock as Dex secured it from the outside.

Sebastian stared at her a moment. His eyes were so bright.

And her throat was way, way dry. "You came after me."

"What the hell else was I gonna do?" He hauled her against his body and took her mouth with his.

# CHAPTER FIFTEEN

*Gentle, gentle, gentle.* Yes, he knew he should be gentle, but his mouth was wildly plundering hers. He was kissing her with frantic, desperate need, and Sebastian couldn't pull back. His control was gone.

That shit happened when a man tracked his lady across town, scaled a building to get to her, and then found a prick holding her hand and leaning in way too close to her.

Jealous? Oh, yes, he was.

Possessive. Sure, he was guilty as hell.

His hands dropped to Alyssa's waist, and Sebastian lifted her up against him. "I'm going to fuck you," he growled. Screw this being the right time or place, he *needed* her. A primitive, savage hunger was driving him like nothing ever had before.

Her arms wound around his neck. "Good."

He almost stumbled. Shit. The woman had a way of making him extra crazy.

She bit his lower lip. "And could you do it fast? Because I don't want to give Dex a show, and I have no idea how long it will be before he's back."

"He sees you naked, and he's dead." Sebastian carried her to the bedroom—the same room that he'd snuck into earlier. He'd scaled the wall, then unlocked the window. Windows on second floors weren't normally wired for security—or at least, not wired the way the ones on the first floor were. Unless glass shattered from a second-floor window, the alarms didn't usually sound. He'd made sure not to shatter any glass.

He lowered Alyssa to the bed and stripped her in seconds. He took care not to jostle her arm. He *hated* that she'd been cut, and he wouldn't get over the sight of her bleeding anytime soon.

"What is it?" She pushed up onto her elbows and peered at him.

His hands went to the waistband of his jeans. "We have a problem."

"I'm naked and you're not? Is that the problem you're talking about?"

"I don't have a condom, and I want to fuck you so hard I'm shaking."

Her tongue flickered out. Pressed to her lower lip. "That's not really a problem. I'm on birth control."

His whole body froze.

"And I'm clear. I'm always very careful. I've never gone without...except, well, I guess with you. Right now."

*Do not pounce. Do not.* "Why with me?" His voice was nothing more than a guttural rumble.

"Because I want you this way." She stared into his eyes.

*I will take you any way I can get you.* "I'm clear, too. You don't have a damn thing to worry about."

She smiled at him.

That was it.

*It.*

He put his gun on the nightstand because, yes, he'd been packing the whole time. He shoved down his jeans, ditched his shoes, tossed his shirt some damn place, and lunged for her. His mouth took hers, and he thrust his tongue past her lips. His cock was aching and eager, and he pushed at the entrance to her body.

*Get her wet. Get her ready.*

His hand slid between them. Eased into the sweet heat between her legs. He stroked her, caressed her clit with his thumb, and worked two fingers into her. He kept going, kept pushing and teasing until her body softened even more for him. Until she was slick and moaning.

Then he replaced his hand with his dick. The head pressed to the entrance of her body.

*Nothing between us. Nothing.*

He sank into her. Lost his freaking mind. She was wet and hot and so tight. For a moment, he didn't move at all because when you suddenly found yourself in freaking paradise, you savored. You enjoyed. You made that shit last.

Her hips arched against him. "Sebastian! I need...*more!*"

He'd give her everything. He withdrew, thrust, and withdrew again. The flimsy headboard banged into the wall and the springs of the mattress squeaked as he became wilder and rougher. As he surged into her and pushed them both toward the pleasure that waited.

She came first. He felt the contractions of her inner muscles around him, and his dick surged into her again and again.

He erupted and poured into her as he came on a release that rocked his whole body.

His breath heaved in and out. In and out.

His eyes were on her. He hadn't looked away. Couldn't look away. She was flushed with pleasure.

Her legs were still around him. Her arms were on his shoulders. Her arms—

Sebastian swore. "Did I hurt you?"

"I don't know. Give me a few minutes to think about it." Her eyes closed.

"Alyssa."

Her lashes lifted. "Yes."

His heart squeezed. He was such a bastard—

"It hurt me on my birthday, when I thought you didn't want me. We'd just met and it shouldn't have mattered, but it did. You did."

He shook his head.

"And it hurt me that I had to pretend over the years that you didn't matter to me. That I had to act like we were...distant friends, at best. Strangers, at worst."

"We're not strangers." His voice was gruff.

"It hurt me to keep my secret," she whispered.

"What secret is that?"

"That every time we met—every awkward party, every tense get-together—I wanted to be close to you."

I was the same way, baby. Being near you was hell. But being away from you? Even worse. "Why didn't you say something sooner?"

"Why didn't you?"

Fuck. Because I was afraid you didn't want me. Because I thought being in your life—even distantly—was better than not having you at all. "Because I can be a dumbass."

Alyssa snuggled close to him. "It's been a long day." Her voice was softening. Slurring a bit.

He pressed a kiss to her temple. "Sleep, baby. I've got you."

"No, I've got you." Her arm snaked around his stomach.

*You always had me. You just didn't know it.*

He reached out and turned off the lamp. Darkness fell into the room. He pulled the covers over her, and a few moments later, Alyssa's breathing evened out as she slipped into sleep.

Sebastian didn't sleep, though. He stared into the darkness, and he thought about what would happen next.

\*\*\*

Dex glowered at the guard before him. "Is this like your first day out of training or some shit? You're here to watch the perimeter. You don't *let* the guy just slip past you."

The guard was sweating.

"You know what? I can't trust your ass. Go switch out with Baylor. He's got better eyes than you, and he's not green."

The guard hurried away.

Dex heaved out a breath. He did not need this crap. Was it too much to hope that the agency would just send him agents who could do their jobs? And not screw up royally?

He glanced up at the second-story window.

The light had just turned off up there.

Not like it took a freaking genius to figure out what had just happened in the apartment. He'd seen the jealousy burning in Sebastian's eyes. The man had barely been able to keep his hands off Alyssa.

*How the hell did you last all these years?* He'd had no idea Sebastian was so very taken with Antony's younger sister. Though, he did have to admit, he could see the appeal. If you went for that type.

Baylor hurried toward him. Even saluted. What in the hell? Did it look like he was a general or something? He'd never been in the army. All those rules and regulations weren't for Dex.

He liked to make his own rules. "If anyone gets in this building without you seeing, I'll wreck you, Baylor."

Baylor nodded. "Yes, sir."

The others were in position. Sebastian was upstairs. No doubt, he was staying very, very close to Alyssa.

If all went according to plan, an attack would be coming soon. He'd certainly left enough breadcrumbs for the perp to follow.

Staying in the shadows, Dex made his way back inside. He and Sebastian needed to have a come-to-Jesus meeting because his gut told him

Sebastian had made some plans that were truly going to screw with Dex's future agenda.

Sebastian could be annoying. He could be arrogant. But the guy got the job done. He was a good agent. Fast and savvy. There was nothing Sebastian couldn't do with tech.

Losing him wasn't an option.

Keeping him, well, that just might require the right leverage.

Luckily, Dex now knew exactly what mattered to Sebastian. And when you knew what mattered to a man, you could control him.

Life, after all, was all about control. So was power.

\*\*\*

The bedroom door opened soundlessly. A faint sliver of light spilled inside, and Sebastian's gaze immediately went to the figure who was trying to sneak into the room.

The figure crept across the carpeted floor and headed straight for the bed.

"You'll want to stop right there," Sebastian told him, keeping his voice a low whisper.

The figure stilled. "Why?" Dex asked. "Is Alyssa naked?" His voice was just as soft as Sebastian's had been.

"You won't find out." But, yes, beneath the covers, she was.

So was he. Hell, he didn't even remember ditching his shirt. The jeans and shoes, yeah, he'd kicked out of those. When had he lost his shirt? Not that it mattered.

"We need to talk," Dex murmured.

"I snuck in the window." The window to the right. "You think I'm going to leave her alone so that some other asshole can sneak in that way, too?"

Alyssa didn't stir. Her breathing remained nice and slow. Her hand was still over his stomach. She was soft and warm. Perfect.

Her scent was on him. His was on her.

"My best guard is watching the west area," Dex groused.

Like that was supposed to impress him?

"And I engaged the upstairs alarm."

"I got *past* the alarm earlier."

"I activated some alarm functions that weren't in place before because I knew you were on the way. No one will get to her without us knowing." He heaved out a sigh. "You'll just be right outside the bedroom door. I'm only asking for a few minutes."

Sebastian's jaw hardened.

"Go," Alyssa told him.

His gaze immediately whipped down to her face.

"It will give me a chance to shower," she added with a yawn.

"How long have you been awake?" He could have sworn she'd been sleeping the whole time.

"Since Dex came in and started his loud whispering."

Sebastian felt his lips pull into a smile.

"I need to shower," she muttered. "Go talk to Dex. Trust me, if anything happens, I'll scream loudly enough for every guard to hear."

"Dex, get the hell out. I'll join you in a minute." Not like he wanted Dex to watch her slip naked into the bathroom.

Dex hurried out.

Alyssa pushed up in bed beside him. "We're going to catch this guy, aren't we?"

"Yes."

She eased from the bed. Wrapped a sheet around her body. Totally unnecessary. It was dark, *and* he freaking loved her body.

She hesitated. "What happens then? As soon as you get him, do I immediately go back to living my life? You know, I get to return to my business and my home and...everything else?"

"You get your life back." He climbed from the bed. Hauled on his jeans. Zipped them. Snapped the button. "But, maybe...just to play it safe...you should keep staying with me for a few days." He moved to stand in front of her. "To make certain everything is okay."

"So...*after* the bad guy is caught, you want me to stay at your place?"

Stay or move in permanently...really, wasn't that just semantics?

"For how long?" Alyssa asked.

Forever didn't seem to be the appropriate reply. He wasn't trying to scare her away, and Sebastian didn't think she was quite ready for that step so he hedged with, "How long do you want to stay?"

The sheet rustled as she stepped back.

He realized she hadn't answered him.

And she was moving for the closed bathroom door.

"Alyssa?"

"I think staying with you will be a good idea. For a few days, anyway. You know, just to make certain things are safe. But, of course, we have to catch the perp first."

She opened the bathroom door.

"We'll get him," Sebastian vowed.

She flipped on the light. Looked back.

"I wanted you from the first moment I saw you." This wasn't the time to confess, but he did it anyway. "I hate that I hurt you on your birthday. You were the most gorgeous woman I'd ever seen, and all I wanted to do was have you smile at me."

Her lips parted.

"I screwed things up then, and I've been screwing things up ever since. I tried to keep my distance because when you get too close to the thing you want so badly, it's hard. Hard not to touch. Hard not to try and take what is right there."

Her head tilted toward him.

"I don't want to screw up with you anymore." That was the last thing he wanted. "Call me on my bullshit."

"You can count on it."

He smiled at her. "Yell at me when I'm an asshole."

"Okay."

"Tell me to screw off when I'm a dick."

"Will do." Soft. Almost tender.

"But, just don't leave me, okay? Because when you walked away in that hospital, it felt like you'd ripped out my heart."

He heard her swiftly indrawn breath. "Some people would say that Sebastian Ridgeway doesn't have a heart."

"But we both know those people are wrong." You have my heart. You have held it for years.

"Yes." Even softer. "They're wrong."

His heart drummed so fast. "So you'll stay? Because I need to make sure you're safe." It was so much more than that. If she would stay with him, after this shit was over, then maybe he could convince her to give him a real chance. He could show her that he had good points. He could wine her, dine her, and basically give her everything her heart desired.

"I'll stay."

Relief surged through him.

"Now go have your talk with Dex. And try not to pull a knife on him this time, okay?" She shut the bathroom door.

He stared at the closed door a moment. "No promises on that one." Sebastian turned on his heel and stalked out of the bedroom.

Dex was waiting for him. Lounging near the wall. He wiggled his brows at Sebastian. "Took long enough. I was starting to think you'd joined her in the shower."

Like that shit wasn't tempting.

"Did you forget your shirt?" Dex asked politely.

Sebastian crossed his arms over his chest.

"Is that a no? You were going for a deliberate fashion choice? Okay. Whatever."

"Get to the point, Dex."

"Right." He cleared his throat. "You're thinking of bailing."

Sebastian stiffened. "The hell I am. I am not going anywhere until we catch the bastard who is after Alyssa."

"Of course. Let me rephrase." A nod. "After we catch the bastard, you think you are going to quit the spy biz."

Yes, that was the plan.

"You think you're going to get your fantasy girl, that you'll turn your back on all the danger, and ride off into the sunset together."

How was that bad? Sounded like an ideal situation to him.

"No? Yes? Any answer at all?" Dex pushed.

"You seemed to have all the answers. Didn't realize my response was required." Sebastian stayed close to the bedroom door. Not that he didn't trust all of Dex's security measures—oh, wait, he didn't.

Dex strode closer to him. "It doesn't work that way."

"Then enlighten me about how things do work."

"You don't just walk away from the agency."

"I think I do." He considered the matter. "In fact, I'm certain that I do. I started working for your bosses when I was barely legal. I did all the work required of me, took more risks than I can count, but I was never in this for the long haul. Your agency isn't my future."

"Because she is?"

He shrugged. "Don't really see where you need to know about that."

"Once you're in, it's for life. You don't walk away from this kind of job."

Was that a threat? It had better not be. "Watch me," Sebastian dared.

"Do you think she'd ever be safe with you?"

What was that supposed to mean?

"I get it. Trust me, I do. I see the others out there. Living their nine-to-five lives. Having families. Birthday parties. Singing their carols at Christmas even when they can't keep pitch for shit."

Sebastian lifted his brows.

"I hate to tell you, but you won't ever have that. Because you will *always* be looking over your shoulder. Always wondering if someone found out what you did in the past. There is a reason that most of the men and women in our line of work don't put down roots. We stay loners because when you connect with others, you put them in jeopardy." A sad shake of his head. "The exact way that Alyssa is in danger now. If she stays close to you—if you do some dumb shit like move in with her or marry her—what message would that send to your enemies?"

"If we stop this bastard, no one else has to know about my past."

"Oh, is that what you think?" Dex laughed. The sound held no humor. "There will be other threats. There always are. You'll look over your shoulder for the rest of your life, and because of that, so will she. Is that really what you want for her?"

What he wanted was for her to be safe and happy. "Antony is involved in this, too. Because of him, because of her tie to him, doesn't that already put a target on her?"

"It does. You know enemies will try to take out family members. Loved ones. It's why she was the perfect target this time. She was important to him and to you. But, see, Antony hasn't quite gotten his hands as dirty as you have."

Yes, he knew that. Antony tended to play the game from more of a distance.

But Sebastian...

"You're the secret weapon, aren't you, Sebastian? The list of your enemies is a mile long. Those who want payback..." Dex exhaled. "Look, I'm not telling you this stuff to be a dick."

"No? Could have fooled me."

"I'm telling you because I like her. You stop this threat. Great. But, as long as you are with her, there will be others. You need to know that. So does she. And *that* is where she gets to decide. If she wants those risks, fine, her choice. She goes into the danger with her eyes wide open. But if she doesn't choose that path, will you let her go?"

That wasn't the right question. Because, hell, yes, if Alyssa didn't want him, he'd never try to force her to stay. The real question...*If I'm putting her in danger, can I ever ask her to stay?*

His phone vibrated. Then pealed with a familiar alarm. An alarm that *shouldn't* be sounding. Sebastian hurriedly yanked out the phone and glanced at the screen. "Someone is in my freaking office again?" On *his* computer? Two break-ins in one night? Hell, no.

"What's happening?" Dex tried to peer at the phone's screen.

"Someone is trying to hack into my computer. *Again.*"

"Is it Antony? Did he go back to your office?"

It could be, but it could also be—

Dex's eyes suddenly widened. He motioned toward his right ear. "*Comm link,*" he mouthed.

Sebastian knew Dex was getting a message from his team. He'd figured they were all wired with Uncle Sam's tiny tech—the better to keep tabs fully on the operation. He'd also known that Dex's team *hadn't* caught sight of him when he slipped inside...or else Dex would have been notified at the time via the comm link.

"Showtime," Dex breathed with a nod. "Incoming."

Sebastian's mind immediately turned ice-cold.

"Spotted on the perimeter." Dex tapped his ear. "Good. Keep eyes on him," he ordered the agent on the other end of the link. "I want to draw the bastard in. Make sure he's close enough for us to take out."

Sebastian shoved his phone back into his pocket.

"Baylor?" Dex paced a few feet away and glanced out a window as he continued communicating with his team. "Check in, now."

Sebastian took slow, careful breaths as battle-ready tension fueled him.

"I see movement," Dex barked. "Anyone with eyes on Baylor? He's not responding."

Had Dex lost contact with one of his guards? It sure seemed that way. Sebastian knew Baylor. A good man, a good agent.

"Copy that," Dex snapped. "Two of them. Detain with any force necessary. You get that bastard down there, and we'll take care of the one coming up here."

Wait. Wait. The one coming up here?

Dex pulled out his weapon as he turned toward Sebastian. "One of my men isn't responding. Another saw movement on the side of the building. Guess you weren't the only one with the idea to scale up to the second level."

Sebastian shoved open the bedroom door. His gaze immediately swept the room. No sign of an intruder. Yet. He rushed for the nightstand and grabbed his gun.

The bathroom door opened. Steam drifted out as Alyssa stood there with her hair wet and a towel wrapped around her body.

At the same time, an alarm blared from below.

"Sebastian?" Fear flashed on her face.

He was already running toward her.

# CHAPTER SIXTEEN

Sebastian caught Alyssa and pushed her back into the bathroom. "Consider the bad guys to be *here*."

Yes, she'd rather been afraid he would say that. "What can I do?"

"Stay down. Stay out of sight." He pushed a gun into her hand. "And if anyone other than me comes in this bathroom door, you shoot, got it?"

She knew how to shoot. Her mom had made sure of it. "Got it."

He turned away.

She grabbed him right back. Kissed him frantically.

His hands locked around her shoulders.

She was pretty sure that she felt the towel fall. Because...of course. Her luck.

"Your towel fell," he whispered.

She nodded.

"Any other time..." He kissed her again. "That shit happens, and I don't leave you."

She almost smiled. Would have, if she hadn't been so terrified.

He bent and scooped up the towel. Gave it to her. "If it's not me, shoot."

Then he was gone. She shut the bathroom door behind him. Locked it. Then she backed the hell away from the door because if bullets started flying, they'd come through the wood and hit her.

She wrapped up in the towel. Wished she had clothes with her. A robe. *Something else.* And she held tight to the gun.

\*\*\*

"What in the hell happened to your weapon?" Dex demanded.

"Alyssa has it."

Dex grunted at him. "Stop this hero complex crap." He bent and hauled a second gun from the holster on his ankle.

It was still dark in the bedroom because they didn't want to turn on the lights and alert the perp, but Sebastian's eyes had adjusted, so he could see easily. He took the backup weapon from Dex.

"The guy is taking one from your playbook," Dex said. "He's scaling the wall. Only he doesn't quite have your stealth."

"Who does?" Sebastian whispered back.

"I'm going to disable the secondary alarm." He tapped on his phone. "See, if I'd had this on earlier, your ass never would have gotten inside. But did you thank me for letting you—"

"Do the freaking job," Sebastian groused.

"It's done. Now you go to the right. I'll go to the left. When he comes through, we take him out."

They both moved into position.

Sebastian flattened his body against the wall even as his gaze jumped to the bathroom door. *No one will get to her.* "You said there were two of them?"

"My team is taking out the second perp now. Still no freaking response from Baylor."

Then there was a soft creak. The window began to open.

Things happened pretty fast after that. The dumbass aimed his gun at the bed. Just acted like he was going to fire from right there.

Dex caught the guy's wrist. Twisted it. The gun fell, bones snapped, and the perp would have fallen his ass right back out of the window if it weren't for the fact that Dex hauled him inside.

The perp twisted and rolled, then he came up, cradling a knife in his left hand. His right hand— now broken, or at least, the wrist was broken— hung near his side.

Sebastian stepped forward and aimed his weapon at the intruder. "Gun trumps knife, asshole. So unless you want me to put some bullet holes in you, you'll drop the weapon, right now."

He didn't drop it. He did *throw* the knife. What in the hell? Sebastian jerked to the side, and he heard a grunt from Dex. Dex had been partially behind Sebastian so—

*Hell.* The perp had turned and was running, but not heading for the bedroom door. He was running straight for the closed bathroom door. The door that had a thin stream of light shining from the bottom, in that thin crack between the wood and the floor. The light that showed someone might be inside.

Alyssa. The perp was going for Alyssa.

*The hell you are.*

Sebastian didn't fire. The last thing he wanted was for a bullet to go through that door. He lunged forward and slammed his body into the perp's. The guy's head pounded into the door. But the punk didn't stop. He twisted his body and came up swinging at Sebastian.

\*\*\*

Alyssa jumped when something—or someone—slammed into the door. She'd wrapped the towel around herself and tucked the edge between her breasts. She crouched in the tub with the gun held tightly in one hand, and she kept her eyes on the door.

She could hear grunts. Thuds.

"I'm fucking bleeding over here!" That had been Dex's bellow.

Then the wood of the bathroom door exploded in as two men—Sebastian and some fellow with sandy blond hair—came crashing inside.

The stranger hit the tile floor. He groaned. And Sebastian's fist slammed into his face. "What in the hell did you do to Baylor?" Sebastian demanded.

"Wh-who?"

"The guard who should have been keeping a watch on this side of the building! What did you—"

"S-stabbed him...dr-dropped his body behind...dumpster..."

Sebastian swore. He leapt to his feet. "Dex, get your team to find Baylor, *now!*"

But the guy on the floor started to laugh.

She didn't think laughing was good. Not at all.

Then his laughter stopped. "Boom," he said.

Boom?

She pointed her gun at him. "Why did you say that?"

Sebastian's head snapped toward her.

"I'm...the distraction," the man on the floor said. He spit out some blood. "My buddy...he was wiring this place."

Sebastian grabbed the perp by the shirtfront and yanked him to his feet. "We have your buddy. He never made it inside the building."

She kept her gun aimed at the fellow.

Another rough laugh. "Didn't...just come with one friend."

She shook her head. Okay. She *had* to be misunderstanding. "He didn't basically say there is a bomb in this building. That's not what he meant, is it?" *Don't be what he meant.*

Dex staggered into the bathroom and pushed past the chunks of broken door. "I'm cuffing the bastard."

"The bastard is saying there's a *bomb*. That he had a third SOB helping him." Sebastian's voice was ice cold.

Dex stiffened. "My team didn't see a third man." His voice thickened as he tapped his ear. "*Did you see a freaking third man?*"

Who was he talking to? Alyssa crept closer to the side of the tub.

Dex nodded, and his hand fell away from his ear. "No sign of a third man." Blood dripped down his side.

She winced.

He bent, groaned, and tried to slap cuffs around the perp. But the perp swung at him—

"I will shoot you," Alyssa announced. She was surprised by how calm her voice sounded. Especially since calm was the last thing she felt.

All three men immediately focused on her.

Sebastian stared with blazing eyes.

Dex blinked. Smiled a little.

And the perp—he glared at her in fury. "Bitch, you're dying!"

Sebastian drove his fist into the guy's stomach, yanked the cuffs away from Dex, and snapped them on the perp's wrists.

Oh. That had been fast.

"Is this building wired?" Sebastian snarled.

"It's probably just a trick," Dex muttered. "They're trying to get us out. Want us to run into the open where an ambush *could* be waiting."

"Boom," the perp said again.

"I don't like when he says that." Alyssa bit her lower lip. Her fingers were all sweaty around the gun.

"I was supposed to be in and out in five minutes. That's all the time I had." The blond-haired man began to laugh. "Guess time is up for us all."

"*Oh, shit,*" Dex growled at the same time. His eyes had flared wide. "Team member just found a device. Timer is counting down. We've got less than two minutes!"

No. Alyssa shook her head. He had *not* said they had less than two minutes.

"Someone sacrificed you," Dex fired at the perp. "Sent you in here to die. You're the distraction, all right, and you're the distraction that's supposed to die with us!"

Sebastian shoved the now swearing perp at Dex. "Get out!"

"Sebastian?" Alyssa called.

His head snapped toward her.

"There isn't really a bomb," she said. "There's not, right?"

He scooped her into his arms. "Baby, hold on. Tight."

Oh, dear God. There really was a bomb.

She held on, tight. Only he didn't take her down the stairs. When he ran into the bedroom, Dex and the perp were gone. Someone had moved *fast*.

Instead of rushing out the bedroom door, Sebastian rushed for the window.

"What are you doing?" Alyssa gasped.

"Getting you out as fast as possible." He kicked out the glass as an alarm blared. "I got in, I'll get you out. Like I said, *hold on*."

And Sebastian started climbing out of the window and freaking down the brick wall. She was shaking and wearing a towel and holding on to him and to her gun, and it was the most insane and terrifying experience of her life. He moved with confident strength, like he was rock climbing or something. Sebastian scared the ever-living hell out of her and then he said, "Jump, baby. Jump and run, *now*."

She jumped. Fell about four feet and hit the ground.

"Run!" Sebastian bellowed. "I'm right behind you."

He'd better be. She held one hand to the front of her towel, barely keeping it in place, and with the other she gripped her gun. Alyssa glanced back.

*Boom.*

This time, the blond jerk didn't say it. That was the sound the explosion made as smoke and flames shot from the bottom of the building. Glass exploded outward. She was looking straight at Sebastian, and the smoke flew behind him. The blast also seemed to lift him into the air.

It lifted her, too. Lifted her and threw her back.

She could see Sebastian's mouth moving, but there was no way she could understand what he was saying. That terrible boom was far, far too loud. And then—

She hit the ground.

Her elbows scraped over pavement because it was not soft ground that she'd hit. A groan broke from her lips. Dammit, that had *hurt.*

Her towel was slipping. Probably the last thing she should care about, but as she flopped there, stunned, the towel seemed awfully and oddly important. She grabbed it, hooked it into place, and—

*Sebastian.*

He was on the ground. Sprawled face down. And there was some guy in all black rushing up behind him. A guy with a gun drawn.

"Get away from him!" Alyssa yelled. Or at least, she thought she yelled it. Something was wrong with her hearing. Everything was muted.

The man glanced up at her. With the flames glowing and darkness around them, she couldn't make out his expression clearly, but she thought he might be smiling.

And she *knew* he was lifting his gun to aim at Sebastian.

"Drop it!" Alyssa screamed as she scrambled to her feet. Again, she thought she screamed but—

He was about to fire.

Sebastian still wasn't moving.

Alyssa had the gun he'd given to her. She lifted it and squeezed the trigger. Her hand jerked as she fired and the bullet flew from the weapon. It hit the man's upper chest. Left side. Close to his shoulder.

He turned his weapon on her.

So she fired again—she fired her second shot at the same moment that Sebastian suddenly rolled over. He came up with a gun gripped in his hand, and he fired, too. The man in black stumbled back. The gun fell from his fingers. Then *he* fell.

Alyssa was still squeezing her gun with a death grip. But as soon as the fellow hit the pavement, she ran for Sebastian. He was already surging to his feet. Weaving just a bit, but getting upright.

"Sebastian!" Her own voice still seemed muted to her. Everything was muted. She was holding her towel, holding her gun, and she was desperate to get to him.

He caught her in his arms. Yanked her against him. "Baby, are you okay?"

She could barely hear his words. She nodded anyway. Then she looked up at him. Blood dripped down the side of his face from a nasty gash over his right eye. "Sebastian?"

He pulled her even closer. "We can't be in the open. We need to move!"

Because there were more threats? She looked around, frantic, but didn't see Dex. She didn't see his guards. Didn't see any other bad guys. She didn't see anyone.

Was that good?

Or, very, very bad? Because Dex had made it out, hadn't he? The others on his team were okay?

Sebastian was rushing with her away from the building. The pavement bit into her bare feet, but she barely felt the sting. Smoke was filling the air. Not a lot of flames—more smoke than flames— and glass was everywhere. She dodged the glass as best she could and—

Was that a buzzing sound?

Her head craned to the left. She could see the blur of lights. Blue lights that were flashing. Wait. That hadn't been a buzzing sound. It had been a siren. One that just sounded funny with her messed-up hearing.

Sebastian was heading toward the lights.

Two patrol cars rushed to the scene. So did a black SUV. Winston jumped out of the SUV. "What in the hell?" His eyes widened as he gaped at them.

"I need her out of here," Sebastian blasted. "Now."

Winston nodded and grabbed a blanket from his vehicle. He ran to them and put the blanket around her. It was such a simple gesture—but, God, she was grateful for it. And for him.

"Get her out of here, Winston," Sebastian said. His voice was clearer to her now. "The scene isn't contained. She's in danger."

She pulled the edges of Winston's blanket closer around her body.

"Get her away from me."

Her head jerked at those words. She'd misunderstood. Surely. Sebastian hadn't just said that? Had he?

"I'm sorry." She read Sebastian's lips because his voice was far too low for her to hear. "It won't happen again."

A bomb? An attack at a safe house? Yes, she doubted either of those events would happen again. This was a whole one-in-a-million situation. Winston motioned toward the uniformed cops, and they surged toward her, even as Sebastian backed away.

"He's bleeding. He needs help." She tried to reach out for Sebastian.

Winston pulled her back.

Sebastian shook his head at her.

Then he turned and raced back toward the chaos and the smoke.

She tried to go after him, but Winston tightened his grip. His cop buddies swarmed in on her.

"I'm gonna need that gun, Alyssa."

She could hear Winston's voice better. Everything was less distorted.

She frowned at him. "I need you to go after him, Winston."

"I will, but I have to take care of you first." More patrol cars zoomed down the road. "Give me the gun. Let me get you to safety."

She looked back toward the warehouse. She couldn't even see Sebastian. "He's hurt."

"And I'm going to protect him, but I want you to give me the gun. Then I want you going with these cops—Isla Burgos and Nico Ricci."

Her gaze darted to them. They nodded to her.

"They're two of the best, and they're going to take you to the station. They're going to put you in my office, and they will stay with you. Got it? They're not going to let you out of their sight. You'll be at the police station. No one will hurt you."

"He was going to shoot Sebastian." She gave him the gun. "You have to watch his back."

"I will, I swear it."

Once more, she looked for Sebastian. He was gone.

*Get her away from me.*

Her heart ached. He hadn't said those words. She was sure he hadn't.

# CHAPTER SEVENTEEN

"They're guns for hire. Their rap sheets are a mile long." Winston rubbed his eyes then frowned at Sebastian. "Look, man, should you even be here? Don't you have a concussion or some shit?"

"I got stitches. I'm fine."

"You've never been fine. You've always been ass crazy, and right now, you're even crazier."

*Tell me something I don't know.* Dawn had arrived. The warehouse—converted apartments, safe house, or whatever the hell Dex wanted to call the place—had been contained.

Two perps were in custody at the police station.

One was in the hospital under guard—the injured bastard who'd been shot.

Dex was okay. So was his team. Well, Baylor had been injured pretty damn badly, and Dex had gone to the hospital with him. But Dex had called Sebastian and told him that Baylor would pull through.

Sebastian figured Dex would be showing up any moment. He'd try to take over the case. Try to take the perps away to some undisclosed location.

*Not happening until I get my chance with them.*

"Put me in a room with them." Sebastian nodded. "Give me five minutes, Winston. You just walk away. Go get some coffee or some of those vegan breakfast things you're always trying to push on me, and by the time you get back, I'll know who hired them." Because that was the big question, wasn't it? Who'd hired the goons?

Winston's lips thinned. "You know I'm not doing that."

"Dammit, man! Would it kill you—just once—to break the rules? To bend them for a friend?" He swallowed and tried to choke down his rage. In his mind, he was still seeing that bastard with the gun. Sebastian had lost consciousness for a few precious moments once he'd had that fun face-first collision with the pavement. When he'd come back to his senses, he'd flipped over and seen that bastard pointing his gun. And he'd *known*—even without looking at the SOB's target—that the man was aiming at Alyssa. "He was going to kill her. I have to find out who sent him. Who sent all of them."

A three-man team. Three men who'd come equipped with a bomb because they wanted to get the job done.

"I will find out," Winston assured him. "Trust me to do my job."

He did trust Winston. One hundred percent. But he also knew that the wheels of justice spun slowly. Very, very slowly. He didn't have time to waste. "Their boss is still out there. If he's out there, then Alyssa is still at risk. I have to stop him."

They were in one of the observation rooms at the station. He was currently staring through the one-way glass at the empty interrogation room.

He wanted one of those perps in that room. He wanted to push that jerk until he broke and told Sebastian everything—

"Have you seen Alyssa since you arrived at the station?" Winston's question was oddly quiet.

Sebastian stiffened. "She's still here, isn't she? You told me you had two officers on her. And the police station should be the safest spot in town." Because Dex's safe house had been shit. As for Dex's grand plan?

*Failure.*

"She's here. I talked to her not fifteen minutes ago." Winston scratched his hand over the stubble growing on his jaw. "She immediately asked about you."

"I'm fine."

"How come you didn't immediately ask about her? You got here, and you started demanding that I let you interrogate our perps. You didn't ask about Alyssa."

But he'd thought about her. Hell, she was *all* he'd thought about.

Winston was studying him with assessing eyes. "I'm surprised you didn't rush right to her side."

That was what Sebastian wanted to do. More than anything. But... "I put her in danger." His confession was low. Hoarse. "When she's close to me, people try to shoot her or she nearly gets blown up."

"Oh. So that's what you're doing." Winston nodded. "Got you."

His eyes turned to slits. "You don't know—"

"That you're trying to pull some seriously stupid martyr BS right now? I'm just hoping its confusion from the concussion and not a serious plan you have." He advanced on Sebastian. "You love her."

He didn't speak.

"You don't have to confirm or deny. I know you. I've been in on the planning stages for *Operation Get Into Alyssa's Good Graces*, remember?"

That operation seemed like a million years ago. "How about we just work on *Operation Keep Alyssa Alive?*" And the best way to do that?

It was for Sebastian to stay away from her.

Once more, he focused toward the one-way glass. The interrogation room door opened. His eyes immediately flew to the man who was being ushered inside. The blond bastard who'd snuck into the bedroom at the safe house. The bastard who'd gotten to safety because of Dex.

"Let me have a run at him," Sebastian urged. "Come on. No one else has to know."

"That is *not* how this situation works. I'm in charge of this case, and I'm going to interrogate him. I'm already seriously doing you a favor just by letting you watch this part."

"You're doing it because Dex pulled rank with your boss and said he wanted an agent keeping eyes on the interrogation in case confidential intel was leaked." He slanted a glance back at Winston.

"That happened, yes." A nod from Winston. "But I'm also doing it because I need you to stay sane. So watch the interrogation from here. If you see something I miss, then we'll deal with it together."

His hands clenched and released. "You don't miss anything." Sebastian knew he was just out of control and being an ass.

"Thanks so much for the praise." Winston offered him a mocking smile. "So remember that, would you? I don't miss jack which is why I know exactly what I'm talking about when it comes to Alyssa."

*You love her.* "You don't understand what's at play."

Winston headed for the door. "Sure, I do. Your heart. Your future. They're both on the line." He exited without looking back.

Sebastian's hands clenched into fists. It's not about me, buddy. It's about her. What if by being with me...she always has a target on her back? If something happened to Alyssa...

He would lose his mind.

\*\*\*

"I need to know what's happening." She had paced Winston's office a hundred times. Or at least, it sure felt that way to her. "When do I get to see Sebastian?"

The cops—a female with beautiful curls and an intelligent, sharp gaze, and a young male with a tense spine and a close-cropped, military-style haircut—both watched her with no expression.

"We don't know, ma'am," the male said. Officer Nico Ricci.

"But he's okay," the woman added. Isla Burgos. "He was treated at the scene, and you heard Detective Lewis when he said that Sebastian was en route to the station earlier."

Yes, she'd heard that. She'd just figured that she would *see* Sebastian soon. Her hands flattened over the front of her jogging pants. Actually, they were Isla's clothes. Isla had given them to her, along with a t-shirt and a pair of tennis shoes that were a little tight, but no way would Alyssa complain about that tightness. Her toes could be pinched all day. She was far too grateful to complain.

*I'm alive. Sebastian's alive. We're okay.*

A sudden rapping at the door had her head snapping up and a wide smile sliding over her face because it had to be Sebastian—

And it was just her brother.

Her smile deflated.

Antony frowned at her. "What's wrong?"

*Nothing's wrong. I was just hoping you were Sebastian.*

He hurried toward her and pulled her in for a tight hug. "Stupid question," he said. "You're probably terrified."

No, she wasn't. She was angry. Furious that those men had attacked. And she was anxious to see Sebastian. She just wanted to make sure—with her own eyes—that he was okay. "Have you seen Sebastian?"

He lifted his head and blinked at her. "Uh, no, I came right to you." He let her go and backed up a few steps.

Sebastian must not have arrived at the station yet. He'd come right to her, too, wouldn't he?

"Can you find him?" She licked her lower lip. "I'm worried about him." Her guards had been adamant that she couldn't leave Winston's office. She knew the perps had been brought in because Winston had told her he'd be taking a run at them in interrogation. He'd assured her that after his interrogations, then they could figure out their next move.

*What is the next move?*

Not another safe house. Not another time trying to lure in the bad guys. Although, the lure trick had worked. Only with nearly disastrous results.

"I want to kill Dex," Antony suddenly declared.

Her eyes widened. Her stare jumped toward the two frowning cops. "He's exaggerating," she hurried to say.

"No, I'm damn well not. This is a serious cluster situation, and the perps should never have gotten so close to you. You were supposed to be safe, off-grid, you were—"

"I knew Dex wanted to lure in the bad guys. He let them find me. The idea was that we'd take them into custody, and all of this would be over."

Antony's face flushed. A very dangerous shade of red. "What?"

Judging by that unnatural color... "I think you heard me."

"I will kill him!"

Again, the cops looked nervous.

Alyssa shook her head. "He's not killing anyone," she assured them. "Just exaggerating. You know how it is."

Their expressions said, no, they didn't exactly know how it was.

Alyssa peered back at Antony. "Watch what you say," she advised softly. "Especially when we are in front of cops."

His clenched jaw flexed. Antony gritted out, "You knew what he'd planned?"

"I suspected back at the hospital."

"And you went with him? Are you crazy?"

Her shoulders stiffened. "I'm not crazy. I am tired of being chased by bad guys. I'm tired of having my whole life turned upside down. I'm tired of running." She could hear the heat in her own words. "So the idea of setting a trap appealed to me. I went in with my eyes open."

"You could have been killed!"

She edged closer to him and dropped her voice even more. "And you're a spy. You could be killed on every mission you take." Her voice was so low the cops wouldn't be able to hear her. She'd also moved and angled her body so that they wouldn't be able to see her lips moving as she asked, "Do you let that stop you?"

"Alyssa..."

"He was going to shoot Sebastian." This part still had her shaking. "Did anyone tell you that?"

Antony's brow furrowed.

"The man was running out of the smoke—some guy dressed in all black. I think he was the one who set the bomb. He aimed his gun, and he was going to shoot Sebastian in the back." Her heart iced at the memory. "I screamed for him to stop. He didn't. So I shot him."

Her brother blinked. "Say that again."

"I shot him. At least twice. I couldn't let him hurt Sebastian."

"You shot a man...to protect Sebastian." Antony frowned, as if he were having a really hard time understanding those facts.

Seeing as how he'd just repeated the events perfectly to her, it was obvious he got what she was saying. "Yes. You know I'm a good shot." Not as good as their mother, but still...she always hit her target.

"You've never shot at a person before!"

"And a person was never trying to shoot the man I love before!"

His eyes became saucers. "No."

Crap. Those words had flown out. *As they always do.* She cleared her throat. "I'm really tired."

"You love Sebastian?"

She'd just said so.

"Since when?" Antony demanded.

She looked away. The cops were watching with avid gazes. Could the situation get any more embarrassing? "Let's talk about it later."

"You can't love him. You barely even seem to like him most days."

"Sometimes, what you see isn't always what you get." She backed away from Antony.

"It's because of the sex." He nodded. "You're confusing good sex and love."

She had to stare at him. An *are-you-freaking-serious* stare.

"What an idiot," Isla mumbled. But her voice was just loud enough to be clearly heard. Alyssa was sure that was deliberate.

"I am absolutely not!" Antony straightened his shoulders. "I will have you know that I am—"

"And I will have you know that I've had sex before," Alyssa stormed right over his words. Obviously, the cops were going to hear it all. Wonderful. "Not like it's my first rodeo."

Now Antony winced. "I don't want to know about your sex partners. That is something a brother should not ever—"

"You're the one who told me I'd confused good sex with love. Newsflash, I've had good sex. I didn't think it was love. I just thought it was good sex. And I don't have good sex with Sebastian."

His brows furrowed. "You don't? I mean, that's great. Then you won't need to have sex with him again and—"

"I have amazing sex with him. *Because* I love him." It was getting easier to say. So what if the cops heard? Maybe it was time to say it to everyone. Or, at least to the person who needed to hear the confession the most.

Sebastian.

"Since when?" Antony seemed truly perplexed. "You've barely tolerated him over the years! Whenever he came into a room, you immediately stiffened! You were always extra tense when he was around and—oh, shit."

Understanding had dawned. She could see it on his face. "Exactly. I was extra tense because he did matter. Because I was nervous around him. Because I wanted to be close, but I didn't know how to make it happen."

"But he's an asshole. Most people don't even like him!"

"That's not who he really is. *You* like him. You know what he's really like, and it's not cool for you to rail about a friend." She paused. "It's even less cool for you to say that stuff about the man I love."

His eyes squeezed shut. "Please, I am begging you, stop saying that."

"Why? The more I say it, the easier it will be for you to accept."

His eyes flew right back open. "Are you using psychology tricks on me?"

Alyssa rolled one shoulder in a shrug.

"Tell me why you love him. Just do that for me. Tell me why, Alyssa."

"How about this...why don't you tell me why he's your friend? Why you've been partners with him for so long?"

"Because he's brilliant." An instant response. "Because I'm an asshole, too, and I understand someone who doesn't bullshit. Because he gets the job done, and I can always count on him to do that. He may drive me crazy at times—lots of times, and in fact, now is one of those times—but I know that he'd have my back no matter what."

She nodded. "I happen to think he's brilliant, too. But I also like that he notices the details about me. All of the details."

"What does that mean?" A furrow appeared between his brows. Antony yanked off his glasses and began to polish the lenses on his shirt.

She put her hands on her hips. "What's my favorite holiday?"

"Christmas." He nodded.

"No, that's *your* favorite holiday. I like the Fourth of July. Because I like fireworks. I love the way they light up the sky."

Now his brow furrowed. "Last summer, Sebastian insisted on spending all that money on the company's annual picnic. I told him that he was wasting money getting that giant fireworks show but he said..." Now his lashes flickered. "He said they were worth any price. I thought he was crazy. Just wasting money. He *was*," he added quickly. "But...did he do that for you?"

"I also like apple pie."

"He had a whole freaking table of apple pies at that Fourth of July picnic!"

Yes, Sebastian had. She held Antony's gaze. "Do you know the scent of my favorite lotion? The lotion I've worn for years?"

"I have no freaking idea. Why would I know that?"

"He knows. It's lavender."

Once more, Antony's lashes flickered.

"Do you know which bakery in town I love the most?"

"Uh, no." Antony shook his head. "Let me guess, though, Sebastian knows?"

She nodded.

He shoved the glasses back onto his nose. "You get that the man has an insane memory? He can remember everything about everyone."

Her brother was trying to say that she wasn't special. That Sebastian remembered the details about all the people he met. "He might very well remember that much about everyone." She nodded. "But when my life was in danger, when he was standing in front of several hundred people about to go live with your newest tech, he left them all because he wanted to save *me*. That means I matter to him. Just like he matters to me."

"I..." Antony's voice trailed away.

For once, she didn't think Antony knew what to say.

That was okay. She had plenty to say. She grabbed his shirt-front. "They won't let me out of this room." She eyed the cops, then peered back up at her brother.

"Uh, that grip of yours is pretty tight, sis..."

"But they'll let *you* out. You're going out now, you're going to find Sebastian, and you are going to bring him back to me. Right now, got it?"

His Adam's apple bobbed as he swallowed.

"Get him. Get him in here. *Now*." Because she had to make certain Sebastian was okay. Because she needed him.

And, as she'd told her brother...because she loved him.

# CHAPTER EIGHTEEN

"I'm not saying a word without my lawyer!"

Sebastian glared at the perp through the glass. Of course, the blond would lawyer up immediately. Bad guy 101, and as the fellow's rap sheet had proven, this wasn't his first brush with the law.

More like his twentieth.

A quick scan of Dwight Granger's file had shown that he'd started getting rough with his enemies back when he'd been a teen. Assault charges had gotten him tossed into juvie, and from there, he'd graduated to bigger game. B and E's, kidnapping, and even a murder for hire charge that Granger had managed to dodge when a witness mysteriously vanished.

"Of course." Winston sat across the small table from Dwight. He nodded. Looked all congenial and calm. "You don't have to say anything. That is completely your option. I was just going to talk so that you'd understand why you will soon be transported."

"Transported?" Dwight straightened in his wobbly chair. "Where the hell am I going?"

"I actually don't know, and I don't want to know. That kind of thing is above my pay grade."

Please. In reality, Winston wanted to know everything. It was just part of who he was.

"Government agents are on the way to collect you," Winston revealed to the perp.

"What?" Dwight laughed. "Like I buy that bull."

Sebastian stiffened. The man's response seemed...genuine.

With a smirk on his face, Dwight glanced around. "Why the hell would government agents be coming to get me?"

"Well, you *did* break into an apartment building, set a bomb—"

"I didn't set the bomb! That wasn't me!"

"And then you assaulted a federal agent."

"Who was the damn federal agent?" Dwight's brows scrunched.

Again, his response seemed genuine. Appearances could be deceiving, though.

Winston looked down at a file in front of him. "I'm not at liberty to divulge an agent's—"

"You're not talking about that rich-boy prick, are you? Because he's no government agent, and you're not about to slam a charge like that on me! No way!"

"You're worried about *that* charge?" Winston cleared his throat. "Maybe you forgot the breaking and entering, the bomb, the—"

"I'm not getting shipped off to some secret government facility, you hear me? That's not happening! I've heard stories about people just disappearing into those holes and never getting out!"

Oh, he'd heard stories, had he?

Winston closed his manila file. "Oh, good, then you're already updated. Here I thought I'd have to go over things for you. But you obviously understand your new living conditions, so we're all set. You'll remain in this room until the agents arrive for your transport." He peered at his watch. "Shouldn't be long. Maybe ten minutes, tops, and then you'll be out of here." He rose. The legs of his chair scraped across the floor. "By the way..." Winston leaned over the table. "That 'rich-boy prick' happens to be a friend of mine, and I don't take kindly to people assaulting my friends."

Dwight swallowed. "You...you gonna hit me, now? Get you some payback?"

"Why would I do that?" Winston smiled. "You're about to be shoved in a hole and forgotten. Your payback will be coming no matter what I do. Same situation for your buddies. You'll all vanish soon enough." He whistled and headed for the door.

"You can't leave me!"

Winston kept walking. "Well, I can't talk to you any longer. You did ask for a lawyer, and the agents are coming and—"

"Screw a lawyer! *Help me.*" Dwight's face mottled. "I wasn't told anything about the people in that place being agents! I was just...shit, the orders kept getting bigger and bigger, you know?"

Winston slowly turned back to face him. "I don't know. Spell the situation out for me."

"Look, first, we were just scaring the woman! I mean, easy money for a scare. Who turns down that kind of job?"

A law-abiding citizen?

Sweat trickled down Dwight's temple. "Those bullets weren't supposed to hit her at the theater, and they didn't!"

*Well, hell.* Winston had worked his magic. Now they were getting some place.

"And we left the message at her place to frighten her. She was supposed to hook up with the rich-boy pr—I mean, with that guy. Your friend. She was supposed to hook up with him. Dammit, I even thought he was our client in the beginning!"

What? Now Sebastian was leaning forward because that last bit made zero sense.

Winston was frowning, too. "What do you mean, you thought he was the client? Why the hell would you think that?"

"Some guys like to play hero." Dwight licked his lower lip. "Me personally? I like to be the bad guy."

Obviously.

"Since the orders were for her not to get hurt, I figured maybe he wanted to act the hero. I mean, the goal was for her to move in with him. We made that shit happen." Dwight nodded.

Yes, they had.

"But then things changed." Winston stalked back toward Dwight. "Want to tell me about the hit at Shark Gaming and Design?"

"Look, if I talk, you've got to keep those agents off me! I'm not disappearing! I'm not having some *X-Files* shit up in here!"

Had that guy seriously just made a flashback reference to—

"I make no promises." Winston tapped his chin. "You know what? Maybe I should go talk to your buddy. What was his name? Oh, yeah, Martin. Martin—"

"Marty don't get a deal! *I* get the deal! I mean, Marty was the one who fired the shot at Shark Gaming and Design. He was also the one who fired at the woman when she was at the theater. I didn't shoot at anyone. You hear me? I never shot at anyone."

Except Dwight had tried to sneak into the bedroom at the safe house and fire a gun at the bed. *The only reason you didn't fire is because Dex snapped your wrist.* A wrist that had already been wrapped up and was currently being cradled on the guy's lap.

"Listen!" Dwight exploded. "If you're making deals, you deal with the guy who didn't shoot!"

And to think, Dwight had been such a confident bastard when he'd been saying, "Boom" over and over again.

Not so confident when he was locked up. Not so confident when he feared he was about to be sent into some secret government prison.

Winston waved his hand. "Why was the hit taken at Shark Gaming and Design?"

"We just got the order that we'd get ten grand if we winged one of the owners. Again, *wing* him. Not kill him."

"Yeah, look, you put a bomb at the last location." Winston's voice dripped sarcasm as he continued, "That screams *kill* to me—"

"It was a small bomb! Shit! It was more of a distraction than anything else—"

The door opened behind Sebastian. He tensed, figuring another cop had come in the room. "Look, I've got permission to be in here—"

"Sure, but knowing you, I figure you'd be watching the interrogation whether you had permission or not," a familiar voice responded.

He fired a fast glance over his shoulder at Antony.

Antony twisted his lips into the rough semblance of a grin. "I kinda thought you'd be *in* the interrogation."

"Tried to be. Winston wouldn't let me." He looked back at the interrogation room. "Things are getting interesting."

Antony moved to his side. They both focused back on the scene.

"You're telling me that you never intended for anyone to get hurt?" Winston shook his head. "Try that line on someone who hasn't seen your rap sheet. You don't care who you hurt. You sell your services to any interested party, and you stopped asking questions long ago." Once more, he made his way for the door. "I think we're done."

"You're right! I do sell my services—and that's what happened this time!"

*Now we're getting to the man pulling the strings.*

Winston slanted a glance back at Dwight. "I'm thinking the government agents would be more interested in your employer than in you."

Dwight's shoulders sagged. "That's gonna be a problem."

"I don't like problems. I'm more of a solution man." Winston returned to the table. He pulled out his chair. Spun it around. Straddled it. "Tell me who hired you."

"I would...if I knew."

Winston waited.

And waited.

"Jesus, I hate the sweat-it-out technique," Antony muttered. "Makes me nervous as hell. By the way, what the hell happened to your face?"

"It's a cut above my eye. Not my face. My moneymaker is just fine."

Antony grunted.

"*It was all online!*" Dwight suddenly cried out.

"You were hired online?"

"That's how that stuff goes down these days, man. Dark Web style." Dwight wiggled his brows.

"Am I supposed to believe this jerk knows anything about operating on the Dark Web?" Antony wondered. "Because I don't. He's more like the hammer you use to bust open a window. Lots of force, but very little finesse."

Yes, he was. But maybe one of the guys he'd been working with had the tech skills to find work online.

"Marty uses the Dark Web, all right?" Dwight said, as if on cue. "He finds the jobs, and when he needs extra help, he comes to me. See, like I told you—Marty is the one you need to send to the agents, not me." He smiled. Some of his confidence seemed to return. Obviously, Dwight was used to making deals and throwing others under the bus. That was why his rap sheet was so long...and his prison stays had been so short.

"This just all got out of hand," Dwight explained.

*Boom.* Sebastian could still hear that bastard taunting him. *Out of hand, my ass.*

Dwight's face hardened, as if a new thought had just hit him. A thought he didn't like. "Can't believe Marty didn't give me more time to get out."

"Guess Marty was double-crossing you." Winston sighed in mock sympathy. "You simply can't trust anyone these days."

Dwight nodded in total agreement. "Damn straight." He smiled again. A flash of yellowed teeth. "So...we good?"

"I don't know who hired you."

"I don't, either, man! That's the problem! It was all online! Never saw him in person, never got a name. Just Player69." He snickered. "And you know what that shit meant."

Winston didn't smile. "How did he contact you?"

"I told you—online! Through the Dark Web and—"

"On your phone? On Marty's phone?"

"On Marty's laptop." His expression became sly. "If I tell you where to find it, will you stop the agents from taking me?"

The interrogation room door opened. A rumpled—and very pissed-looking—Dex filled the doorway.

"Aw, damn, not him again!" Dwight craned his head and glowered. "What is that no-dick SOB doing—"

"He's the agent who will be transporting you," Winston told him. Now, he did smile. "Have a fun trip."

Dwight didn't just slump. He shriveled.

Antony's shoulder brushed against Sebastian's arm. "We need that laptop."

Hell, yes, they did.

"If we have it, we can track the mystery boss down in five minutes. Five minutes, and the bad guy is ours." Antony turned toward Sebastian. "I'll wait and make sure Winston gets the laptop's location. You go and talk to my sister, then we can meet up and—"

"I'm not talking to Alyssa."

"What? Dude, she's being held in Winston's office. The cops with her are under strict orders—probably from you and Winston—that she can't leave. If she tries to walk out, they might cuff her or some BS like that. She needs to see you. So walk in there, let her know you're all right, and then we can—"

"I think it's better if I don't see her." *It's better if she never sees me again.*

Antony didn't blink. He barely seemed to breathe.

Sebastian cocked his head. "You okay? Your face just went all red."

Through clenched teeth, Antony snapped, "Why aren't you going to my sister's side?"

"Uh, why are you even asking? Since when do you *want* me around your sister?" He tapped his chin and deliberately kept his voice flippant. "Aren't you the one who told me to keep my hands off her? Should have listened to you sooner. From here on out, consider my hands to be one hundred percent *off* her—"

Antony grabbed him and shoved Sebastian back against the one-way glass.

"Easy," Sebastian warned him. "You're not the one who gets all crazy." *That's me.*

"I am when we're talking about my sister!" Antony glared at him. "She shoots a man to save your ass, and now you're dumping her? Are you kidding me?"

*She shoots a man to save your ass.*

Hold up. He'd shot the guy to save *her*. Right?

"This is why I wanted you to stay away from her. The challenge is over, isn't it? You got what you wanted, and now you think you're moving the hell on." Antony's gaze burned. It was so hot that Sebastian was surprised the man's glasses weren't fogging.

"Antony—"

"This is *my* sister! You don't hurt her. You don't pull your crap on her!"

"You seem a little angry," Sebastian pointed out softly. "For all you know, Alyssa will be glad to see me walk away."

Some hard emotion flashed on Antony's face. There one moment, gone the next. Too complex and too fast for Sebastian to figure out what the hell it had been.

"She's had nothing but trouble since I got close to her," Sebastian continued as he fought to keep his voice from giving anything away. "Maybe me staying away from her is exactly what she wants."

"I don't think so." Antony still held him in a tight grip.

Sebastian had the feeling that Antony was holding back on him.

"If she shot a man to save you, I think that's a pretty clear statement on what Alyssa wants."

"Okay, that's the second time you said that. What the hell are you talking about? The guy was going to shoot *her*. That's the reason I fired, and the reason she had to shoot, too. She was in danger, and I'm damn sorry about that." More than sorry. He was ripped open, torn apart with regret. *I don't want to put her in danger.* "Don't you see that's why I need to step back? Because as long as I'm close to her, she will—"

"Dumbass. Listen to my words. She shot him to save you. Alyssa told me that while your ass was unconscious—from that freaking face-first slam into the pavement that people keep whispering to me about—the perp was going to shoot you in the back. She stopped him. She shot him—twice—and how do you thank her for saving your life? By breaking up with her?" Disgusted, Antony released Sebastian and stepped back. "You don't deserve her."

*The perp was going to shoot you in the back.*

Antony spun on his heel and headed for the door.

"I never deserved her," Sebastian said quietly. "That was the problem. I knew it even as I wanted her."

Antony glanced back at him. "If you walk away from her now, then hell, no, you didn't deserve her. Because if a woman is willing to kill for you, if she's willing to go to those lengths to keep you safe, then you hold tight to her. You don't let anyone come between you."

There was nothing he wanted more than to run right to Alyssa. "But I'll keep bringing danger to her. She won't ever be safe with me."

Antony's savage expression softened. A small, super tiny bit of softening. "Is that what this crap is about? You think you can keep her safe by walking away?"

"I'm a spy—"

"Then quit! How about just be the billionaire asshole that everyone thinks you are? Everyone but my sister, by the way. Because she spouted lots of craziness about how you really saw her and how you knew her favorite holiday—"

"Obviously, the Fourth of July," he said. "You know how her face lights up and she gets that big smile whenever she sees fireworks."

Antony's eyes narrowed. "And how you know what kind of ridiculous body lotion she wears."

"There's nothing ridiculous about lavender. The lotion smells fantastic. *She* smells fantastic."

Antony's arms crossed over his chest. "What's her favorite bakery?"

"Over the Moon." He shrugged. "She likes their chocolate chip muffins."

"Since when?"

"Uh, since she opened her jewelry business? Remember when we were helping her to set up the website—"

"*You* did that. I told you we could just send a tech over."

"Well, I had to make sure it was done right. Anyway, she was eating their chocolate chip muffins and she said that she liked them far better than any other—"

Antony held up his hand. "What's *my* favorite holiday?"

"Christmas."

"And my favorite restaurant?"

"The Italian place down on Fourteenth. Rizzoli's."

Disappointment darkened Antony's eyes. His lips twisted. "I was right. You remember the same shit about everyone. She's not special to you." He turned away. "You're good at spouting the right words, but Alyssa doesn't get that you can spout those words to anyone. Because you remember everything." He reached for the door.

Yeah, he did remember everything. When it came to Alyssa, every single memory he possessed was in sharp focus. "On her twenty-first birthday, she was wearing faded jeans, black converse shoes, and this blue top that fell off one shoulder. I thought she was the sexiest woman I'd ever seen, but you were standing at my side, breathing down my neck, and telling me that I had better keep my hands off your sister."

Antony stiffened. "Sometimes, you make me want to punch you in the face."

"She was blowing out her candles and making a wish, and it was stupid, but I made a wish, too."

Antony looked back at him. "If you tell me that you wished you could fuck my sister, I will break your pretty-boy face."

"I wished that she'd always get whatever she wanted. I wanted her to always smile because she had the most amazing smile I'd ever seen. It lit up her eyes."

Silence.

Sebastian looked away. His gaze darted to the one-way glass. Shit. Dwight was being escorted out. He'd missed the last part of the interrogation.

"You get that I'm a spy, too, don't you?" Antony spoke haltingly. "Like, you haven't somehow missed that important point?"

Sebastian raked a hand over his face. "Of course, I get that."

"Since she's my sister, the sister of a spy...you *get* that puts her at risk, right? I mean, isn't that how this whole mess started? Because you thought I'd sent you a text saying my cover was blown? That Alyssa was in danger?"

"Being the sister of a spy is different than being married to spy." He looked back at Antony, just in time to see Antony's eyes flare in surprise. "What?"

Antony turned to fully face him. "You thought you'd marry her?"

*In my fantasies, hell, yes.* "No. I mean, why would she want to marry someone who would have to lie to her about the jobs he does? Someone who keeps secrets and who would bring danger *into* her home? And if she really did shoot that guy to save me—"

"She did. Why are you having trouble wrapping your mind around that? It's weird."

He swallowed. Because if she did...if she shot someone for me...

The observation room door opened behind Antony. Winston stepped inside and shot a frown at them both. "What the hell is this? Party time? I'm in there, working my ass off, and you two are just standing around and shooting the breeze?"

"Give us a chance to work for you," Sebastian said. "We need the laptop." His voice was wooden. "Give it to me or Antony and we can figure out who hired the perps in minutes."

"Uh, yeah, I already have cops going out to collect the laptop. Didn't you see that part?" Winston motioned toward the glass. "Or were you busy with something else that was more important than the investigation?"

Antony pointed to Sebastian. "This idiot doesn't get that my sister shot a man to keep him alive."

Sebastian lifted his chin.

"Oh, didn't I tell you that bit?" Winston nodded. "My bad."

His bad?

"Alyssa told me all about it," Winston continued in his seemingly casual tone. "The perp even backed up her story while he was drifting in and out of consciousness in the ambulance. Guy got chatty with the EMTs and the cop who'd been assigned to stay with him. While you were on the ground, the fellow was going to shoot your ass in the back because he'd gotten word he could eliminate you. But Alyssa shot him instead. I believe she actually wound up shooting him twice."

Sebastian couldn't move.

"Isn't he acting weird about that?" Antony peered at Sebastian with squinted eyes. "Shouldn't he...I don't know...rush to her side and say how eternally grateful he is to her for saving his ass?"

"Sure, he's being all weird. But I know why. He's scared." Winston nodded and stalked closer to Sebastian. "Because when a woman saves your life, when she's willing to kill for you, a smart man holds tight and *never, ever* lets go."

"Everyone says he's smart." Antony shook his head. "To me, he's acting like a fool."

"Again, scared."

Sebastian growled.

Winston tossed a glance toward Antony. "He's scared because he wants to run to her and he wants to keep her with him, but if she shot a man this time, what happens next time?" Winston's voice softened as his stare returned to Sebastian. "I know you, Sebastian. And I know that's what you're thinking. She shot the perp this time. But what happens next time? Does she try to jump between you and a bullet? Does she *kill* the bad guy? Does she get herself killed?"

Another growl escaped from Sebastian. Harder. More savage.

"If she's hurt while she tries to save you..." Winston's lips curled down. "What do you do?

You know, other than lose your ever-loving mind."

The two men were between him and the door. "Get out of my way," Sebastian ordered.

Neither man moved. "Why?" Winston put his hands on his hips. "You suddenly got somewhere you need to be? Like I told you already, I sent cops to retrieve the laptop. You'll be notified when it gets here. In the meantime, your buddy Dex said he'd be moving Alyssa to a new location. He's got her, so you can just mark that item off your to-do list."

Sebastian's heavy breathing huffed in and out.

"Hey, this way, you don't even have to see her." A shrug from Winston. "Don't have to say thanks for saving my ass."

Sebastian lunged forward. "Dex isn't taking her anywhere. He screwed up with her last time—"

Antony put a hand on his chest. "And you're screwing up with her now."

"I want her *safe*."

"Maybe being with you *is* the safest place for her to ever be." Antony's voice was more subdued. Less *go-to-hell* angry.

"Alyssa isn't supposed to shoot people. She's supposed to be happy. Blowing out birthday candles, making wishes." He swallowed. "I wasn't supposed to drag her down into my world."

Surprise flashed on Antony's face. "Is that what you think you did?"

"I dragged you down. Brought you into this mess when you had no business being a spy."

"*I* made my choice. I did it. Not you."

"You want out. You think I don't see it? You want—"

"*You* want out," Antony threw right back. "You want out because you want a different life. I've seen it for a while." Antony cocked his head. "Is that why you were taking fewer and fewer cases? Because you thought you could slip out and try to make a life with Alyssa?"

If he'd cut out the danger, if he'd put it all behind him... "It doesn't work that way." Dex had been correct on that point. Sebastian had been blind. "The enemies I made won't just forget me. I'll always be looking over my shoulder and wondering if my secrets have been discovered. I can't ask her to live that way."

A sly expression slid over Antony's face. "So you're just gonna give up on her?" He looked at Winston. "He's gonna give up on her."

Winston nodded. "Obviously."

"He's going to let Dex take her to some undisclosed location."

"*The hell I am!*" Sebastian's denial exploded before he could hold the words back. "His guards are crap—"

"He's going to let Alyssa walk away," Antony plowed on. "Let her go out and date some random guy. Get married. Have kids."

A low, dangerous rumble slipped from Sebastian. Not a growl. Much, much rougher. Primal.

Antony paid no attention to the rumble. He waved vaguely to Winston, as if they were just having a grand old talk, and added, "Because you know, it will be fun when he shows up for holiday parties and he gets to watch Alyssa with her husband and kids, and no way will Sebastian ever think... 'That could've been me. That *should* have been me. That could have—'"

Sebastian shoved past his friends. "I'm stopping Dex."

"Yeah, and while you're off being such a badass, be sure to tell me sister that you're done with her. Tell it to her face! I *dare* you!" Antony called as Sebastian yanked open the door.

Sebastian didn't answer him. He was dealing with one fire at a time.

Fire one...

Dex.

*You are not using her again.*

\*\*\*

"I don't think that went well," Winston announced.

Antony's shoulders dropped. "He's always had that stupid martyr complex. Thinks that he has to do the right thing. That he has to save people from themselves. Gets old, real old."

Winston glanced at the open door. "You don't think he'll be able to tell her goodbye."

"Hell, no, he won't. You are right, he is scared. But the whole reason he wasn't going in there to see her? It's because the moment he takes one look into her eyes, he's done. He'll probably drop to his knees and propose to Alyssa then and there."

Winston didn't look convinced. "He doesn't want her in danger. He'll put her safety above everything else."

But you couldn't protect someone from every single danger in the world. "Life is unpredictable. That's a problem for Sebastian. He wants to control everything because when he was a kid, he could control nothing. No, scratch that. He could control numbers. Coding. That's why he hacked."

Winston let loose a low whistle. "Didn't ever look at it that way. From the outside, control seems to be the last thing Sebastian wants."

"The Bad Boy of Tech." Antony shook his head. "Control is what he wants most. But with Alyssa, I think it's the thing he has the least. He wants to control every threat to her."

"Like you don't want the same thing?" Winston sent him a knowing glance. "Isn't that why you told him to stay away from her?"

Originally, when he'd first asked Sebastian to stay away...*I just didn't want her hurt.* She was his sister, and Sebastian had been introducing him into a world of spies and danger. Keeping Alyssa away from that world had seemed necessary. But then time had passed, and he'd learned so much about Sebastian. *I thought Alyssa hated him, though. Until today. Until she told me how she really feels.* Now, everything had changed. He damn well didn't want his sister to have a broken heart. He wanted her *happy.* So he'd just needed to move a few pieces around on the chess board. Needed to push the knight toward the queen. "Sebastian and I are very much alike on a whole lot of things." And that was why he knew, with utter certainty, that when Sebastian saw Alyssa again...

*You can bluff a good game, my friend. You can say you'll walk away.*

*But if you wanted her for all these years...*

*You won't let her go.*

Especially not when Alyssa dropped her little bombshell on Sebastian.

Antony had deliberately not told Sebastian that Alyssa said she loved him. That was for Alyssa to reveal, not him. But once Sebastian heard those words, once he knew Alyssa was crazy about him...

*He'll never let her go.*

"So you're okay with Sebastian hooking up with your sister?"

Antony winced. "I don't want any visuals."

"I'm sure you don't."

"I didn't want him to hurt her. That was always my worry. It was my mistake because I didn't get the full situation between them. I didn't see the real picture." *I didn't realize how Sebastian really felt.*

Winston cocked one eyebrow. "You need a new prescription for those glasses or are you seeing clearly now?"

"I think I finally am."

"Good. When this investigation is over, when everything settles down, remind me to tell you about *Operation Get Into Alyssa's Good Graces.*" He turned away. "You will laugh your ass off because Sebastian has been *that* far gone for a long time."

A smile tugged at Antony's lips. "Operation what?"

\*\*\*

Two cops were waiting outside Winston's office. A male and a female. "Thought you were supposed to stay with her," Sebastian said as he saw them and immediately tensed. He knew the cops. They were two of the best on the force. That was why Winston had sent them to watch Alyssa.

"The special agent in charge wanted alone time with her." Isla Burgos propped her shoulders against the wall. "But we're not moving from this position."

Nico Ricci nodded from his spot on the other side of the door. Then he chided, "She's been asking about you. Was wondering when you'd show up."

Guilt twisted inside of Sebastian as he reached for the doorknob. He swung the door open, not bothering to knock because...whatever. *Dex can deal with me interrupting.*

When the door opened, he saw Dex sitting on the edge of Winston's desk. Dex was leaning toward Alyssa as she sat in a nearby chair. Dex's hand was curved under her chin.

"Tell me..." Dex was saying. "Have you ever thought about being a spy?"

"Seriously?"          *Un-fucking-believable.* Sebastian kicked the door closed. "You bring her into the spy world, and it will be the *last* mistake you make."

# CHAPTER NINETEEN

Five minutes before Sebastian stormed into Winston's office...

"So...that whole takedown at the safe house didn't go as planned." Dex blew out a long breath and angled to half-sit on the edge of Winston's desk. "My bad."

Alyssa sank into the chair near him. "Your bad? Is that the best you've got?"

He pursed his lips and considered the matter. "My very, very bad?"

"That's not funny."

"I know, but see, I don't exactly get how to handle apologies. I don't do apologies a whole lot in my line of work. I tend to break rules and plot missions, and I don't screw up nearly as much as you would suspect. You know, given our history."

Her eyebrows arched. "They put a bomb in the building."

"Yes, but I'd like to note that it wasn't a very *big* bomb. It was more bang and flash. If they'd wanted to take down the building, they would've needed a lot more power. I think it was more about distraction than anything else."

That didn't make her feel better. "I was bait, and the entire situation went to hell."

"Granted, that did happen." He winced. "But I'm not sure...after a review of the situation...that *you* were so much the target."

"Excuse me?" He'd lost her.

"I just came from an interrogation with one of the suspects. Dwight Granger. A real 'save his self' kind of guy. And I'd already had a brief chat—back on scene—with another perp, a not-so-upstanding fellow named Marty."

She waited.

He blinked. "No questions?"

"I figured you would keep talking. Not just stop dramatically."

"Fair enough." A nod. "Marty and his little gang didn't storm the place until *after* Sebastian arrived."

She already knew that, but... "Sebastian said he didn't lead anyone to us—"

"No, I don't think he did. I believe the perps followed the breadcrumbs I'd deliberately left. But I think they were watching the building, and I think they were waiting. They wanted Sebastian to arrive, and it was only *after* he got there that they made their move."

Her heart surged in her chest. Now she got what he was saying. "And one of them tried to kill Sebastian."

He nodded. "Heard about that. Really nice shooting you did, by the way." A pause. Then he leaned forward. His hand slid under her chin.

Alyssa tensed. "What are you doing?"

"Planning for an arrival. Should happen in the next sixty seconds or so. I'm usually good at predicting things like this."

"Uh, okay."

"But my question to you will be legitimate. Because that truly was nice shooting, and I liked the way you handled yourself when things went to hell. And all in a towel, no less."

Her eyes narrowed on him. "I will never live that down."

"No, the legend will live on. At least in my mind."

Her cheeks flushed.

He smiled. "Tell me...have you ever thought about being a spy?"

"Seriously?" A disgusted snarl.

A door slammed.

She jerked.

"You bring her into the spy world, and it will be the *last* mistake you make."

Before she could speak, Sebastian stormed forward. "Get your hand off her, man!"

Dex slowly pulled back his hand.

Alyssa grabbed for the sides of her chair, physically rooting herself to the spot. On one hand, she wanted to surge to her feet and grab Sebastian. Hold tight. On the other hand... "It sure as hell took you long enough!"

The anger faded from his expression. He blinked and seemed bemused.

"I mean, I've just been sitting in here for a few hours. Hoping you were alive and not slumped in a gutter somewhere."

Dex coughed. Or smothered a laugh. Hard to be sure. "Um. It's just terrible that he let you worry that way," Dex added with a hard nod. "So selfish."

Sebastian's gaze cut to him. "Do not start with me."

Dex lifted his hands. "This feels like a private conversation. I'll give you a minute—or five—then come back so that Alyssa and I can finish our discussion." His stare swept back to her. "I meant what I said."

He wanted her to be a spy?

"No." Sebastian shook his head. "Absolutely not. She is not interested so go ahead and walk away."

That was it. Alyssa let go of the chair and jumped to her feet. "You don't know what I'm interested in!"

"You *want* to be a spy?"

Dex began to sidle away.

"Maybe," Alyssa snapped. "Not like I've considered it before. But Dex says I have a flare for it."

Dex was almost at the door. He stiffened. Glanced back. "I don't think I used the word flare. I did say that you were a nice shot. You are."

Sebastian blocked her view of Dex. "Because you shot that bastard to save me."

"Yes. And I didn't even get a thank you." Scratch that. What was she saying? She squeezed her eyes shut. "I don't want a thank you. I just wanted you to be okay, and I was going crazy being away from you." Her eyes opened. Accusingly, she charged, "You sent me away."

Pain flashed on his face. "I am not good for you."

"Who says I want you to be good?"

He frowned.

Wait. Wrong words. She'd blurted the wrong stuff. "You *are* good for me, all right? I feel good when I'm with you."

"You're running for your life when you're with me."

"And who is protecting me? Who's watching out for me? It's not Dex. He's waving me around like a red flag and basically shouting, 'Come and get her! Bait over here!'" She craned around Sebastian so that she could glower at Dex, but he was gone. The door was closed again. It was just her and Sebastian. Good.

"You could have been killed because I brought you close to me." Sebastian's voice was so wooden. "That can't happen. I can't put you at risk. I *won't*. I—"

"Stop." Her stomach had just twisted into a very unpleasant knot. "If this is the scene where you say that you're going to leave me in order to protect me, you stop right there."

He stopped.

"Because that crap doesn't work. You leave me, then guess what? Suddenly I don't have my own personal spy at my beck and call."

"That's...true," he spoke haltingly. "But...beck and call? I mean, is that really—"

"If I called you and told you that I was in trouble, what would you do?"

"Run to you." An immediate reply.

The right reply. "That's what I'd do for you, too."

The faint lines near his eyes deepened. "The kind of danger I face is different than what's normally in your world. It's deadly. You never would have been targeted at all if it wasn't for me."

"You mean if it wasn't for the fact that you and my brother are spies?" She tilted her head. "Are you *sure* about that? Because Isla and Nico and I were talking—see, we had a whole long time to chat while I was waiting in this room for you to come and show me that you weren't dead."

He winced.

"They told me the guys arrested had rap sheets that stretched for days. That they sold out their services to the highest bidder. Call me crazy, but it seems odd for your super spy enemies to hire out the job to local thugs." Pair that up with what Dex had told her about the thugs rushing to the safe house only *after* Sebastian had arrived...

At her words, Sebastian's face went blank.

"You're not calling me crazy," she pointed out.

"You've never been crazy a day in your life. Keep talking."

"Well, okay. Since you're here...finally." She would share all of the ideas she'd had. "I swear, I can't help but wonder if this whole mess might not be about the spy game at all. Sure, the first text came to you saying that Antony's cover was blown, but...other than that reference, why are we so sure it's about spy town?"

"Spy town?"

"You got the text during your big PR launch. You had to leave the launch and rush to my side—

which was very nice, by the way. It's one of the reasons I'm not super pissed at you for leaving me hanging in Winston's office for so long."

His hand lifted, as if he'd touch her, but then his fingers clenched.

What was up with that? She wanted him to touch her. Alyssa soldiered on and said, "When you left the PR launch, it caused quite the stir. At least, that's what seems to have happened on social media."

"Yeah. But my team had the situation under control. They did their job."

"Still, when both of the big bosses cut out, that makes the company seem...a little uncertain, doesn't it? Antony wasn't there. You rushed away..." She could see he was understanding where this train of thought was leading. "Maybe someone wanted Shark Gaming and Design to appear unstable."

His gaze seemed to peer right through her. "Antony was shot at while he was on Shark Gaming and Design property."

"That hit wasn't aimed at me, not at all. And then the guys who stormed Dex's safe house? They only arrived *after* you got there. As in, right after you. The timing was suspicious to me." Dex's information had just helped to deepen her worries that this might not be about spy secrets.

"Timing." He frowned. Reached for the pocket of his jeans, as if he were searching for something.

For the first time, she actually focused on what he was wearing. She'd been so happy to see him a moment before that she hadn't really taken in all of the details.

Now, she saw that his jeans and sneakers were stained with what looked like soot. He wore an Asheville PD t-shirt that stretched across his powerful chest.

He tapped his front pocket again. "Lost my phone. Probably dropped it at the safe house."

"I doubt you'll be getting that back anytime soon. It could be completely destroyed. I'm sure you can get another." She slipped closer to him. "Most things are replaceable."

His head lifted. "You're not."

Alyssa tensed.

"Not that you're a thing. You're not a thing. You're a person. *The* most important person in my life. The only one I can't let down."

That sounded promising. She put her hands on his chest.

"I'm so wrong for you," he told her. His voice had gone ragged. "Antony had that part right from the very beginning."

"No, he didn't." She wanted his mouth. She wanted to kiss him and pretend that everything was all right, just for a little while.

"I bring danger with me. You don't need danger."

"Did you see me screaming my head off?"

"No. Not even when I had us scaling down the wall."

"Did you see me abandoning you? Trying to save myself?"

"No. No, dammit, you—"

"I fought for you. You would fight for me. I get that I don't have super ninja skills, but don't act like I can't handle a little bit of danger. Not saying I want us getting shot at every day, but..." She rose onto her tiptoes. "I know what I'm getting with you. I accept any risks."

Her lips pressed to his. For a moment, his mouth softened beneath hers. His lips started to part—

"No." His hands closed around hers, and he gently, but very firmly, pushed her back. "I can't take the chance. I can't stand the idea that something could happen to you. I *have* to keep you safe." Each word was low and guttural. "I'm sorry. I should have kept my hands off you from the beginning. Fucking fantasy."

"I'm not a fantasy. I'm flesh and blood. So are you. Neither one of us can ever be called perfect, and that's good. Real life will never be perfect. It's messy and it's scary and it's crazy, and, yes, sometimes, it's dangerous. But *sometimes*, real life is all about happiness. There's so much joy you can't stand it." Did he get what she was saying? "I can handle the good and the bad." With him, for him, she'd handle anything.

His gaze dropped. "What if you get tired of dealing with my bad?"

Her spine straightened. "Is that what you're worried about? That I'll get tired of the drama that surrounds you, and I'll leave?"

"I'm worried I can't protect you. I'm worried—" His gaze rose. Pinned her. "I'm worried that I will love you so much I can't breathe without you. I won't be able to protect you or you'll get tired of the danger that stalks me, and you'll leave, and then I won't know how to live without you."

Her chest warmed. Those intense, rumbling words were just pure Sebastian.

He cursed. "Now I've probably scared you. I'm sorry. You never got how much I wanted you. How much every single time I was near you, I just wanted to pull you into my arms."

She looked around. "I'm near you now, but you just pushed me away."

"Because I'm *trying* to do the right thing—"

"If you were doing the right thing, you'd be kissing me now. You'd be lifting me up, sweeping everything off Winston's desk, and making love to me." She put her hands on her hips. "That's what you'd be doing instead of this whole BS routine. I mean, really, what's the point of it? Is it a test? You think I'll walk? Not happening. In fact, I'd go so far as to say that will never happen. Know why? Simple. Because I'm in this for the long haul with you. I'm not going to get scared away. I know what you are—I know *who* you are—and I'm standing with you."

He blinked. His face...hardened.

He didn't say anything.

That was unfortunate. He'd been so intense before. She'd rather thought for sure he'd come back with his own big declaration. Or, maybe she'd just hoped that he would.

"You shouldn't have said that," he rasped.

"Well, we both know I have a tendency to blurt out what I'm thinking." She shrugged. "Sue me."

"I'd rather fuck you."

Alyssa glanced over at the desk. "Ahem."

"*You shouldn't have said that.*" He pulled her tightly against him.

"Why not?"

"Because I was trying to give you up." His hands curled around her waist. He lifted her up. Swept some stuff off Winston's desk. Put her on top. Spread her legs. Stepped between them.

"Wh-why would you want to give me up? Why were you trying to do that?"

"Because if I didn't let you go now, I'd never be able to do it. And when you tried to leave later, when you got sick of the spy game, what was I supposed to—"

She put a fingertip over his lips. "You worry too much."

His tongue came out. Licked her finger.

A shiver slid over Alyssa's body. "How many times do I have to say it? I'm not going any place." Her voice had grown husky. "Neither are you. We're in this together, from here on out. I mean, didn't you hear Dex? I'd make a killer spy."

"I don't think that's what he said."

"I don't care what he said." Her finger traced over his lower lip. "Kiss me."

He did. His mouth took hers with a savage hunger. Or maybe she was the one with the savage hunger. It was hard to tell. Their lips met. Their mouths parted. Need exploded.

She couldn't get close enough to him.

He caressed her with frantic hands.

His tongue thrust into her mouth. She moaned because, God, she did love him. And she loved everything that he could do with his tongue.

"Can't lose you," Sebastian grated.

"Then don't try getting rid of me."

"Fucking *can't*." His mouth fed on hers. Deep, drugging kisses that had her arching toward him. The t-shirt was in the way. Hers. His. She needed to throw them across the room.

*Across Winston's office?*

A little bit of sanity raised its head. This was probably not the best place.

But he was kissing his way down her throat. Sucking and licking and—

She moaned.

*Are the cops still outside? If so...I should...* "Yes, right here." Her hands sank into his hair. What he was doing with his mouth felt *so* good.

Someone knocked at the door.

Because...*right*. They were in a police station. Other people were close.

Sebastian stiffened. His head lifted.

"I'm opening the door," Winston barked. "You know, the door to *my* office."

"*We will finish this,*" Sebastian whispered to her.

In the next moment, he'd lifted her off Winston's desk, spun her around and put her in the chair she'd originally been sitting in a few minutes before. Sebastian crossed his arms over his chest, blew out a ragged breath, and straightened up as he assumed a position near the desk just as Winston threw open the door.

Winston eyed them suspiciously. "What in the hell did I interrupt?"

"Alyssa was telling me her take on the crimes." Sebastian's voice was rough, a wee bit raspy, but other than that, he seemed totally in control.

Good for him. Meanwhile, Alyssa's heart was about to jump out of her chest and her lips were tingling because she swore she could still feel his kiss.

"Uh, huh. You were just talking." Winston shut the door and sauntered inside. He frowned at his desk. "What happened? Who knocked over my stuff?"

"Dex," Sebastian supplied immediately. "Such a bastard. Found him in here, *sitting* on your desk, if you can believe that."

"What an asshole." But Winston glowered at Sebastian.

"Absolutely."

Alyssa shifted in her seat. "How did the interrogations go?"

"It's looking like the perps have zero clue that they stumbled into a spy web. We've got a very solid lead on the person who hired them, though. I've got cops retrieving a laptop that should take us straight to the ringleader."

That was good news. She nodded.

"That's in line with Alyssa's suspicions," Sebastian said.

Winston's focus sharpened on her. "Tell me."

Okay. She did. She told him all about how she wasn't so sure this case had anything to do with spies and that, instead, it seemed to have a whole lot more to do with Shark Gaming and Design. Or at least, that was the way it seemed to her.

Another knock banged on the door.

She wasn't at all surprised to see her brother stroll in. His gaze was considering as it drifted from her to Sebastian.

"Did you get that shit worked out?" Antony wanted to know as his stare lingered on Sebastian.

"Oh, they got it worked out. Trust me," Winston muttered.

She flushed. So they'd gotten a bit, um, carried away.

Sebastian took a step toward Antony. "Were you on my computer last night?"

"Yes, sure, I was." He gave Sebastian a *you-should-remember-this* frown. "You were there. You burst in and nearly scared the hell out of me. That was right before Alyssa saved me from getting shot."

Sebastian waved an impatient hand. "*After* all of that. After we left the hospital and split up, did you go back to access my computer?"

"No. I hit the streets to talk to some contacts I have."

Winston lifted his brows.

"I have contacts," Antony mumbled when he caught Winston's doubting expression. "You and Sebastian are not the only ones with connections. I get that my connections might not seem as cool as the ones you use but—"

"You *weren't* on my computer again?" Sebastian's expression had darkened.

"You hit your head. I get that." Antony nodded. "Heard all about that header you took into the pavement and that's why you're asking the same question over and over again." He smiled patiently at Sebastian. "No, I was not on your computer a second time last night."

"Someone was."

Everyone's attention locked on him.

"Got the alert on my phone, right before that jackass climbed in the window at Alyssa's safe house. Literally right before." Sebastian's voice was flat. "Then I was fighting that jerk, he was saying there was a bomb, and we had to escape as quickly as we could. During the escape, I lost my phone."

Alyssa pushed out of the chair. "You almost lost your life."

"Yeah, that fits, too." He didn't seem concerned.

She was plenty concerned. "*It fits?*" Wow, her voice had just risen way too much. But nothing about him nearly dying fit for her, thank you very much.

"Sure. I was the only one who knew that someone had hacked into my computer. That alert goes straight to me, no one else. I didn't get the chance to report it or check on it, and if I'd died, then no one else would ever have known that someone at Shark Gaming and Design was hacking into my files."

She reached for his hand. "Good thing you didn't die."

He squeezed her fingers. "Good thing I had you watching my ass."

She smiled at him.

His dimples started to—

"This is really sweet and all," Winston interrupted. "But from where I'm standing, it looks like Alyssa is right. This isn't about your spy BS at all."

Antony had taken a step back. "No, it's not. Hell, it's about the oldest reason in the book, isn't it? The oldest reason to turn on those close to you. The oldest reason to kill..."

"Money," Sebastian supplied. "Someone was trying to steal our tech to make a freaking killing. That someone started by using Alyssa to distract you and me both, Antony. Then he stepped up his game and went straight for us. He tried to shoot you. He tried to kill me."

"Sonofabitch." Antony's mouth dropped open. "We need to get to Shark Gaming and Design!"

"Hell, yeah, we do." Sebastian pulled Alyssa toward the door. "Let's go."

"Right." Antony was in their path. He nodded quickly. "She's going now. Gonna be constantly at your side. Got it. Good decision." Another nod. A satisfied one, this time. "Knew you'd get over that whole leaving her crap as soon as you found out she was in love with you."

Alyssa immediately dug in her heels. *"Leaving me?"* Her heart ripped open. Or, at least, it sure felt that way.

Sebastian's head swung toward her. He gaped at her in shock. *"You're in love with me?"* he asked at the same time.

Winston whistled. "Well, this got even more awkward."

# CHAPTER TWENTY

"We're going to talk," Sebastian told an obviously unsettled Alyssa as the elevator climbed to the top floor of the Shark Gaming and Design building. "And I'm going to clear the air, and I will apologize to you a thousand times if necessary."

"*You were going to leave me?*" Pain creaked in her words. That gutted him. If he had his way, Alyssa would never know a moment's pain.

But...

*I'm the one who hurt her.*

The elevator hurtled up. He'd used his key pass in order to get access straight to the top floor. "Baby, I can explain..."

The elevator stopped. The doors dinged.

Antony coughed from his position in the corner. "Try explaining later. Let's crime solve now."

Sebastian and Alyssa both tossed a glare his way.

"I'll check my office first," Antony offered quickly. "I'll see if I can find the guy's tracks on my system. You review yours." He hurried out of the elevator and away from them.

Alyssa jumped out of the elevator, too.

Ella and a group of guards were waiting in the top floor's small lobby for them. "What's happening?"

Sebastian raked her with a quick glance. "I guess you're working twenty-four-hour shifts, now, huh? You must have pulled an all-nighter. I know you didn't expect all this when you signed on with us."

"Antony was almost shot last night." Ella's gaze darted to his retreating figure. She motioned with her hand, and one of the guards immediately moved to tail Antony. "On *my* watch. So, yes, I'm pulling a twenty-four-hour shift. I'm doing anything necessary to help." Her gaze came back to Sebastian. "What can I do?"

"Keep the building locked down from this moment forward. No one leaves, but Detective Winston Lewis and a fellow named Dex Ryan will be arriving ASAP." Arriving with the laptop. Dex had already pulled rank at the police station. As soon as the cops Winston had sent retrieved the laptop that they all needed, Dex planned to bring it straight to Sebastian so that he could work his magic on it.

One way or another...this mess was ending.

"They'll have ID, and they will be armed." Just so she knew. "But they're on my side. Send them straight to me."

Ella nodded. "I met Dex last night. Kind of an unforgettable ass of a guy."

Most people tended to think that way about him.

Her gaze flickered to the wound over Sebastian's eyebrow. Ella winced. "Do I want to know what happened?"

"A collision with pavement. Could have been worse, though. At least I didn't get shot in the back." He wrapped his arm around Alyssa. "Thanks to Alyssa."

Ella's eyes widened as her attention flew to Alyssa. "You saved him?"

"Apparently," Alyssa's voice was cool. "It's what I do."

"Damn, girl. Good for you."

Then Ella got moving. So did her guards. Sebastian hurried and—

His assistant Doug walked right out of Sebastian's office. Sebastian frowned at him. "What in the hell were you doing in there?" And why hadn't Ella mentioned that Doug was in his office?

Doug stopped. Stared. Then rushed forward and threw his arms around Sebastian. "I'm so glad you're okay!"

"Why were you in my office?"

Doug pulled back. His red bow tie was a bit crooked. "I always put the weekend mail in your office on Monday mornings."

Wait. Was it Monday? Seriously?

"You normally let Doug in your office." Ella had come back. Now she frowned worriedly. "Has the procedure changed? You didn't tell me to stop him—when you called, you just said to have guards ready to act."

"Our stock is tanking." Doug's voice dropped. His body trembled. "Did you see? Apparently, it's bad news—*major bad news for the market*—when one of the company's founders gets shot at on Shark Gaming and Design property. Added to the fact that you pulled that disappearing act at the big press promotion—"

"Doug. Get your shit together," Sebastian ordered. "Your body is shaking."

Doug slumped. "I don't want to be fired. I don't want us going bankrupt. I like this company." He twisted his bow tie. "This is so bad."

"Doug."

Doug puppy-dog stared at him.

Ella frowned suspiciously at Sebastian's assistant.

And Sebastian tried to figure out if he was staring at an enemy. "Doug, what time did you arrive this morning?"

"Seven a.m.," Ella piped in. "Just like he always does." Her hands went to her hips. "You think he's involved in what's happening? Want me to interrogate him?"

Doug backed up. "I-I just dropped off mail! I was doing my job!"

Alyssa sidled closer to Sebastian. "Let's get on your computer. Every moment that passes wastes more time."

She was right. "Keep Doug in the building," he ordered Ella.

"What?" Doug paled. "Oh, God. Oh, God." It almost looked as if he might faint.

"Doug, get some coffee," Alyssa advised him. "Coffee and deep breaths, and we'll all talk soon, okay?" Now she wrapped her hand around

Sebastian's. "Right now, I need to be alone with Sebastian, so excuse us."

"I could use some coffee," Doug mumbled.

Ella spoke softly to a guard, and then the guard advanced on Doug. "Come with me," the guard ordered, "and we'll get that coffee."

Sebastian knew the guard would also make sure Doug didn't leave. *Do I really suspect my assistant?*

No, but Sebastian couldn't take chances.

Alyssa cleared her throat. "Sebastian, you ready?"

Ready to end this? Hell, yes. But...from the corner of his eye, Sebastian saw Isaac Swain appear in the corridor that led back to Research and Development. He held a brown box in his hands and appeared utterly dejected.

*Isaac.*

It was startling to see the guy. Mostly because the last time that Sebastian had come face to face with the fellow, Isaac had been on a date with Alyssa.

Now he was...

Isaac was slowly starting to glare at Alyssa and Sebastian. "I knew it!" Isaac crowed. "I knew the two of you were sleeping together!"

Sebastian took a hard, aggressive step toward the crowing dick.

"Nope." Alyssa tightened her hold on him. "Not worth it. Don't."

Isaac stalked toward them, still clutching the box of what appeared to be his possessions. "You came to that theater, jealous as hell, busting up our date—because you'd been sleeping with her the whole time!"

"I wish," Sebastian fired back.

Isaac frowned. "What?"

"I wish I'd been sleeping with her the whole time." He hadn't stuttered or mumbled. Sebastian thought he'd been quite clear.

Isaac squinted at him.

"You were swinging out of your league," Sebastian told him flatly. "So the hell am I, but for some reason, Alyssa wants me."

*She may even love me. God, I hope she does. We are circling back to that one ASAP. As soon as I can smooth things over and get her to stop glaring at me.*

"I'm not staying here." Isaac straightened his shoulders. "So you don't have to fire me."

Sebastian peered down at Alyssa. "Was I firing him? Was that on my to-do list?"

"You're jealous because Alyssa went out with me!" Isaac accused. "Because she wanted *me!*"

Alyssa didn't look over at Isaac. "I don't think we even talked about him after the theater. We were distracted by other things."

She wasn't just talking about sex, obviously. Because, hello, a whole lot had gone down. But her words still made Sebastian smile.

"Though he did call once to check on me," Alyssa added.

Wait, he had? When?

Isaac cursed, then said, "Excuse me, but I'm on my way out."

Now Sebastian did look at him. "Yeah...no." With his free hand, he motioned to Ella and her crew. "Detain the guy. Put a guard on him and make sure he stays in his office until I can have a little one-on-one time with him."

"Consider it done." Ella advanced on Isaac. A bulky guard followed her steps.

"What?" Isaac gripped his box even tighter and backed up. "You can't force me to stay here."

Sebastian headed toward his office with Alyssa at his side. "Sure, I can. Haven't you heard? I'm a selfish prick. I do what I want all the time."

"Oh, God." Isaac's voice was horrified. "I knew you heard me say that at the theater! That's why I was packing up. I know my job is over. I'm sorry! Jeez, I'm *sorry!*"

Sebastian ignored him because Alyssa was right. They needed to get to work and stop the distractions. He swept into his office and went straight to his computer. Alyssa tried to step away from him, but he pulled her right back to his side. "I work better when you're near."

He booted up the system. Ignored the stack of mail on his desk.

"Since when?" Alyssa asked softly. "I could actually swear that you've been barely aware of my existence for the last few years."

His fingers were flying over the keyboard. Some bastard had been in his system. Good work, but...a little sloppy in places. The wrong places—places that would have sent alarms blaring for Sebastian.

*But then, I wasn't supposed to find his footprints on my system. I was supposed to be dead.*

He kept typing. Hunting. Pulling up every piece of data that the unknown bastard had accessed.

*Nothing about spy work. This is all pure Shark Gaming and Design. Schematics. System plans. Future development ideas.*

"I'm always aware of you," Sebastian said as he followed the footprints. "Anytime that you're in a room, I know exactly where you are. And when you're close to me, that's when I'm at my best. *That's* the reason I want you close right now. I can sure as hell hunt and think better when you're near. You just make me better."

"But you were going to leave me."

For an instant, his fingers faltered. "You make me better," he said again. "But I'm not sure what I do for you." His gaze darted to her. "Turn you into a killer? Make you live a life full of danger?"

She slowly shook her head. "You don't turn me into anything. I do what I want. And if I want to protect you, I will. If I want to have sex with you, I will. If I want to get married and have kids with you..."

He stopped breathing.

"Well, I guess that's something we'll talk about later. You know, way after all of your apologies and your declarations about how you love me and stuff."

"I...I haven't said I love you."

"And I haven't told you that I love you, either. Antony said that. I haven't told you anything directly. Maybe because I'm waiting on *you* to make the big move. You kind of owe me, don't you think? Since you were going to—"

"Don't you already know, though? Don't you know how I feel?"

"How would I? Am I supposed to be a mind reader?"

No, of course not. "I'm sorry." He was. "It's simple. It's just...been you, Alyssa. For me, there's only...you."

***

"I need to talk to Antony," Isaac snapped as Ella and the security guard—some big, muscle-bound jerk with a sneer—tailed him down the hallway back to the Research and Development area on the top floor. "He'll listen to me. He understands me!"

"That's not going to happen," Ella responded.

Isaac whirled to glare at her. "I'm not trying to leave the facility! I'm trying to talk to someone with reason!"

Ella lifted her brows. "Are you yelling at me?"

He was. Because this was bad. "I came to this company because of Antony. He is the one who hired me, not Sebastian. Sebastian has always disliked me and because I made the mistake of taking Alyssa out on *one* date, now the guy straight-up hates me."

"You took the boss's girl out?" The massive guard laughed. "Idiot."

Isaac felt his cheeks burn. "I don't know what's happening here. I heard about the shooting, yes, and this morning when I arrived early, Doug told me there are rumors the company is in trouble. Maybe Sebastian is looking for some kind of fall guy—*I don't know!* But Antony can help me. I just need to talk to him for a few minutes. *Please, Ella.* I am begging you here."

Her lips pursed.

"Five minutes," he added quickly. "Just five. Look, I'm not leaving the building! I swear! I'm just going to talk to Antony. You and the guard can stand right outside of his office the entire time."

"*If* Antony wants to talk to you, then you can see him," Ella relented. "For five minutes. But if Antony doesn't want to see your ass, then you'll be cooling your heels in your office."

"It's not an office," he mumbled. "More of a cubicle."

*** 

"Your fingers aren't moving," Alyssa pointed out as she tried to keep her breathing slow and steady.

"No."

"You're supposed to be finding out what the bad guy did to your system."

"I already figured it out. He accessed upcoming projects. Got his greedy fingers in all my tech and schematics. He copied the files, probably put them on a tiny flash drive so that he could get them out undetected, and now he's planning to sell the info to the highest bidder."

He'd already found out all of that? But he'd only been typing for a few moments. "You work fast."

He reached for her hand. "I told you, I work better when you're near."

"I think that's a lie."

"I don't lie to you. I lie to other people. I bullshit other people. I tell them what they want to hear, and yes, I am even an extremely selfish prick to the rest of the world. Back at the theater, Isaac had that part right."

She swallowed. His touch made her whole body feel heated.

"I was trying to stay away at the police station because I hate that I put you in danger."

"You were going to leave me."

He shook his head. "Did you see how long that shit worked? I walked into Winston's office, saw you, and knew I could never stay away."

"You tried, though." And that *hurt*.

"You were in my head every second that I was away from you." He pressed his lips together, then he told her, "I'm sorry."

"Couldn't hear you." She could hear him perfectly. She just wanted to hear the words again.

"I'm sorry. I'm an asshole. I'm very, very sorry."

\*\*\*

Ella rapped on Antony's door. "Antony?" she called. "I need to talk to you."

"Come in!"

She opened the door. Found him hunched over his keyboard. "Isaac Swain is demanding to see you."

Antony looked up at her. Squinted behind the lenses of his glasses. "Who?"

"Isaac Swain," she repeated and ignored the fact that he looked stupid cute with those glasses. Why did she always go for men in glasses? Keeping her voice brisk, she added, "Sebastian ordered all staff to stay on the premises."

"Yes." A nod. "They should. No one should leave."

She waited. He didn't say more. Had he missed the first announcement she'd made? "Isaac is demanding to speak with you for five minutes."

"I'm working so *no—*"

"Please!" Isaac called from behind her. "It's about *covert intel!*"

What in the hell did that mean?

But Antony had stiffened. "Send him in, now."

She'd never heard quite that tone from Antony before. It put Ella on instant alert. "What's wrong?"

His eyes—normally so warm and dark—were flat and cold. "I'd like to tell you, but it's classified."

She rolled her eyes. "Seriously, spy boy, I'm the head of your security. You need to tell me everything."

He leapt to his feet. "Why did you call me that?"

She stormed forward and slammed her hands down on his desk. She would *not* notice how sexy he looked with his tousled hair. "I called you that because you're acting like some kind of spy wanna-be with your classified talk. I get that the tech intel here is important, but I can't do my job efficiently if my hands are tied behind my back!"

"Your hands aren't tied. They're on my desk."

She narrowed her eyes at him. "Sometimes, you drive me crazy."

"*Antony!* We have to talk!" Isaac cried.

Right. Isaac. Not exactly employee of the year over there.

She motioned him forward. "Lucas, stay outside the door," she told her guard. Maybe she'd stay in there with Isaac and Antony and monitor the situation—

Her phone buzzed. She looked down. Read the text.

"Dex and Winston are on the way up. I need to go meet them." She nodded to Antony. "You good?"

He still had that hard, dangerous look about him. Weird. Because the man normally looked like a handsome nerd to her. This was different...

He was different.

"I'm good," he assured her.

She brushed by Isaac. Isaac was still gripping his precious box of, well, whatever. Staplers? Coffee cups? "Five minutes," she reminded him. "And then you're done."

Ella hurried outside. She made sure that Lucas kept his position, and then she went straight for the elevator.

These men were getting on her nerves. How was she supposed to protect the company if Sebastian and Antony kept leaving her in the dark?

# CHAPTER TWENTY-ONE

"I'll give it up."

Alyssa's brows drew together. "What are you talking about now?"

"As soon as I see Dex, I'm telling him that I'm out. I'll walk away from the spy world. It won't eliminate the threats. I hate that. When I signed on, I didn't know—couldn't plan on *you*. If I could go back in time, I'd stop. If I knew you were in the future for me, I'd do everything right. I wouldn't ever do anything to put you in danger, I swear it."

She leaned forward and brushed her lips against his. "Stop." Alyssa kissed him again.

His hands rose and curled around her hips.

"I think you did a whole lot right," she whispered. "I'm not asking you to give up the spy life for me. I'm not asking you to change for me."

"Baby, I would give up everything if it meant I got you." He pulled her back for another kiss. A longer, drugging kiss. "I don't want to be off in another country, I don't want to be bringing danger to our door. I want to be with you. I want those kids you mentioned. I *will* find a way to keep you safe."

"Wait." Her eyes searched his. "You skipped a step. A big step."

"Where? When?"

"You went from kissing me to having kids with me. I think there's a step in between that whole process."

"I will make love to you as soon as—"

"The love part." She nodded. "That's the part you missed. You should go over it again."

He swallowed. "I love you."

Alyssa smiled at him. "Was that so hard?"

"One of the hardest things I've ever done."

She kissed him. Stroked his mouth so softly with her own. "Well, you did a stellar job," Alyssa murmured against his lips.

"*Sebastian!*" Ella announced through the door. "Your detective friend and that Dex guy are here with a laptop."

Sebastian's mouth lingered against Alyssa's. She enjoyed the kiss, but she pulled back and said, "Send them in!"

Winston came in first. He sighed when he saw them. "Every time I open an office door, you two are making out."

"Guilty." Sebastian let her go and made a grab for the laptop. "Let me at it."

Winston surrendered the laptop.

"Great." Dex nodded. "You get to work. Winston and I are going over your security cams."

"I accessed them as soon as I arrived. Could do it on my computer." Sebastian was already working on the laptop. "Guy cut into the system. Whole thing went dark for several minutes. Just the way it did when Antony came in last night."

Alyssa saw Dex and Winston share a long look before Dex said, "Then we'll be going to talk to the security guards who *should* have been watching that feed at the time. Surely they would have noticed a glitch like that."

Ella straightened. "They absolutely *should* have noticed and reported to me immediately." A brisk nod. "Come this way." Then she paused. Slanted a suspicious glance at Dex. "You sure you're FBI?"

"Isn't that what my badge said?"

Alyssa caught the deliberate wording of Dex's reply. How about that? He wasn't straight up lying, he was just letting the false ID do the job for him. Because, no, he wasn't FBI. She hadn't exactly gotten a ton of specifics, but weren't spies under the CIA's giant umbrella?

Ella cleared her throat. "You just...you don't quite remind me of a Fed. I mean, you told me last night that the FBI was involved because of contracts that you'd worked with Shark Gaming and Design in the past, but—"

"Ella," Sebastian said her name firmly.

She looked over her shoulder at him.

"Don't push on this one. Dex has clearance from the government. We're cooperating with him fully. That's all."

She nodded but didn't look happy.

Winston glanced at Alyssa. "You good?" he asked softly.

She moved toward him.

Sebastian reached out with one hand and pulled her toward him.

Winston frowned.

"He works better when I'm close," Alyssa explained.

Winston didn't smile, but he nodded. "Keep an eye on him."

"You know I will."

A moment later, the door closed behind him.

She felt Sebastian's eyes on her. She was frowning because Winston's demeanor had been different. He'd seemed tense. Alarmed. And the way he'd rushed to talk to the guards...

*He thinks the man we're after is here.*

Sebastian was typing on the laptop.

"Is he here?" Alyssa asked softly. "As in...does he work for your company?"

Sebastian's jaw hardened. "Based on the trail I'm following...fucking, *yes*. He sent these messages from Shark Gaming and Design."

She inched closer. "But *who* sent them?"

His fingers moved faster.

***

"Sebastian is out of control," Isaac fumed. "He's locking up employees! And he's dragging your sister around with him! Your *sister!*"

Antony stood behind his desk. A tension headache throbbed in his right eye. "Why did you say 'covert intel' a moment before?"

Isaac swallowed. "Because that's what you do, isn't it?" He glanced over his shoulder at the closed office door. "You didn't want Ella hearing the truth. And I thought maybe she knew. Guess not, huh?" His gaze swung back to Antony. "So let's talk." He hurried forward, still gripping his precious box.

Antony's right hand slowly moved toward his desk drawer.

Isaac dropped the box on Antony's desk. Then he drove *his* hand into the box and came up holding a gun. "Were you looking for this?"

Antony yanked open the drawer. The drawer that *should* have contained a gun. Only it didn't.

"Because I found it when I was in your office earlier. It was locked in your drawer, but I'm good with locks. Heck, I'm the one who picked the lock before and took the phone you'd left behind." Isaac smiled. "I'm good with secrets, too. Found out yours pretty quickly."

*Keep him talking.* Antony's hand slid back to his side. "Which secrets are we talking about?"

"We're talking about the fact that you're a spy. Like I said, found out real quick. Well, not *super* quick, but once I was on your computer, digging around, I was able to put some puzzle pieces together." He bit his lower lip. "To be honest, it was a hunch at first, but it made sense, you understand? I noted places that you and Sebastian had both traveled to, and I also monitored for reports of any incidents. Tech incidents. The kind of incidents that can embarrass governments."

"A lot of those incidents *aren't* reported."

"You'd be surprised at what's on the Dark Web."

*He's got the gun aimed at my heart.* As soon as Isaac had said "covert intel" in that grating voice of his, Antony had known he was looking at the guy who'd been working to steal Shark Gaming and Design secrets. While Antony had been searching on his computer, he'd realized his files had been compromised.

*The bastard who compromised everything is right in front of me.*

Yes, he'd realized he was staring at his enemy, but Antony had needed to get Ella out of the office because she couldn't find out that he was a spy. Her text about Dex and Winston had arrived just in time.

Antony knew Ella thought that he was just a tech nerd. If he tried pulling some Jason Bourne shit in front of her, things would not go well.

*And I didn't want her anywhere near this jackass.*

Because, yes, dammit, Ella was his head of security. She was smart, tough, savvy, but...

*I don't want her hurt.* When it came to Ella, he tended to not always think rationally. A problem he had. He was dealing with it. Sort of.

"Did you hear what I said?" Spittle flew from Isaac's mouth.

Antony's fingers skated over the keyboard. "Yes, I did. Dark Web. Scary stuff." He kept his eyes on Isaac as he slowly typed. "You know, I've even heard you can hire killers on the Dark Web. Guns for hire, just like in the Wild West."

Isaac paled. "They don't know who I am. I never told them!"

*Way to confess.* "Yes, but Sebastian is about to get their laptop, and you know once he has it, he'll be able to trace the communication back to you so—"

"*If you hit send on the message you just typed, I will put a bullet in your heart.*"

"Calm down," Antony said.

Too late. The man was obviously *way* past calm.

Isaac pulled the trigger.

\*\*\*

*Bam.*

Sebastian's head jerked to the side when he heard the distinct sound of a gunshot firing.

"That's...my brother's office." Alyssa's voice shook. "That came from right next door. *Antony's* office!"

She lunged for the door.

He caught her around the waist. "Faster way. One that won't be expected." *Not expected by whoever just fired that shot.* He pulled out his weapon from the back of his jeans. Went to the passageway that connected his office to Antony's. "Stay quiet," he told her. "He won't see us coming."

Alyssa nodded. He opened the secret passageway. Barely breathed as he made his way to Antony's office. The outer door silently slid open, and Sebastian saw—

Antony, lying in a pool of blood.

And crouched over him...with his gun still drawn...Isaac.

Sebastian aimed his own weapon. "Step the hell away from him."

Isaac whirled. "What? How the hell did you get in?"

"Secret passage, asshole. Every good billionaire-prick, Batman wanna-be has one." He heard a gasp behind him and knew that Alyssa had seen her brother.

Isaac's gun shook as he aimed it at Sebastian. "Wasn't supposed to go down like this."

"You mean you weren't supposed to be the one who pulled the trigger? Because you sent other people to do your dirty work? That what you mean?"

Isaac flushed. "I just wanted the tech. Do you know how much money it's worth?"

"I've got an idea. Considering I fucking made it."

"You're such a bastard—"

Was the guy for real? "I'm a bastard? You just shot one of my best friends! Drop the weapon right now, or I will shoot *you*."

"No, you won't." Isaac's gaze darted to Alyssa. "You won't do it in front of her. You want her to see you as the hero. The hero doesn't shoot. He doesn't kill. He—"

"He does when his friend—her brother—is lying in a pool of his own blood."

Antony let out a groan. "Just...shoot...him...already!"

"He can't." Isaac's chin notched up. "Because he wants to know what I did with his precious tech. He won't shoot me. Not until he can figure out what I did with—"

Alyssa grabbed the box on the desk. She shoved her hand inside. Rooted around a bit and came back up holding...

A small flash drive. "Found it." She cut a glance at Sebastian. "Or at least, I'd bet that this is the drive he used on your computer, seeing as how it was tucked in his special box."

Isaac snarled and lunged for her. When he lunged, Isaac pointed his gun at her.

*No fucking way.*

Sebastian fired. The bullet blasted into Isaac's shoulder, and the weapon fell from Isaac's fingers as he screamed in pain.

"*You shot me!*" Isaac gaped at Sebastian. "OhmyGod!"

"Bastard..." Antony rumbled from the floor. "Hurts...doesn't it?"

Sebastian rushed for Isaac. He kicked the gun away from its position near Isaac's foot and slammed the SOB into the desk. He wrenched Isaac's arms behind his back.

Isaac screamed even louder.

"Now who's the prick?" Sebastian demanded.

"You...still are," Isaac huffed.

The door flew open.

Winston, Dex, and Ella burst inside. Their expressions were locked and tight and Ella—she immediately ran for Antony.

"You're hurt!" She dropped to her knees beside him.

Alyssa hurried to her brother and knelt to examine him.

Sebastian kept his tight grip on Isaac and cocked his head toward Winston. "Tell me that you have cuffs on you."

Winston held them up.

"Please arrest this asshole. Right before he shot Antony—"

Antony groaned, cutting through Sebastian's words.

"*You were shot?*" Ella gasped. "You aren't supposed to be shot! You work on a computer all day! That is a *safe* job!"

Sebastian shook his head. The woman had no clue. And she sure was tenderly running her hands over Antony.

What was that about?

"The bullet is still in Antony's side." Alyssa's voice was high. Afraid. "He needs an ambulance."

Dex whipped out his phone. Sebastian heard him calling for an ambulance and for his team.

Winston approached with cuffs.

"As I was saying," Sebastian continued grimly, "right before he shot Antony, I found out that Isaac was the guy who'd hired our thugs from the Dark Web. Isaac was the mastermind. All that stuff went down because he wanted to steal Shark Gaming and Design secrets."

Dex looked over at Sebastian. Then Isaac.

"Shark Gaming and Design," Sebastian emphasized. This whole mess had never been about spies.

It had been about secrets, yes, tech secrets.

It had been about greed.

It had been about money.

Now, finally, it was over. His gaze darted to Alyssa. She was crouching over her brother and talking softly to him. Her hair fell over her shoulders.

Dex crept close to Sebastian. "We'll need a private briefing, ASAP."

Yes, they would need a briefing because Sebastian had some plans he needed to discuss with his handler.

*Get ready to handle the changes that are coming.*

# CHAPTER TWENTY-TWO

"You're quitting?" Dex gaped at him as they stood in Sebastian's study. "We've been over this before. You can't just walk away!"

Sebastian crossed his arms over his shoulders. Twenty-four hours had passed since they'd caught Isaac at Shark Gaming and Design. Sebastian was currently enjoying being back at home, while Isaac was raging in a jail cell. Though Isaac needed to stop the raging and get used to living behind bars.

Not like he'd be getting out any time soon.

The fact that Isaac had discovered Sebastian and Antony were spies? Well, that meant he was getting special attention from Uncle Sam. The kind of attention you didn't want. The kind of attention that meant you were in for a whole new level of pain.

*He won't be sharing those secrets with anyone.*

"Look, Antony is okay," Dex pointed out—as if Sebastian had somehow forgotten what was happening with him. "The docs dug the bullet out. He'll heal, and he'll be back in the game in no time."

"Yeah, that's the thing..." Sebastian exhaled. "I don't see it as a game. I see the spy world as a problem. It's standing between me and what I want."

*"Her."*

Why deny it? "I'm making changes. You were right, I can't eliminate all the threats, but I also can't keep her safe when I'm halfway across the world on missions."

"You actually think she's going to be okay with the risks you bring to her?"

The door to Sebastian's study opened. Alyssa stood there, clad in faded jeans and a black top that hugged her breasts. Her long hair slid over her shoulders, and her eyes seemed even bigger and darker.

*Gorgeous.*

"Why don't you ask her?" Sebastian invited.

Dex immediately put his hands on his hips and spun toward her. "Do you have any idea what you're taking on with him? You're prepared for the fact that he might have enemies who show up, gunning for him?"

Sebastian tensed.

She sighed. "You're trying to scare me."

Dex nodded. "Maybe you should be scared. Isaac found out the truth. Others could, too."

"Yes. And if that happens..." Alyssa walked straight to Sebastian. Her eyes lit up as she approached him. "If that happens, we'll deal with it. Together."

*Together.* Yes, that was exactly where he wanted to be—with her.

"Life is full of risks," Alyssa continued quietly. "If you let those risks stop you from living, then you'll miss out on some pretty important things. The best things."

Sebastian's hand lifted and curled under her chin. "I will do everything I can to protect you."

She gave him a slow smile. "And I will do the same for you. I kinda have a vested interest in watching that sexy ass of yours."

He laughed. God, she made him feel good.

"You two...you're trouble. Like, seriously, do you know how much trouble this is going to cause me?" Dex groused. "You have skills that I need Sebastian! It's not like I can just replace you at the drop of a hat."

Sebastian glanced Dex's way. "You still have Antony."

"For the moment." He heaved out a frustrated breath. "But what's he gonna do? Fall in love, decide he wants to give up the spy life, and then screw me over, too?"

Now Sebastian shook his head. "You know, it's not always about you."

Alyssa turned toward Dex. "It's not."

He frowned. "Are you sure?" Dex tapped his chin. "I thought it was."

Sebastian almost smiled at the guy. Yes, Dex could be a pain in the ass but, deep down, Sebastian liked him.

Dex studied them both for a moment. Then he nodded. "I will do everything I can to erase you from the system. I have a lot of pull, so...pretty soon, you'll be like a shadow there. It will make it a whole lot harder for your enemies to find you.

*Harder,* but not impossible. Like I warned you before, quitting isn't the way it works."

But Sebastian understood what Dex was saying. Every precaution would be taken. "Thank you."

"No, thank you. Thanks for your service. And good luck. I mean that." His attention shifted to Alyssa. Sharpened on her. "He loves you more than anything. You get that, don't you?"

She nodded. "I do now."

"How do you feel about him? Because he's not a prick. Or at least, not always, and he deserves someone who cares."

Aw. Dex sounded like *he* cared. Now Sebastian did smile at him.

"Stop that shit," Dex immediately snapped.

Sebastian laughed.

"Don't worry," Alyssa assured Dex. "I more than care." She faced Sebastian. Gazed up at him. "I love you. I want to spend the rest of my life with you. I'm ready for risks. I'm ready for adventures. I'm ready for everything that will come our way."

From the corner of his eye, Sebastian saw Dex slip away. The door clicked closed behind him. Sebastian waited a beat then gruffly asked, "You even ready for marriage? Maybe those kids you talked about?"

"I don't know...are you asking?"

He would be asking. Very soon. He had plans. Hopes. Dreams—dreams that had started the day he'd first seen her.

"Say it again," Sebastian urged her.

"Say...I don't know?" Her dark eyes warmed with a teasing gleam. The gold flecks flared.

Sebastian shook his head.

"Oh, you mean the part where I said I love you?"

He pulled her even closer. "Yes."

"I love you."

He kissed her. Took her mouth with all the fierce hunger and need that roared through him. She kissed him back the same way. With need, wild desire, and...love.

He loved her so much. Dex had been right. There was no one in the world Sebastian loved more. For him, Alyssa was it.

"You know," she whispered against his mouth, "there is a perfectly good desk about two feet away."

"And there's a perfectly good bed upstairs." He kissed her again. He loved her mouth. Loved to nip her lower lip then sweep his tongue inside her mouth and taste all of that sweetness.

*I just love her.*

"How about we start here..." Alyssa sensually invited. "Then work our way up?"

Any plan she wanted was perfect for him.

But Alyssa pushed against his shoulders. "Give me just a second."

*I will give you forever.*

She walked away from him. Went to the door. Turned the lock. Alyssa glanced back at him with a sensual smile. "We tend to get interrupted a lot."

He smiled at her.

For a moment, she faltered. "The smile does it to me. Every single time."

His head tilted.

"I don't know if I've ever told you, but I love your smile."

Sebastian shrugged. "I don't know if I've ever told you, but I love every single thing about you."

Slowly, she stalked back toward him. "You can't know that for certain."

But he nodded. "I do, trust me."

Her hand slid down his chest. A sensual caress that ended at the snap of his jeans. "But there are some things about me that you don't know yet."

"I'm sure I'll love them."

"How about we find out?" Alyssa unsnapped his jeans. "Why don't we find out...just what it's like when I get my turn to pleasure you?" She lowered the zipper.

His over-eager cock sprang toward her. No underwear in the way. "Baby, you already give me more pleasure than I can stand." Sex with her was better than sex with anyone else. No competition.

"But we should make sure." She was stroking his dick. Making every muscle in his body tighten eagerly as she pumped him from root to tip. "You know, be very certain that you love what I do." She looked up at him through her lashes. "Because if you don't like something, tell me. I can be a quick learner."

Then she lowered to her knees.

*Fucking hell.*

The sight of Alyssa on her knees before him...

She brought her mouth close to his cock. Blew lightly over the tip.

Then took him inside.

His hands clamped around her shoulders. She sucked him. Licked him. Moved her head back and forth in a rhythm that made him crazy as she took his cock deeper and deeper, and she sucked him and—

"*Fucking love it.*" Loved it so much he was about to come.

*No, she has to come, too.*

Her mouth slid off him. She licked her lips. Beamed up at him and started to go right back—

He yanked her upright. Got her those two feet to his desk. Shoved everything else off the desk and put her up there. Hey, if Alyssa wanted to use the desk, why the hell not? The bed was way too far away.

Alyssa kicked away her shoes. He hauled off her jeans and underwear, then pulled her to the edge of the desk. His cock shoved at the entrance to her body. He wanted to sink deep and never let her go.

"Alyssa." His voice was guttural.

Her nails bit into his shoulders. "You're making me wait!"

"I love you."

Her breath caught. Her gaze locked on his. "I love you, too."

He drove into her.

They both moaned. She was tight and hot and perfect. The best dream he'd ever had. Only she wasn't a dream any longer. She was real. She was his. She was—

Wrapping her legs around his hips and telling him to go faster. Harder. So he did. He let go of his control and just held on to her. Primal desire exploded through him. He kissed her deep and long. Devoured her mouth even as he pounded into her. Over and over.

Then he was blazing a path down her neck, licking her, biting her lightly, sucking her skin.

"Sebastian!" Alyssa cried out his name even as he felt her sex contract around him with the pulses of her release.

She felt so freaking good. But he didn't come, not yet, because he was too busy enjoying the way she felt when she climaxed around him.

Her breath heaved in and out. "I love you," she whispered.

He came. A release that blew right through every cell in his body. So powerful that he was swept away and all he could do was hold on to her.

\*\*\*

He was carrying her up the stairs.

Alyssa cracked one eye open. Smiled slowly. "Are we moving on to phase two?"

His hold tightened around her as he gave a low, deep chuckle. "Absolutely."

"Good." His neck was kissably close, so she leaned her head forward and kissed him. Licked the skin right over his pulse point.

He hissed out a breath. "We could always have phase two right here on the stairs."

She licked him again. "Tempting." Her head slid back. "You didn't tell me...how did you feel about having my mouth—"

"Baby, I fucking loved it. Go down on me anytime. Consider it an open invitation. Please, go for it. Over and over again."

She laughed. "I will."

He was smiling, too, but then as he carried her up to the landing, his smile slowly faded. He paused at the top of the stairs and gazed down at her. "I love you."

It made her heart warm every single time that he said those words.

"I will love you until the day I die," Sebastian promised.

Her heart squeezed. "Let's just plan on you not dying for at least a hundred more years, okay?"

"I'm not going anywhere."

"Neither am I." She was exactly where she wanted to be. In his arms. "I love you."

When his dimples flashed again, Alyssa felt her heart melt.

She'd always known that Sebastian would be dangerous to her.

She'd been right.

He'd stolen her heart, and, from here on out, he'd always hold it in the palm of his hand.

Only fair because Alyssa knew she had his heart, too. She'd keep it safe. She'd treasure it— him—always.

"I think there was promise of a phase two," she reminded him. "You know, hint, hint."

His laugher made her whole body feel warm as he turned and carried her to the bedroom.

# EPILOGUE

"Don't even think about it." Antony Kyle had a warm, charming smile on his face, but his eyes were ice cold.

Sebastian took a sip of the ridiculously expensive champagne and fired a quick glance at his buddy. "I have no idea what you're talking about."

"You know exactly what I'm talking about. I see the way you're staring at my sister. You're about to pull some serious shit here, aren't you?"

"I wouldn't call it shit." He'd call it romantic planning. Sebastian shrugged. "I mean, it *is* her birthday. I would be an incredibly crappy boyfriend if I didn't have some sort of big plan in place for her." He glanced across the room. Alyssa was hugging her mom. Her dad stood by her side, smiling warmly. And a few feet away, one of the caterers was carefully arranging the birthday cake that Sebastian had ordered for Alyssa.

As he watched, the caterer placed the birthday candles on top of the icing.

Almost show time.

"Just so you know, I have one rule," Antony announced.

*Here we go again.*

Sebastian pulled his gaze away from the cake and focused on Antony.

"Make her happy." Antony slapped his hand on Sebastian's shoulder. "Because if you don't, then I don't care if you did save my life, I will fight you."

A laugh tore from Sebastian.

Winston appeared at Antony's side. He was sipping his champagne. "What's so funny?"

Antony turned toward him. "Hey, buddy! Congrats on the promotion."

Winston smiled.

Sebastian saluted him with his champagne flute. "You deserve every accolade. Asheville—hell, the whole state—is lucky to have you."

"Aw, now you're just trying to get on my good side."

"You only have a good side," Sebastian told him, being completely honest. "You're one of the best people I've ever met. I'm lucky to call you my friend." He cleared his throat. Motioned to Antony. "Lucky to have you both."

Winston slanted a look at Antony. "Is he drunk?"

"He has been hitting the champagne pretty hard. But I think it's just because he's nervous."

"Why's he nervous?" Winston wanted to know.

"Because I think he's about to ask my sister to marry him, and his crazy ass is scared she'll say no. Like that will happen."

The candles were being lit.

*Time to do this.* He shoved his champagne flute to the side. Began marching for the main table and for Alyssa.

Everyone was closing in on her. People started to sing.

"Great party, man," a voice murmured at his side. "Thanks for the invite."

His gaze darted to the right. *Dex?*

Dex winked at him. "Like I'd miss this. Always fun to see the mighty fall."

He couldn't deal with Dex, not right then.

He had bigger priorities.

Sebastian made it to Alyssa's side. The candles were lit, glowing softly, and the *Happy Birthday* song was almost over. Alyssa turned toward him with a warm smile.

*I love you,* she mouthed.

His hand shoved into his pocket. She looked back at the cake. Leaned over the table. Just as the voices stopped singing, she pressed her plump lips together, closed her eyes...

And he knew she made a wish.

Then she blew out all of the candles as everyone cheered.

He sank to one knee.

The cheers stopped. In fact, everything went dead silent.

Frowning, Alyssa glanced around. When she saw him and the small box he'd just opened and offered to her, Alyssa's eyes widened in surprise.

"I don't know what you wished for," Sebastian told her gruffly, "but you've always been my wish. Will you please do me the honor of marrying me?"

Then, dammit, he held his breath because hell, yes, he was nervous. This was Alyssa, and she mattered. *More than anything.*

Her smile came, slow and sweet, and her dark eyes lit up. "You do know what I wished for," she told him. Her voice was warm and confident and so very sexy. "I wished for you."

"You've got me."

She took the ring. Slid it on her finger. "A perfect fit."

"Is that a yes?"

"Yes."

He surged up and scooped her into his arms. His mouth pressed to hers even as his heart raced in his chest.

People were clapping and cheering, but he didn't look at them. He couldn't.

He was too busy holding on to his wish.

*I will protect her. I will love her.*

*And Antony doesn't need to worry because I'll gladly spend the rest of my life making sure she's happy.*

\*\*\*

"That is so friggin' sweet." Dex helped himself to a full champagne flute. "Guess you're about to get a brother-in-law, huh?" He frowned at Antony. "Are you crying?"

Antony sniffed. "Absolutely not."

Dex still stared at him with suspicion.

"I'm going to congratulate the happy couple." Winston shouldered past Dex. "Excuse me."

"I need to congratulate them, too," Antony quickly said. He was smiling now.

But Dex moved into his path. "You're really okay with Sebastian marrying your sister?"

"He'd die for her. More importantly, he'd kill." Antony nodded. "I wanted Alyssa to wind up with a man who loved her more than anything, and she did. So, yes, I'm more than okay with it." He side-stepped around Dex.

Dex turned and glanced across the large room.

Well, looked like that group had gotten their happy ending.

Good for them.

*Too bad we can't all get endings like that.*

Dex noticed that Sebastian had finally let go of Alyssa. Sebastian turned to shake Winston's hand. Alyssa hugged her brother.

Then Sebastian glanced across the room. His gaze met Dex's.

Dex inclined his head. He hoped Sebastian realized what a truly fortunate bastard he was. Most people didn't find a love like the one he and Alyssa had.

When you did find it, you did everything necessary to protect it.

So, yes, he got why Sebastian was leaving the agency, and he'd do his level best to always watch out for the happy couple. He wasn't a total bastard, after all. Despite what most folks thought, he did have a heart.

Dex raised his flute to Sebastian.

*Best of luck.* But it wasn't really about luck, was it? It was about fighting for what mattered. Fighting for the people close to you.

Sebastian had always been one hell of a fighter.

A fighter who'd just gotten his wish granted, even though it wasn't even Sebastian's birthday. Dex laughed and drained his champagne.

It was time to party.

**The End**

# A NOTE FROM THE AUTHOR

Thanks so much for taking the time to read NEVER GONNA HAPPEN! I hope you enjoyed the hacker spy and his adventures! I wanted to write a fun romance because times have been so very stressful for everyone. Books have always been my favorite method of escape, and my wish was that this story would help you escape, too.

If you enjoyed this book, be sure to check out my "Wilde Ways" series—all of those stories are fun romances with a side dose of suspense.

If you'd like to stay updated on my releases and sales, please join my newsletter list.

*https://cynthiaeden.com/newsletter/*

Again, thank you for reading NEVER GONNA HAPPEN.

Best,
Cynthia                                        Eden
*cynthiaeden.com*

# ABOUT THE AUTHOR

Cynthia Eden is a *New York Times*, *USA Today*, *Digital Book World*, and *IndieReader* best-seller.

Cynthia writes sexy tales of contemporary romance, romantic suspense, and paranormal romance. Since she began writing full-time in 2005, Cynthia has written over one hundred novels and novellas.

Cynthia lives along the Alabama Gulf Coast. She loves romance novels, horror movies, and chocolate.

## For More Information

- *https://cynthiaeden.com*
- *http://www.facebook.com/cynthiaedenf anpage*
- *http://www.twitter.com/cynthiaeden*

# HER OTHER WORKS

**Wilde Ways**

- Protecting Piper (Wilde Ways, Book 1)
- Guarding Gwen (Wilde Ways, Book 2)
- Before Ben (Wilde Ways, Book 3)
- The Heart You Break (Wilde Ways, Book 4)
- Fighting For Her (Wilde Ways, Book 5)
- Ghost Of A Chance (Wilde Ways, Book 6)
- Crossing The Line (Wilde Ways, Book 7)
- Counting On Cole (Wilde Ways, Book 8)

**Dark Sins**

- Don't Trust A Killer (Dark Sins, Book 1)
- Don't Love A Liar (Dark Sins, Book 2)

**Lazarus Rising**

- Never Let Go (Book One, Lazarus Rising)
- Keep Me Close (Book Two, Lazarus Rising)
- Stay With Me (Book Three, Lazarus Rising)

- Run To Me (Book Four, Lazarus Rising)
- Lie Close To Me (Book Five, Lazarus Rising)
- Hold On Tight (Book Six, Lazarus Rising)
- Lazarus Rising Volume One (Books 1 to 3)
- Lazarus Rising Volume Two (Books 4 to 6)

## Dark Obsession Series

- Watch Me (Dark Obsession, Book 1)
- Want Me (Dark Obsession, Book 2)
- Need Me (Dark Obsession, Book 3)
- Beware Of Me (Dark Obsession, Book 4)
- Only For Me (Dark Obsession, Books 1 to 4)

## Mine Series

- Mine To Take (Mine, Book 1)
- Mine To Keep (Mine, Book 2)
- Mine To Hold (Mine, Book 3)
- Mine To Crave (Mine, Book 4)
- Mine To Have (Mine, Book 5)
- Mine To Protect (Mine, Book 6)
- Mine Series Box Set Volume 1 (Mine, Books 1-3)
- Mine Series Box Set Volume 2 (Mine, Books 4-6)

## Bad Things

- The Devil In Disguise (Bad Things, Book 1)
- On The Prowl (Bad Things, Book 2)
- Undead Or Alive (Bad Things, Book 3)
- Broken Angel (Bad Things, Book 4)
- Heart Of Stone (Bad Things, Book 5)
- Tempted By Fate (Bad Things, Book 6)
- Bad Things Volume One (Books 1 to 3)
- Bad Things Volume Two (Books 4 to 6)
- Bad Things Deluxe Box Set (Books 1 to 6)
- Wicked And Wild (Bad Things, Book 7)
- Saint Or Sinner (Bad Things, Book 8)

## Bite Series

- Forbidden Bite (Bite Book 1)
- Mating Bite (Bite Book 2)

## Blood and Moonlight Series

- Bite The Dust (Blood and Moonlight, Book 1)
- Better Off Undead (Blood and Moonlight, Book 2)
- Bitter Blood (Blood and Moonlight, Book 3)
- Blood and Moonlight (The Complete Series)

## Purgatory Series

- The Wolf Within (Purgatory, Book 1)
- Marked By The Vampire (Purgatory, Book 2)

- Charming The Beast (Purgatory, Book 3)
- Deal with the Devil (Purgatory, Book 4)
- The Beasts Inside (Purgatory, Books 1 to 4)

## Bound Series

- Bound By Blood (Bound Book 1)
- Bound In Darkness (Bound Book 2)
- Bound In Sin (Bound Book 3)
- Bound By The Night (Bound Book 4)
- Forever Bound (Bound, Books 1 to 4)
- Bound in Death (Bound Book 5)

## Other Romantic Suspense

- One Hot Holiday
- Secret Admirer
- First Taste of Darkness
- Sinful Secrets
- Until Death
- Christmas With A Spy